THE INTERN'S HANDBOOK

A THRILLER

SHANE KUHN

Simon & Schuster

NEW YORK   LONDON   TORONTO
SYDNEY   NEW DELHI

90

Simon & Schuster
1230 Avenue of the Americas
New York, NY 10020

First Simon & Schuster hardcover edition April 2014

SIMON & SCHUSTER and colophon are registered trademarks of Simon & Schuster, Inc.

For information about special discounts for bulk purchases, please contact Simon & Schuster Special Sales at 1-866-506-1949 or business@simonandschuster.com.

The Simon & Schuster Speakers Bureau can bring authors to your live event. For more information or to book an event contact the Simon & Schuster Speakers Bureau at 1-866-248-3049 or visit our website at www.simonspeakers.com.

Jacket design by Roberto de Vicq Cumptich

Manufactured in the United States of America

1   3   5   7   9   10   8   6   4   2

Library of Congress Cataloging-in-Publication Data
Kuhn, Shane.
The Intern's handbook : a thriller / Shane Kuhn. — First Simon & Schuster hardcover edition.
        pages cm
1. Law firms — Fiction.   2. Internship programs — Fiction.   3. Impersonation — Fiction.
            4. Assassins — Fiction.   I. Title.
                PS3611.U394I58 2014
                    813'.6 — dc23
                    2013034014

            ISBN 978-1-4767-3380-7
        ISBN 978-1-4767-3385-2 (ebook)

For Amanda D.

. . . Ma Ville Lumière. You are the dream that came true.

Interns are invisible. You can tell executives your name a hundred times and they will never remember it because they have no respect for someone at the bottom of the barrel, working for free. The irony is that they will heap important duties on you with total abandon. The more of these duties you voluntarily accept, the more you will get, simultaneously acquiring TRUST AND ACCESS. Ultimately, your target will trust you with his life and that is when you will take it.

—The Intern's Handbook

PRIORITY MEMORANDUM
ALL INFORMATION HEREIN IS CLASSIFIED

To: All field agents
From: William Cummings, director
Subject: JOHN LAGO
    Case File #36-F42
    Age: 25
    Ht/Wt: 5' 10" / 175 lbs.
    Hair: Brown
    Eyes: Blue
    Whereabouts: Unknown

The United States Department of Justice has issued a nationwide and international arrest warrant for John Lago. Lago is believed to be a senior operative in a network of contract assassins working within a shell organization known as "Human Resources, Inc." Human Resources, Inc. (HR, Inc.), presents itself as a placement agency for office interns. However, it is believed that these interns are actually assassins trained to infiltrate multinational corporations and government agencies in order to eliminate heavily guarded executives and principal employees. The number of contract murders HR, Inc., is responsible for is unknown.

    This organization has been the subject of an ongoing FBI investigation. Our objective has been to identify and apprehend the head of HR, Inc., and its chief financiers, and effectively terminate all operations. Until recently, our audio and video surveillance efforts have yielded hundreds of hours of raw data, but no actionable evidence.

Eighteen hours ago, we intercepted an electronic communication from suspect John Lago. It was addressed to several individuals believed to be new recruits at HR, Inc. It is titled *The Intern's Handbook* and it appears to be an informal guide for assassins in training. In light of new evidence found in this document, I am placing a priority mandate on the investigation. A manhunt coordinated by the FBI and CIA is under way. *The Intern's Handbook* is included in this case file as mandatory reading for field agents pursuing suspect Lago.

As he is now the focus of this investigation, I am also providing transcripts from audio and video surveillance tapes in which Lago is a subject. We are attempting to identify the victims and associates referred to in the transcripts, whose names were previously censored. Any persons known to be in contact with Lago are now suspects or material witnesses and should be brought in for questioning.

It is my hope that this case file will facilitate Lago's capture before more lives are lost.

Best of luck and Godspeed.

—William Cummings, director

SUSPECT JOHN LAGO IS CONSIDERED ARMED AND VERY DANGEROUS. FIELD AGENTS ARE REQUIRED TO FOLLOW STRICT PROTOCOLS AND ONLY ATTEMPT TO APPREHEND HIM WITH A FULL STRIKE TEAM AND LOCAL LAW ENFORCEMENT BACKUP.

THE INTERN'S HANDBOOK

by

John Lago

1

IT'S THE HARD-KNOCK LIFE

If you're reading this, you're a new employee at Human Resources, Inc. Congratulations. And condolences. At the very least, you're embarking on a career that you will never be able to describe as dull. You'll go to interesting places. You'll meet unique and stimulating people from all walks of life. And kill them. You'll make a lot of money, but that will mean nothing to you after the first job. Assassination, no matter how easy it looks in the movies, is the most difficult, stressful, and lonely profession on the planet. From this point on, whenever you hear someone bitch about his job, it will take every fiber of your being to keep from laughing in his face. This work isn't for everyone. Most of you are going to find that out the hard way because you'll be dead by the end of the month. And that's still just the training phase.

If you're having second thoughts, that's a natural reaction. The idea of killing people for a living is what second thoughts were made for. In response to all of your questions regarding whether or not you'll feel bad, lose your nerve, live in constant fear, or even want to kill *yourself*, I can provide one simple answer: yes. All of your worst nightmares will come true in ways you never imagined. And either you'll get over it, or you'll be gargling buckshot. Either way, you're covered.

When you reach your darkest hour—which will arrive daily—take comfort in the fact that you never really had much of a choice in the matter. Like me, you're gutter spawn, a Dumpster baby with a broken beer bottle for a pacifier. We've been described as "disenfranchised." Our diagnosis was "failure to thrive." We were tossed from county homes to foster homes to psych wards to juvenile detention centers—wards of the state with pink-slip parents and a permanent spot in line behind the eight ball. Little Orphan Annie would have been our homegirl. So, what were you going to do with your life, starve on minimum wage, greeting herds of human cattle at Wal-Mart? Sell your ass to Japanese businessmen? Peddle meth to middle school kids? I think not. For the first time, you're going to be able to take advantage of being a disadvantaged youth because everyone knows that orphans make the best assassins. Try humming "It's the Hard-knock Life" while you empty a fifteen-round Beretta mag into Daddy Warbucks's limousine and you'll see just how sweet revenge can be.

If you're reading this, you are a born killer and the people that recruited you know that. You have all the qualifications. First off, you've never been loved, so you feel no empathy for loss. To experience loss, you have to have had something to lose in the first place. Since love is the most important thing you can ever feel, and you've never felt it, then you are bereft of just about every emotion except anger.

And let's talk about anger. Have you ever heard of Intermittent Explosive Disorder? Even if you haven't heard of it, you've experienced it. It's that blinding, uncontrollable rage that turns you into a violent, sometimes homicidal, maniac. Maybe you beat your foster brother half to death for drinking the last Pepsi. Or maybe you fully unleashed it on your juvie cell mate and granted him an early release in a body bag. All the social workers, corrections counselors, and psych doctors, with their nicotine-stained fingers and permanent caffeine twitch, have classified you as dangerously antisocial with a footnote about how you have nothing constructive to offer society. But at Human Resources, Inc., everything that made you a pariah will now make you a professional.

Now let's talk about brains. You've been kicked, thrown, and dragged out of every school you ever attended. But if you're reading this, you are of genius level intelligence, even though you probably beat the shit out of every bumper sticker honor student in your town. How else would you have survived? Only someone with wits beyond her years can stay alive when the whole world thinks she'd be better off dead. You're at the top of the evolutionary food chain, adapting to things in ways that would have made Charles Darwin soil his Harris tweeds.

———

Finally, you may have noticed you have some extraordinary physical abilities. I'm not talking about superpowers, for those of you whose only male role models came from a comic book rack. If you had been raised by something other than wolves, you might have played football or basketball or earned your black belt in something. You would have excelled because you are stronger, faster, and more agile than the average person. Your reflexes are like lightning and your field of vision captures everything down to the finest detail. Incidentally, that's why you avoid crowds. Simultaneously concentrating on every movement made by hundreds of people is not only overwhelming, but it also makes you hate humanity even more than you did before. Bottom line: you did not choose this career, it chose you.

This is your handbook. *The Intern's Handbook.* It's not a part of your new-hire welcome packet. In fact, if they catch you reading it, you will be dead before you can turn the page and your faceless, fingerless corpse will be divided into six trash bags and dissolved in a vat of sulfuric acid in some nameless New Jersey chemical plant. So, please be discreet, because there's a good chance this handbook will save your life.

My name is John Lago. Of course, that's not my given name because my biological parents were too busy disappearing from my short life to sign my birth certificate, which said "Male Baby X." My foster parents called me whatever they managed to blurt out between backhands and booze. So when I was old enough to scrape up a hundred bucks, I paid a guy to forge me a new birth certificate and make a man out of me.

Why John Lago? I could have chosen anything and it's not every day that you get the opportunity to name yourself. It all started with my love of classic cinema. The only friend I ever had growing up was Quinn, the projectionist at the local porn theater. When the place closed for the night and all the pervs slithered home, Quinn would spool up some amazing films from his extensive collection. I grew up on Stanley Kubrick and Akira Kurosawa. I knew who Clint Eastwood was before I knew who was president. For me, film is the great escape (which is also an amazing movie), and I recommend you cultivate an appreciation for it because you're going to need something other than hideous, soul-eating nightmares to occupy your mind. Monsters like us can learn to be human beings from watching movies. All of the experiences we never had are covered in film, and they can be our emotional cave paintings, guiding our path among the ranks of normal society. So your assignment, should you choose to accept it, is to try watching something other than epic fails and donkey porn on YouTube. Just avoid assassin movies, because they'll give you all kinds of bad ideas.

Back to my self-inflicted, Hollywood-inspired moniker. My surname is born out of the greatest era in American cinema—the 1970s. "Lago" is the name of the doomed western town in Clint Eastwood's *High Plains Drifter*, a film that is, without question, the story of my life. I chose "John" because, even though I'm guaranteed eternal damnation, I'm a big fan of John the Baptist. He prepared the unwashed masses for the coming of the Messiah, is given props in the Qur'an for his Purity of Life, and unlike Jesus, he never asked God for a get-out-of-jail-free card before Herod served his head up on a silver platter. I learned all of this by watching Chuck Heston bring the fucking brimstone when he played headless John in the biblical epic *The Greatest Story Ever Told*.

As for the rest of the meat puppets in this tragic parable, some of the names have been changed to protect the guilty. I didn't manage to stay aboveground and out of a supermax hellhole by broadcasting the identities of my contacts at HR, Inc. or my targets. And I'm not going to start now. In keeping with the theme, their names have been pulled from the venerable celluloid of classic and contemporary cinema. If you can figure out what films they come from, you'll get extra credit.

I've been an employee of HR, Inc. since I was twelve years old. I'm now twenty-four, soon to be twenty-five. I have "completed the cycle," as they say. When I started here, my recruiting class consisted of twenty-seven smart-ass punk motherfuckers with two feet in the grave, including myself. There are three of us left. So you might say I know a few things. Or in what is undoubtedly your parlance—that of a *modern-day* smart-ass punk motherfucker with two feet in the grave—"Dude's got mad skills, yo." Hip-hop, you have fucked the king's English for life. Good on you.

If you're anything like I was at your age, you're probably convinced you're going to live forever. I have news for you, brothers and sisters. The shortest distance between truth and bullshit is six feet straight down. It doesn't matter if you believe me or not because there's no greater reality check than a 230 grain .45 caliber hollow point hitting your forehead at 844 feet per second.

So swallow your pride and *read this book*. I don't have to write it. I'm doing you a favor. In fact, I'm risking my neck for you, and I've never even met your sorry asses. The thing is, no one ever gave me the heads-up on anything when I started this gig. Of course,

I had my training. But I never got the inside scoop. In most businesses, you learn the ropes from those with more experience. Not this one. Bob, our intrepid leader, wouldn't talk dirty to his wife unless she was on a need-to-know basis. In my opinion, Bob's tight-ass approach to secrecy is the reason why many of my classmates now have tree roots growing out of their eye sockets. He calls himself a "big picture guy." This is a Business 3.0 way of saying he doesn't give a shit about anything but the bottom line, least of all you. There are more where you came from, and when you whack one mole in this business another invariably pops up. Protecting the interests of his "clients"—the bloated, scotch-guzzling frat boys of the *nouveau* American aristocracy—is his first and only priority. Everyone else is expendable.

You are my priority. If I can save some of you—the most pathetic human punching bags next to the orphans in India that swim in rivers of human excrement—then maybe I'll only end up in the seventh circle of hell instead of the eighth. And if you live through all of this, maybe you can make some kind of name for yourself, shrug off the filthy rug you've been swept under, and create a legacy that transcends trailer parks, drunken beatings, and fucking for food. We will probably never meet. However, in our own twisted way, we are the family that none of us ever had and we have to stick together. It might not be much, but this little handbook is the only proof you've got that someone has *your* back.

Despite the fact that absolutely no one ever had my back, I'm rapidly approaching the ripe old age of twenty-five, a milestone that very few of you will ever cross. While most young professionals are just getting their careers started at twenty-five, that is the mandatory retirement age at HR, Inc. According to Bob, it is the cutoff point at which people begin to question anyone who would be willing to work for free. And I quote: "Even if people believe you are still an intern at twenty-five, you will call attention to yourself as a loser who is way behind in his or her career path. And calling attention to yourself is a death sentence."

The whole philosophy behind HR, Inc., is that an intern is the perfect cover for an assassin. Again, quoting Bob:

"Interns are invisible. You can tell an executive your name a hundred times and that executive will never remember it because they have no respect for someone at the bottom of the barrel, working for free. The rapport they have with their private urinal far exceeds the rapport they will ever have with you. The irony is that all you really have to be is an excellent employee with a strong work ethic and they will heap important duties on you with total abandon. The duties that their lazy, entitled admins and junior execs wouldn't do without guns to their heads are actually critical day-to-day tasks that keep a business running. They also open the doors to proprietary data, personal information, and secure executive areas. The more of these duties you voluntarily accept, the more you will get, simultaneously acquiring the keys to the kingdom: TRUST AND ACCESS. Ultimately, your target will trust you with his life and that is when you will take it."

As much as I hate to stroke Bob's ego, the concept is fucking genius. But why, you may ask, do we go to so much trouble just to whack someone? *La Femme Nikita* can pop a guy with a sniper rifle from a hotel window while she runs a hot bath. Couldn't we park ourselves on a rooftop with an L115A3 long range sniper rifle and shoot our targets like fish in a barrel? A British commando in Afghanistan took out two Taliban soldiers from over eight thousand feet with that baby. That's like drilling someone in Battery Park while you're eating dim sum in Chinatown.

There are many reasons why we don't do things like they do in the movies or on the battlefield. First off, even a Navy SEAL sniper is going to miss once in a while, and they're the best in the world. Bullets and physics are a real bitch, and *we* can't afford to miss.

Second, when high-profile mucky mucks start getting splattered all over the streets of the biggest city in America with military-issue weaponry, that's called a *pattern*. Patterns are one of the FBI's favorite pastimes. Mix that with politics and you've got so much heat you can't whack a pigeon without getting black-bagged and taken to Guantanamo Bay for the all-inclusive interrogation and torture package. It's ironic, but this work requires the utmost finesse. That's what separates the professionals from the shirtless hillbilly dipshits you see on *Cops*.

If one can provide a high-quality product for a reasonable price, there's a huge market for assassinations. As long as you avoid patterns and make it seem like your target's enemies are the hitters, you can — yes I'm going to say it — *get away with murder and make a killing*.

The key to success in this business is quality personnel. That would be you. Here at HR, Inc. we are trained very well. It takes years to perfect this so-called craft, which is why they recruit us when we're young. But excellent training does not guarantee success or even survival. I've seen recruits that were considered stars get that smug look wiped off their face with both barrels on their first job. The most important thing I'm going to try to teach you is this: solid training will give you the skills you need to be good at this work, but good and dead is still just dead. Knowing when to set that training aside and allow your instincts to take over will make you unstoppable.

I am unstoppable. I owe much of that to experience. So, in order to truly prepare you for what you're getting yourself into, this handbook will chronicle, in great detail, my final assignment. Within this account, you will see the job as it really is, not as it is in Bob's theoretical world of "typical scenarios." I'm sorry, but there are no typical fucking scenarios when you're planning and executing the murder of a high-profile, heavily guarded individual. Bob will train you and then train you to rely on your training. This is a military approach, and it works well in military operations—for the most part. I will teach you to think like a predator and master the improvisational tracking skills predators use to execute a clean kill and survive. There's a big difference between these approaches, and the only times I've really come close to death were in the beginning, when I was drinking Bob's Kool-Aid by the gallon.

In addition to providing a play-by-play of my final assignment, this handbook will also be a field reference manual with some simple, memorable rules to follow, backed up by real-world examples. In my nearly eight years of active assignment—yes I started wasting people at seventeen—I have thirty-four kills. I may not have seen it all, but pretty goddamned close.

2

"WE'RE ALL GOING TO MISS YOU, JOHN."

Today I'm going to get my final assignment from Bob. It's a little weird, thinking this is the last one. I've been working here since I hit puberty, and in a few weeks, it's all over. I'll receive my final wire payment and they'll burn everything that ties me to this place—ID cards, weapons, clothing—everything. I won't even be able to go back to my apartment. I'll be given a new identity, some traveling money, and clothes. The only evidence I'll have of my former life with HR, Inc. will be my bank account numbers, aka my best friends. I'll have all of the money I've saved over the years, along with a seven-figure retirement bonus. This will be more than enough for me to disappear and completely reinvent myself for what I hope is the last time.

The few of us that make it to retirement almost always continue with the same work, just as freelancers. Not me. This may be the only type of work I've ever known, but I'll be damned if I'm going to stay in it just because I'm too much of a pussy to learn something new. It's like that old convict in *The Shawshank Redemption* that finally gets out of prison after being in there for fifty years and hangs himself because he doesn't know how to tie his own shoes without some bull poking him with a stick. The writer should hang himself with his own heartstring. Only household pets think that way. I've had to convince some of the smartest people in New York City that I was qualified to perform menial tasks at law firms, hedge funds, military tech companies, security firms, commercial real estate companies, multinational oil and energy conglomerates, and the list goes on. I can bullshit my way into a lot of different fields, so I'm going to choose one and go kick as much ass there as I did here.

The difference is I'll be a normal working stiff, eating bad microwave food, bitching about taxes, and sucking at golf. And I'll love every minute of it. No more living in constant paranoia about being caught or whacked. I won't have to wash the stink of gunpowder and blood out of my clothes. I can have actual friends that I won't have to kill if they find out what I do. And the best part? I'll never have to look at the shark eyes of another "early retiree" whose severance package just blew his brains out on a filthy bathroom wall.

———

"We're all going to miss you, John."

That's Bob, and that's the first thing he says to me when I sit down to be briefed on my final assignment. It catches me slightly off guard. Bob likes catching people off guard, especially if it's an attempt to show them that he's just another guy who considers the feelings of others, which I can assure you he does not. For a split second, I feel a wave of nostalgia pass over me.

Maybe Bob will miss me. Maybe I'm the son he never had, I think.

Then he deploys the cynical grin I've come to loathe over the years, and my wave of nostalgia turns to nausea. What he meant was it's going to be hard as hell to find someone as merciless and bulletproof as me. He's right. He's going to miss having a human button he can push that will rain down Old Testament destruction without leaving so much as a carpet fiber for the cops to sniff.

"I'll miss you too, Bob," I lie.

"How many law firms have you worked?" he says, ignoring my equally false parting sentiment.

"Off the top of my head . . . seventeen."

"Still feel comfortable and well versed in that space?"

"I've passed the bar exam four times in the last five years . . ."

"I don't take anything for granted, John. You know that."

"I know, Bob. What's the gig?"

"Anxious to get out of here?"

"Anxious to get to work."

"Good. Because this one is not going to be easy."

"Are they ever?"

"Why the attitude?"

"Senioritis I guess."

"You should avoid telling jokes. You're not funny."

He hands me a thick file. I glance through it, finding what I like to call my *bullet points*—target profile, location layout, target's known enemies, vulnerabilities, etc. I raise an eyebrow because Bob is sending me to Bendini, Lambert & Locke, possibly the most famous law firm in New York City. They are notorious for representing elite clients and peddling an enormous amount of political influence. Now it's getting kind of interesting. I keep scanning and everything seems to be in order except for one small detail.

"Who's the target? Not seeing that in here, Bob."

"That's because it's not in there."

I look at him, expecting the grin. Instead his face is slightly apologetic. This is as close to embarrassment as Bob can get.

"That's . . . irregular," I offer.

Side note: never openly protest any aspect of any assignment in front of Bob. He was a first platoon Marine, and whiners of any stripe make him physically ill. You may comment on "irregularities" so that (a) he knows you're paying attention and (b) you can get the intel you need to cover your ass. However, you must only seem to be casually inquiring because he needs to believe that if he asked you to whack someone blindfolded with one hand tied behind your back, your only question would be "Which hand?"

"My apologies, John. This is a complex case, more than usual. The target is one of the three partners. He's gone out of his way to keep his identity hidden . . . for obvious reasons."

I read some more of the profile.

"I see what you mean, Bob."

Another side note: try to say Bob's name as often as you can without going over the top. Men like Bob are in love with themselves, and the mention of a lover's name floods their cerebral G-spot with endorphins.

"Selling the FBI's witness protection list to the highest bidders. Definitely something you'd want to keep on the down low."

"His 'clients' are what you might expect," Bob adds. "Mafia families, gangbangers, foreign drug cartels."

"All the best people."

"Your cynicism concerns me, John."

"How so?"

"A cynic is a man who knows the price of everything and the value of nothing."

"Oscar Wilde. You're waxing poetic, Bob."

"At least we've given you culture here, if not sophistication."

"How does he get the names?"

"The same way anyone gets anything they want. Money, privilege, and the right golf partners."

"*That* sounds a bit cynical to me, Bob."

"You start Monday. Address and contact names are in the file, along with your cover dossier."

"Hmm. Who am I this time?"

I read a bit, pretending to give a shit.

"Michigan Law School. Top ten in the country but not very flashy. Nice touch."

"You'll be surrounded by Ivies. They know their own kind."

"They all had 'fathers' but instead I had a 'dad.'" I sigh.

"Interesting quote. Twain?"

"Kurt Cobain."

"Get out, John."

3

THE FIRM

I'm going over my identity dossier, spending the weekend with my new self. They gave me a new surname, but as always, I get to go by "John." Quite frankly, there is no other name that's more perfectly anonymous, and I'm always glad I don't have to learn how to answer to some new name like a fucking rescue dog or Chinese exchange student. My new self went to public high school (self-starter), college at Notre Dame (salt of the earth), and then Michigan Law (smart but not connected). I was the perfect equal opportunity quota candidate without being ethnic — a white Catholic without a drop of blue blood. Firms like Bendini, Lambert & Locke want to appear progressive, but let's not get carried away.

Thanks to Bob, my soda cracker profile is the perfect cover. I'll be ignored and considered socially irrelevant by my wealthy Ivy League peers but not despised. I'll be tolerated by my superiors, who will wait for me to make some obscure error that *they* make regularly, at great peril to their clients, so they can summarily shit-can me and, in their words, "Send me back to Peoria with the rest of the hicks." This will enable them to maintain their bullshit PR front without having to worry about me being around long enough to kick the Lilly Pulitzer out of all these paunchy drips on the squash court. But they don't have to worry. I'll be gone soon enough.

After studying the file and burning it, I quietly thank Bob as I watch my final assignment go down in flames. Killing a guy that wears tasseled loafers and eats Steak Diane for lunch is a cupcake of a gig, and I might actually have some fun for a change. Sure it might have been nice of him to give me a bit of a challenge as a proper send-off, but that's Bob for you. He's already written me off and put me on some low-priority rodent hunt so he doesn't tie up any of the new talent. Fine with me. I'll put this pin-striped bass on my stringer and be eating a cheeseburger in paradise by the end of the month.

The only rock in my flip-flop is that I don't even know who the fucking target is. I'm not a detective. I don't sit on stakeouts in beige sedans with empty coffee cups and burger wrappers on the dash. And I sure as shit don't stick my nose where it doesn't belong. In other words, I'm not a dog, trotting around sniffing crotches, trying to separate good guys from bad guys. I see ALL people as threats, even the ones that become assets and help me, unwittingly mind you, to accomplish my objective. It's just cleaner that way. And growing up in foster homes, as I'm sure most of you have, you learn to think that way in order to survive. Everyone is guilty until proven innocent but still perfectly capable of being guilty at any given moment.

None of that matters though. The job is the job, and I have no choice but to get it done. Bitching about it will only distract me, and let's be honest, has bitching about *anything* ever helped *anybody*? This job is about action without judgment, and I advise you to re-main focused on that at all times. Failure is not an option. I've seen recruits walk away from jobs for a number of reasons, many of them very good, only to end up taking a bullet before cocktail hour. It sounds harsh, but I have actually learned to like this kind of clarity. Until I started working at HR, Inc., everything about my life had been maddeningly uncertain. Now it's very clear. I have to either kill the target or die trying. Clarity equals victory. Look at successful people. Do you really think they have seven effective habits? Fuck no. Who's got time for that? They have one effective habit: DOING. When you are a "doer" you lap the rest of the rats in the race.

So, I fully accept the gig without reservation or judgment and go about the tedious business of navigating the Internet circus to read up on the partners. Let's start with Bendini. His grandfather was a wealthy Sicilian that built most of Bensonhurst. His father went to Princeton and carried on with the family business until he got into some bad spec housing deals with the mob and blew his own brains out. Bendini's grandfather sent him to prep school and he went on to Yale and Harvard Law. The rest of it is about his legal career, which would put you to sleep faster than a bottle of Ambien. I do like Bendini for his dad's mob connection, but it's thin at best.

If you thought Bendini was boring, Lambert makes him look like P. T. Barnum. Lambert moved to the United States from Germany with his parents when he was an infant. Evidently he's quite the supernerd because MIT accepted him after middle school. He went on to get a PhD, an MD, and a JD. After working as house counsel for a big pharma company, Bendini poached him and made him the youngest partner in the history of the firm. He brings them millions in revenue from drug companies and biotech. It's unlikely he's the target, but that's what makes me like him so much. Getting your hands on witness protection program data is the kind of caper a smart bastard like Lambert could pull off. Unlike his partners, he flies way below the public radar, which means he could make a lot of moves without drawing attention to himself. It's always the quiet ones that invite you in for an iced tea and end up stacking your body parts like cordwood in the crawl space.

Finally, I do a rundown on Locke. Ex-military, two tours in Vietnam, awarded the Purple Heart, honorably discharged in 1975. Went on to Penn, like his father, and then Harvard Law, like his mother. Became one of the most successful defense attorneys in New York history. Definitely the firm's biggest PR hook but almost never grants interviews. The press calls him "the man in black." I leaf through all of the clippings from his cases—movie stars, pro athletes, rock stars.

Seems weird that he would take the time to rat out informers hiding out in Iowa, but I like the defense attorney angle. Witnesses for the prosecution are like cockroaches to a defense attorney. They can't get them under their heels fast enough.

What's fucked-up is that these guys are all wildly rich and powerful and definitely knocking on the door of a sweet retirement. I can't believe any of them would be so terminally stupid as to get involved in such a dirty business. Whoever it may be is risking generations of future wealth, his life, and the lives of his family when you think about the vermin he has to get in bed with to make these sales. But greed and power could turn Gandhi into a Kardashian, and we're talking about lawyers here, so I guess I shouldn't be surprised.

4

THE PERKS OF BEING A WALLFLOWER

In some ways, getting into character is the most difficult part of the process. Your whole life, you have been one person. In this life, you will have to be many people. If that sounds fun to you, then you'll do just fine. The secret is to immerse yourself so well into your new persona that even *you* believe you are this person. If you believe it, then you will never feel like you are lying and you will never exhibit any "tells."

The Look is one of your greatest weapons and it's critical that you nail it. You might be thinking, *How hard can it be to look like an office nerd?* Answer: really fucking hard. And you can't be perceived as a nerd anyway. Nerds are noticeable. They are the subjects of ridicule, despite the fact that Hollywood and TV Land try to tell you otherwise. I remember the faces of each and every nerd I beat to a pulp in my three glorious years of public school because I was angry about my shitty life and wanted to take it out on someone I knew would not fight back. The point is that you have to be more of a wallflower than anything else. You have to blend into your surroundings and be ultimately forgettable.

To quote Bob: "Interns do not have a face. They may occupy the same space with you for years, but for the life of you, you can never remember their names."

If you want proof, go to any high school reunion. The popular people will be approached multiple times by wallflowers. These inconsequential nobodies actually believe they might, as an adult, have the equal opportunity to become friends with someone who still can't pick them out of a lineup. "What was your name again?"

There is a simple reason for this approach. Wallflowers have zero traits that stimulate the brains of other people and string together enough synapses to make memories. You always remember the things that rub you the right way or the wrong way. The positive and negative are both powerful memory reinforcement tools. Negative is more powerful than positive, which is based on your survival instincts. But you can't remember something that doesn't touch you in a positive or negative way. And this is our ultimate goal. We must learn from the wallflowers, life's most perfect unintentional losers.

Rule #1: Act neutral.

My fifth job was one of my hardest. It was a big fashion house, and you can imagine how everyone dressed. I asked Bob for a sizable clothing allowance so I could fit in once I started my internship, and he flat out refused. He said that no matter how hard I tried to be on the same level as my coworkers, they would still never see me as one of their own. In fact, I would become subject to the circle of brutal judgment that goes on every day as employees whisper evil shit about their so-called friends. In short, I would no longer be invisible.

So I watched the employees whose names the fashion insects could never remember, and Bob's advice started to click. Eventually I discovered the most invisible guy in the place—the one that everyone in the office would see and interact with every day, but whose name they could not recall even if they had a gun to their heads: The UPS guy.

I bought a few books on color theory, and sure enough, brown sparks the smallest neurological response of any color in the spectrum. It also elicits feelings of reliability and security, traits that are critical to gaining access and trust. So I built my wardrobe around this pillar of blandness, never straying too far. Brownish gray, brownish green, brownish black, etc. All of these colors are easily found in the sale rack of every department store because people do not intentionally buy clothing that will erase them from the universe. And when you put an entire outfit together with these colors, it's like you are a chameleon wearing the perfect camouflage for every background in existence.

For hair, go to Supercuts. That cut-by-numbers place is the Mecca of ordinary. And I highly recommend getting glasses, because people tend to make more of a connection to you when they can clearly see your eyes. What you need are nondescript, ubiquitous frames—thin, dull metallic finishes and clear glass. Go to LensCrafters—*totally forgettable glasses in about an hour.*

Back to the fashionistas. They had a CEO who was producing and trafficking child pornography out of his textile factory in Thailand. Did I mention that killing this piece of shit was my favorite job? Getting to work on his floor was easy because everyone in that business is lazier and more entitled than usual, and it's amazing that anything gets done. The hard part was figuring out an enemy profile. Bob is big on killing folks in a manner befitting the target's enemies. Bombs, guns, bludgeoning, poison, electrocution, knives, fire, drowning, etc. Assassins just have their preferences. The IRA would rather blow you to bits than stab you and have to smell the bangers and mash on your last breath. The cartels like beheading. Goodfellas like piano wire, ice picks, and the occasional live burial. Bob studies these things ad nauseam, no pun intended. But this case was different. Creepy pedophile fashion magnates with deformed pinky fingers are hated and reviled by many, but they don't typically have high-profile enemies—at least no enemies with the balls or the money to put out a contract on someone . . . until now.

So I got creative. I asked him if I could bring my eleven-year-old "nephew" Andy visiting from the Midwest to work so that I could show him around. I'll be damned if he didn't drool a little into his espresso cup. Of course, Andy was part of our crew. Guy had some kind of disease that stunted his growth. Looked just like a kid. Bob only used him for specialty jobs like this because eleven-year-old interns are most definitely going to be noticed anywhere outside a NASA think tank.

When I brought him in, the CEO had arranged a "private tour." Told me I could just leave the boy with him and he would take care of everything. He even had pink frosted elephant cookies and pineapple punch set out. Sick bastard must have been raped by clowns on a circus train at some point in his sorry life. Fifteen minutes into his Willy Wonka routine, our sawed-off operative injected him with enough Adrenalin and Viagra to blow up his cocaine-scarred heart and leave him with an erection that the coroner would have to get a logging crew to cut down. Now, that's what I call a triumph in improvisational warfare. We put Uncle Plooker in front of his computer, fired up his private stock of kiddie porn, and slipped out with root beer Dum Dum suckers in our teeth.

5

THE BULLSHIT EXPRESS

I'm spending the day boning up on all the law clerk nonsense I learned at different legal intern jobs. It's not difficult. Mostly you're there to make sure the actual lawyers are not fucking things up royally with poorly written language, utterly incorrect language, language copied from other contracts but never customized for the new contract, etc. And let me tell you, you are *always* busy. Being around lawyers is like being in a classroom full of kids with severe ADHD and low blood sugar. They have learned to despise detail so much that they subconsciously, or consciously, ignore it. For the most part, they are gunslingers, painting the town red with broad strokes, and they rely on the help to make sure the ship doesn't sink and take their house in Montauk with it.

In addition to my crash course in wills and torts, I am also immersing myself in the warm bath of my new persona. Let's recap on why orphans make great assassins. All of our lives we've never been given the opportunity to develop our own identities. Many of us never had a real name and we certainly never had real parents or any kind of connection to our genealogies or cultures of origin. We never even had a room of our own—the great diorama of developing personalities festooned with posters, photos, tchotchkes, and all of the icons and totems that represent our every feeling, hope, and dream. We are the blank slate. Aristotle's tabula rasa. And we are the masters of being a wolf in sheep's clothing.

Becoming someone else is one of my favorite parts of the job. It puts a silencer on my inhibitions and allows me to do and say things I would never say to people as my real self. That can be an extremely amusing exercise with the opposite sex. And it gives me a sense, although fleeting, of what a normal life might be like. It's weird, but just having a taste of that has saved me from the rubber room on more than one occasion. As an added bonus, this well-developed skill will come in very handy when I finally molt out of my John Lago skin and slither into the real world of retirement.

Tonight I'll be taking a ride on the Bullshit Express. It's one of my rituals when I prep for a job, and I strongly suggest you adopt it. I'll go to a bar, buy anyone a drink, and start talking. When you buy someone a drink, they will almost always chat you up and ask you all about yourself, mainly because they want you to ask about them in return. People love to talk about themselves, especially white people. The Bullshit Express is how you field-test your knowledge of your cover dossier. You'll be surprised at how well you do this when you have a real context. The more drinks you buy, the more practice you will get *and* the more you will find yourself adding to the story. This is a strong memorization technique that I like to call "owning it." When you own it, you get to a point where you actually think it's true, and then you are golden. Lies are, after all, the only things we tell ourselves that we truly believe.

I spend a few hours casing the law firm building, a venerable, old money fortress holding court in the storied enclave of Central Park South. I pop into a local bar around quitting time. The dark wood paneling, $15 Heinekens, and $1,500 call girls lead me to believe there's a good chance this is a Bendini, Lambert & Locke watering hole. This would be the best possible scenario for me to put my cover through the paces, so I roll in, looking for an ear to chew.

Sitting at the bar, my favorite hunting ground, is a woman in her mid to late twenties with blond hair and brown eyes that make her beautiful in a *Roman Holiday* meets *True Romance* kind of way. Her features are somewhat conventional, but there is something exotic underneath it all, something dark and sexy that reminds me of a young Liz Taylor. Her expensive shoes and pocketbook, at odds with her underwhelming suit and briefcase, tell me that she is a working stiff with the right priorities. Not to mention she is a woman sitting at a bar alone. This is a baller move in any town, and only girls with serious chops even attempt it. I like her immediately. All aboard.

ALL INFORMATION HEREIN IS CLASSIFIED
SURVEILLANCE TRANSCRIPT: AUDIO RECORDING—
MOBILE PARABOLIC REFLECTOR MIC

Location: Bull on Thames Pub, Central Park South, Manhattan
Subjects: John Lago and Alice (censored).

SUBJECT ALICE IS SEATED AT THE BAR.

Lago: Is this seat taken?

Alice: Do people really say that anymore?

Lago: I say it. But I say a lot of things people don't say anymore.

Alice: Really? Like what?

Lago: For me, music will always be on an album.

Alice: I like vinyl. Have a seat. What else you got?

Lago: Truck versus SUV.

Alice: Not bad. But that's a little bit provincial. Give me a really good one and I'll buy you a drink.

Lago: One-night stand versus hookup.

Alice: Mike! He'll have what I'm having.

Lago: What are you having?

Alice: Wild Turkey. Neat.

Lago: A highly underrated brand.

Alice: And somewhat misunderstood.

SOUND OF GLASSES PLACED ON BAR.

Bartender: Two middle fingers. Enjoy.

Alice: Thanks, Mike.

PAUSE. LAGO COUGHS. ALICE LAUGHS.

Alice: I'm Alice.

Lago: John.

Alice: You live around here? Wait, don't tell me anything. Let's just guess everything about each other. You game?

Lago: Sure. Ladies first.

Alice: Ladies first, huh? Definitely not from Manhattan.

Lago: What makes you think—

Alice: Stop! You're going to give something away.

Lago: All right. Carry on.

Alice: I'm going to guess you're from the Midwest but very well educated.

Lago: And I'm going to guess you're from the East Coast because you said I was from the Midwest BUT very well educated.

ALICE LAUGHS.

Alice: I may be a snob, but guess what?

Lago: What?

Alice: I'm from the Midwest.

Lago: Bullshit. You don't have the ass for it.

SOUND OF ALICE HITTING LAGO.

Lago: Ow! Damn! That was really . . . enthusiastic.

Alice: You think that hurts? Keep talking about my ass, buster.

Lago: Buster? You are from the Midwest. What are you doing in New York? Besides beating up dudes in bars?

Alice: I came here for work. Finished law school recently. Go ahead. Get them out of your system.

Lago: Get what out of my system?

Alice: Lawyer jokes.

Lago: I don't know any.

Alice: Bullshit.

Lago: Not into them. Probably because I'm a lawyer too.

Alice: No way.

Lago: Way.

Alice: What firm?

Lago: [censored]. I'm just out of school as well, so I'm starting an internship there.

Alice: Get out!

SOUND OF ALICE HITTING LAGO AGAIN. SOUND OF LAGO GROANING IN PAIN.

Lago: Okay. That one really hurt.

Alice: That's my firm—where I work!

Lago: Really? Cool. For how long?

Alice: I'm actually just finishing the intern program. Hoping to get an associate job.

Lago: Good luck. I hear getting hired . . . for actual money . . . is next to impossible for most people.

Alice: True. But I'm not most people.

Lago: I can see that.

Alice: You want to see more?

Lago: Meaning?

Alice: I think you know what I mean, counselor. By the way, no one ever says "counselor." That's just a TV thing.

Lago: I think I know what you mean, and if I'm right either you're a serial killer or I have some great astrological shit happening right now.

Alice: Maybe both. Come on.

Lago: Uh . . . Maybe not.

Alice: Don't you want to be my next victim?

Lago: As much as I'd love to say yes . . . we're going to be working in the same office and . . .

Alice: Okay, okay. Please stop. You're killing my buzz, and I don't handle rejection well.

Lago: I'm not rejecting you.

Alice: I'm offering and you're saying no, right?

Lago: Yes, but not "no" in the pejorative sense.

Alice: You're going to be a great lawyer.

Lago: Wait. Finish your drink.

—END TRANSCRIPT—

6

GET YOUR SHINE BOX

Monday morning. It's a brisk autumn day, my favorite time of the year. New York is spectacular. The summer garbage smell has finally drifted off to Europe via the Gulf Stream, replaced by the smell of wet leaves decomposing in the gutter. Sounds nasty, but it's one of the best smells I can imagine. It's musty, earthy, and it reminds me of the first time I felt okay knowing I was alone in the world and would be that way for the rest of my life.

I was six years old and I was languishing in some home for wayward youth outside Reno, Nevada. The changing leaves would float down from the Sierras and land outside my window. I remember thinking that the leaves were more beautiful dead than they were alive. And I stopped crying about the things I would never have, because I knew they meant nothing.

First day of my last job and it feels a little strange. I'm trying not to get sentimental about a life that has been defined by the size of its body count, but I can't help it. It's what I know. But I also know that the sooner I can just get this job done, the sooner I can get out of this business and get on with my new life.

Now, let's go kill someone, shall we?

———

I show up for work at Bendini, Lambert & Locke in my grayish greenish brown suit, matte black cap toe shoes, and LensCrafters specs. The building is your typical titans of industry monolith that burns old money in the two-hundred-year-old boiler. That reddish hue in the tap water is the blood of the Irish laborers that broke their backs to build the place.

I'm waiting in the marble and platinum lobby, making detailed mental notes about every aspect of the main building security system, when I notice the receptionist looking at me—over and over again. She looks the way you would expect a receptionist to look at an office run by old, pasty white men who count their money more often than Ebenezer Scrooge. Pretty but severe. Double Z's up top but with rail thin hips that just don't anatomically match. Christmas bonus? Despite my petty judgments, I am, after all, just a man, and she's checking me out, occasionally smoothing her dress or hair—preening like a tropical bird. Even though I would like to offer her the shagging I know she desperately wants, I don't like it when people are focused on me, especially when I'm in character on the first day of a gig.

But then she does me a big favor. She speaks. With a voice so annoying that dead men would rise up just to silence it. And I'm relieved, because that voice might as well be a can of ugly spray, emptying itself all over her.

"So . . ."

Sweet Jesus it's awful, like a cartoon child after a round of hormone treatments. I note that she's a smoker too with the witchy grit that rattles across her larynx.

" . . . You got into the internship program, huh?"

"Yes."

"Impressive."

"Thank you."

I need to throw her off the scent, so I do the rudest thing I can imagine in the company of an attractive woman vying for my attention—I pull out my phone. And I bury my face in its colorful screen, like a crow mesmerized by Christmas tinsel. You know that face. It's the social networking sneer you see on every app junkie getting a fix. It's one of the most loathsome cultural phenomena in contemporary society and I can see that she has gone from digging me to wanting to dig her nails into my eyeballs.

"You won't last a week."

No answer from me. This is the kind of conversation that could make me one *memorable* motherfucker.

"Toughest internship in the city. Impossible to get. Impossible to keep. I'm surprised they let a hick like you in. Where you from, Peoria?"

Actually, this is good. She is now underestimating me because she believes I am too timid to challenge her opinion. As long as I keep my mouth shut and smile, I will not make an impression on her. By the way, never smile and show your teeth. The pageant people have it wrong. Showing your teeth is *always* a sign of aggression. This is why Miss America is one of the most hated human beings on earth.

Ding. The elevator door opens and my savior, a wretched little swollen zit of a woman carrying an iPad, looks around for me over her reading glasses.

"John?"

"That's me."

"You're fifteen minutes late. Not good."

———

Rule #2: Just tell us who shot Mr. Lincoln.

First impressions are everything. How you look and what you say in the first moments of meeting someone will instantly tell them more about you than they would learn if they knew you for a lifetime. Sounds like bullshit, right? Love at first sight is not a romantic notion, it's an axiom based on the power of first impressions. This is why speed dating is the only dating that's worth a damn. A dog only has to sniff another dog's ass to know exactly where he stands. The point is that you have roughly sixty seconds to provoke affection, hatred, or indifference.

Indifference is what we interns are striving for. This is why I recommend speaking from what is called "the top down." It's an old journalism thing. The inverted pyramid. And it is the pinnacle—albeit an inverted pinnacle—of objectivity. The journalist top loads the story with the most important facts, so if you only read the first paragraph, you got it. This style is bereft of what they call "editorializing"—a phenomenon wherein the journalist feels that we give a fuck about his opinion and we have to listen to it the entire time he reports the story. Tune into Bill O'Reilly or Anderson Cooper and you'll see what I mean. Now download some old PBS NewsHour shows with Jim Lehrer. He does not offer opinions. He does not change his delivery the least bit, whether he's talking about a minor tick down in the market or full-blown ethnic cleansing. This makes the listener focus on the story and not the person delivering it. Ironically, this whole approach came about through assassination. When Lincoln was shot, the telegraph story about his death at the hands of Booth was the first scoop ever for Reuters. "AMERICA. ASSASSINATION OF PRESIDENT LINCOLN." A smoking gun of objectivity.

What this means to you is that you speak only when spoken to. You do not volunteer opinions, make casual observations, or crack jokes. All of these actions would make you a person that the brains around you would want to analyze. I'm not saying be a mute. When someone else cracks a joke, you smile but do not laugh. Your laugh may sound ridiculous and then you are "that guy or girl with the fucked-up laugh"—a memorable title.

When people offer opinions, you nod or let them know you're listening. In the end, they'll think you're shy—an innocent wallflower that they have no interest in pursuing. Do any of the kids on the playground even *look* at the shy kid sitting by himself in the sand? Hell no. And when you are asked for your opinion or even just asked a question, you answer like a telegraph journalist. Top-level facts, delivered in an even, relaxed, and emotionless tone. Once they get what they want, they will leave you alone. And the beauty of it is this: they will always remember that someone *else* gave them the information, someone they like. Our minds are not interested in truth. They are our private twenty-four-hour news cycle putting a constant spin on reality. It's like *The Matrix*. Everyone is plugged in to the Bullshit Express.

———

"You fucking maggots make me want to puke."

That's Hartman, the fifty-something office manager and wannabe drill sergeant in charge of the interns. He wants us to think he's some kind of ex-military hard case with his flattop and shiny black boots. I've seen Cub Scouts with more Oorah. Bob would eat him for breakfast, then eat his own guts, and then ask for seconds. This guy would soil his pants right now if I pulled my ankle piece. It's a tiny .22 caliber holdout special that looks like a toy, but Hartman would evacuate his bowels at the mere sight of it.

There are twenty-three well-scrubbed spawn of the white power elite, one Asian woman, and me standing in what Hartman calls "the Barracks." Basically, it's a small, dank-smelling cafeteria with soda machines and a dorm fridge and it's reserved for office plankton like us. Hartman strides around it like Patton.

"Twenty-five of you stand before me today—which is a world record for consecutive shit stains."

He walks along the wall we are all standing in front of like firing squad victims, inspecting the ranks.

"I see there's still no shortage of lazy white people in the world."

He stops at the Asian woman.

"Do you speak English?"

"Yes," she says, too afraid to be pissed off by the racist question.

"Good. Then you're already ahead of the curve."

"Yes, sir."

"Shut up. Here you speak when you are spoken to. You listen and take notes. No one cares about your opinion. No one cares what you think about anything. You are a fly on the wall, and if I hear you buzzing, I will swat you with yesterday's news."

He stops and looks at me, sizing me up. I look past him, not down like the others. Looking down means you are feigning subservience, and this guy knows we are all a bunch of egomaniacal assholes. So, I don't disrespect him by looking him in the eye and I don't call attention to myself by pretending to be afraid of him.

"Military?"

"No, sir."

He scowls. Whatever he thought was special about me just flew out the window. His contempt quickly turns to beautiful indifference. In his mind, I am already lower than the wad of gum full of cockroach eggs wedged next to his heel.

"Three of you will actually be interns at Bendini, Lambert and Locke when it's all said and done. The rest will be cleaned off my shoe by the African American gentleman with the shine box at the end of the block."

I'm fucked. Either Bob was unaware that intern boot camp was part of the program here or, more realistically, he knew about it and kept his mouth shut to get back at me for my "attitude." Either way, I'm in deep shit. I know a lot about the law, but these people are Ivy League law school graduates. They are probably smarter than most of the fucking associates already working at the firm. And ambitious? Forget about it. They would sell their parents to a zombie slaughterhouse if they thought it could get them a meeting with Mark Zuckerberg.

For a brief moment, I think about killing them one by one to get my own leg up. But even though HR, Inc. condones "collateral damage" if it ensures a kill, that is something I have worked hard to avoid over the years. How would you like to be going about your business, busting your ass to pay the bills and take your kids to Disney on Ice, and have some dick like me put a bullet in your head? Not cool. Not cool at all. So, I have to suck it up. And that's exactly what Bob will tell me later when I casually remark that the intel had not included information about me being a character in a Mike Judge remake of *Lord of the Flies*.

"You will each be randomly assigned to different departments. And you will work like you've never worked in your life. You will not sleep. You will barely eat. And don't be surprised if the gallons of rotgut coffee you drink make you piss blood for a week. I will weed out all nonhackers in my beloved intern corps. Do you understand me, maggots?"

"Yes, sir!" we all bellow.

"Good. Now get to work or I will eat your balls and shit out what family you have left. And if you don't have balls, you might as well start picking out your Starbucks apron."

After all of the good assignments are passed out, I get the "let's put the hick in the basement" assignment. If this were a first-person shooter, I'd be standing buck naked on level one with a ball-peen hammer to defend myself against cyborgs bristling with exotic weaponry. I have to find a way out of this shit detail as soon as humanly fucking possible if I'm going to have a shot at this.

Then light dawns on Marblehead and I remember my latest trip on the Bullshit Express the other night. Over stiff pours of Kentucky's finest paint thinner I met Alice, an intern who'd been working for the firm for nearly a year. She's pretty, ambitious (but not annoying), and, like my persona, she's a boot strapper street fighting her way out of middle-class mediocrity. I didn't think much of her as an asset at the time, but beggars can't be choosers, and I need to make a move.

7

THE RABBIT HOLE

As I sit in the records morgue, counting the number of massive black mold patches growing on the ceiling, I wait for a fish to bite on the little morsel of bait I sent up to the main office earlier via the mailroom. I paid a guy down there to send the aforementioned Alice a bogus case file request so that she would have to pay me a visit in the morgue. Which reminds me of one of the first rules I learned at HR.

Rule #3: Go postal.

The mailroom of any corporation is the center of the universe when it comes to access. It is the eye of the hurricane and the central nervous system, all rolled up into one dark, stinking, blue-collar slave ship. And the men and women that make up the flora and fauna of its bowels will do just about anything for a few bucks.

I used the mailroom to complete one of my first assignments. I was sent on what Bob likes to call "a bug fogger." Of course, you'll have your share of these as new fish. These are the lower paying, lower profile gigs that Bob likes to take in high volume. Over time, their cumulative pay is bread and butter, and they relieve Bob of the burden of having to think of ways to train you every day.

The reason they're called bug foggers is because they're like trying to kill a roach with a can of Raid. The targets are usually reclusive, due to their inability or unwillingness to hire proper security. So you can either blast the place to kingdom come (waste of time) or find a way to strategically fire a kill shot right into the thorax. It's an excellent aptitude test. If you are an impatient blaster, then you are far more likely to get exterminated yourself than if you wait for your prey to come nibble on your salacious piece of bait.

My assignment, whom I affectionately called "Rosebud," was the sole heir to a Serbian billionaire. He lived like Howard Hughes in the penthouse of a Midtown office building that looked like it had been built by the legions of hell. It was axle grease black, blazoned with imported Romanian gargoyles, and was rumored to be haunted by the three hundred–odd workers that were crushed and burned when the first fifteen floors collapsed during construction in the early 1920s.

I am not always privy to the "why" of every target, but Bob did mention in passing that the guy's family wanted him dead due to his "unsavory lifestyle." The rumor mill, also known as the *Post*, had printed a lot of far-fetched things about him being a serial killer, a cannibal, and even a vampire. They weren't far off. His father was an infamous Serbian war criminal, and Rosebud had been his right-hand man. These fuckers were Serbian military brass in the genocide of 1995 and managed to emigrate to the U.S. with an oil tanker full of cash. Daddy fancied himself a player in New York's Russian mob scene until they found him floating without a face in a bathtub full of rats. Brothers and sisters, you do not fuck with Russians. But Rosebud was just a coked-out shut-in. The whole thing stunk to me of an old money hostile takeover—most likely being perpetrated by someone else in the family who wanted his turn at the trough, now that Daddy was worm food.

But that is neither heir nor there. Back to the whole mailroom center-of-the-universe thing. Around the time of this assignment, some jagoff had "gone postal" and shot up a post office in Chelsea. The *Post* had printed the headline "DEAD LETTER," and that gave me an idea. The mailroom in this ancient pillar of greed was still employing the gas tube system of mail delivery. Mailroom jocks would stuff letters, and contraband, into the little plastic mail capsules, shove them into the humming, eager mouth of a long acrylic tube, and the capsule would be sucked off and spat out in some other part of the building. It just so happened that my target had his own tube, exclusive to his penthouse office. One person was assigned to it—a crusty old ex-cop with a huge gut and a mustache full of soup. That fat goldbricker fuck got paid to sit there all day and shove maybe two or three capsules into the penthouse tube.

Remember how I said mailroom workers will do anything for money? I paid one of the younger ones to dissolve a box of Ex-Lax in goldbricker's favorite beverage—hot cocoa with about a pint of dollar store whiskey. After three or four minutes, you could hear Sherman's march in his lower intestine. He tried to hold it as long as he could but eventually ran screaming to pay tribute to the nearest porcelain god. That was when I slipped Rosebud a mail tube containing what he thought was his afternoon snack—a gram of uncut cocaine. I found out that part of goldbricker's charm was his access to drugs, and Rosebud basically lived on a couple of eight balls a week.

My specially modified capsule had been outfitted with a small camera so I was able to see the gaunt, heavily bearded Rosebud cut fat rails of what looked like Bolivian marching powder but was actually a powder form of A-232, the most powerful military-grade nerve agent ever created. He snorted the lines like a sorority girl in Cancun and within seconds he was violently convulsing and hemorrhaging profusely out of every orifice while he thrashed through the stacks of filthy magazines and newspapers he had hoarded over the years. Predictably, the *Post* headline the next day read "POISON PEN PAL," and the Russian mob took the blame.

———

"I got a mailroom order requesting case files for . . . Oh shit."

Alice is standing outside my cube, looking at me like she might look at some foul insect. This is not the friendly reception I was expecting. As my first-class passenger on the Bullshit Express the other night, she suffered what was probably the only rejection she's ever experienced, and she still appears to be smarting from it. My bad. I overestimated the charm my playing slightly hard to get would have on her. And now she's in my dark forest of archive hell on a fool's errand.

"Hi, Alice."

I hand her a large stack of useless files.

"So *you're* the hick from Peoria everyone's talking about."

"That's me."

"Still white and uptight?"

She *is* feeling stung. That means she gives a shit, and I can work with that.

"I'm sorry about what happened at the bar. I hope you don't take it personally."

"Don't flatter yourself."

I laugh alone.

"I'm sure you weren't all that heartbroken," I attempt.

"Heartbroken, no. But I felt pretty sorry for you, missing out on my unorthodox, yet devastating sexual technique."

"Rain check?"

"We'll see, cowboy."

"You won't be turned off by the fact that I'm one of Hartman's new maggots?"

"Maybe I want to sleep my way to the bottom."

"You've come to the right place. How do you like my office? The decor is new-century dungeon."

"Pretty sweet. I've never seen him put a *live* human being down here. He must really like you."

"I'm special."

"Needs?"

Now we're both laughing.

"You should quit, you know?" She grins.

"Why?"

"The black mold down here is going to give you a brain tumor."

"Thanks for the pep talk. This is turning out to be an amazing first day."

She laughs. Even better.

"So have you made any headway in your vision quest to become a junior associate?" I ask. Women like to know that you remember things.

"I'll know soon. Word on the street is that it's down to me and another guy from my intern class."

"Let me guess, a white frat boy that went to Harvard?"

"Actually, he's a Yalie douche."

"Circle Jerk doesn't stand a chance."

"Why do you say that?"

"Your shoes. You could nail a man to the cross with those."

"Glad someone noticed," she says, softening a bit. "These fuckers cost more than my rent."

"They have 'hire me or I will firebomb this fucking place' written all over them."

Always compliment a woman's shoes or handbag. It makes you seem slightly metro, which translates to emotionally available. Also, it tells them that you aren't looking at their body (God forbid), which means you are not as much of a creep as they were automatically assuming you were by even talking to them in the first place. I prioritize shoe compliments over handbags because many women are self-conscious about their feet, and if you sound genuine, you'll score big points. She takes a seat to relax for a moment, always a good sign.

"I was serious about you getting the hell out of here. You're going to get lung cancer from the asbestos."

She removes a shoe and rubs her foot suggestively.

"Yeah, but I prefer that to getting career cancer from being immersed in complete irrelevance."

"There's no cure for that. Just slow, painful death."

"And a lot of terrible self-help books sent by concerned family members."

We laugh and she puts her shoe on, getting ready to leave. I need to make a move.

"Maybe you can get me on the upper floors so I can beg someone to make me their indentured servant."

"A favor? We barely know each other," she says as she looks around my completely blank cube.

"I know, but us maggots need to stick together. You never see just one of us hanging around a rotting corpse do you?"

She looks me in the eye and smiles. This is unexpected. It feels predatory. I look away, cursing myself. Then I look back and find her searching gaze still hanging in the haze of my cubicle.

"I work in Wills and Trusts. Bendini's turf. I guess I could order a bunch of bullshit files be exhumed from this pit of despair and delivered up there."

Sounds familiar, I think.

She smiles and the look grows more intense. I'm not sure if she wants to kiss me or eat me. At this point, I might be persuaded to accept either.

"That would give you some face time up in the big show. After that, it's up to you. Sound good, cowboy?"

We look at each other for a beat. I want so badly to go toe to toe with her, but that is light-years away from how my persona is supposed to be. I swallow a bitter pill of pride and stay in character.

"I would owe you big-time if you could pull that off," I gush.

"When I skin that Yalie douche, you can take me out to crush some beers and pull the wings off a few chickens."

"Deal. I know the best wing place in town."

"Hicks from Peoria always do."

With that, she walks away, ensuring I have a full view of her ass as she heads for the elevator. That went well. Not only did I rise above my drooling-hunchback-in-the-dungeon status, but I also made our meeting seem like a *chance encounter,* one of the most powerful aphrodisiacs known to man. Thanks to chick flicks, the concept of true love being orchestrated by the rough, construction worker hands of fate is an easy sell.

8

ACCESS

Later that afternoon, Alice throws me the bone I've been waiting for: access. It comes in the form of multiple file deliveries to the upper floors, giving me the chance to suck up to someone who might give me some real work. Sweet Alice. I wheel an ancient cart full of foul-smelling, oddly stained files to the higher floors and loiter my ass off for as long as possible. Then I see my opportunity. One of the senior associates is calling for his assistant to get him some coffee. Said assistant is in the break room, gossiping with the rest of the cake-fed cube farm heifers. I slip into his office, my hands pressed together like Hemingway's valet, bowing ever so slightly.

"Good morning, sir."

"Fuck you, Howdy Doody."

"Coffee?"

"You heard me say it. Should have just gotten it before you walked in here like a mental patient in your grayish brownish greenish fucking . . . what kind of a goddamned suit is that? Don't answer. I don't care. Just go. And kick my assistant in her fat ass on your way back."

"How do you take it?"

"Black. And it had better not taste like it's been scraped from the bottom of a crematorium oven."

I leave without a word. ALWAYS let them have the last word in every conversation. If you trail off with some useless acknowledgment, they will hate you for assuming they give a fuck about any word that comes out of your mouth other than *yes*.

———

Rule #4: Learn how to make the perfect cup of coffee.

This is the single most important part of your job as an intern. Go ahead, laugh. You can make copies and do runs until you're blue in the face and an exec will not give a shit. You make him the best goddamned cup of coffee he's ever had and he may not remember your name but he will make damn sure you are at his desk every morning for a repeat performance. That's repetitive exposure, which begets access and trust. Forty-four percent of my kills came from my superior coffee-making ability. It's simple, puts you in direct contact with the target, and it can be a vector for a variety of weapons. This opportunity presents itself more often than you think. Admins HATE making coffee, even though it's part of their job. That's because all of them are "just doing this job while they pursue a career in _____." Fill in the blank: actress, singer, porn star, reality show freak—same shit, different day job.

Example—Job #20. I was working an exec at a military satellite software company for months. He was in the heavily secured upper floors of a ninety-story office building. Every access point I put into the scenario was a dead end. Fucking guy went to the gym with armed security. Then I saw him standing in a long line outside Starbucks one morning with his goon detail. So I stepped up to talk to him, and one of his goons almost curbed me in the bus lane. I showed him my key card and told him to go to his desk, that I would handle this for him and that he shouldn't be drinking the monkey piss they serve at Starbucks anyway. The goons thought that was funny. The nerdy exec chilled out. Instant connection. Since this was a particularly difficult access scenario, I had to bring in the big guns, so to speak. So I brought him a cup of El Injerto from the Huehuetenango region of Guatemala—150 euros a pound and not available for purchase in this country. Ground the beans myself. (I keep an entire coffee service case in my cube at all times.) Served it with unpasteurized French cream and raw sugar cane lumps. Guy looked like he wanted to kiss me or be my bunk mate in a Turkish prison.

I brought him that same cup of coffee every day for three weeks and he waited for it like Lou Reed was waiting for his man. Anyway, he finally got tired of having to escort me into his office and gave me full access to the highly secure eighty-sixth floor. Access. Trust. Do you know how many people would love to waterboard this guy to get their hands on his fucking BlackBerry? But he lets some intern, whose name he could NEVER remember, have unescorted access to the floor? Keys to the kingdom. And don't think for a minute that his being on the *eighty-sixth* floor was lost on me.

Three days later, I made him a special cup. Mixed in a little isopropyl nitrate and laced the sugar lumps with a catalyst I'd rather keep to myself. You can't have all my secrets, grasshopper. Per the routine, I brought him the coffee; he dropped in the lumps, etc. But while he mixed it, I pulled on the Kevlar poncho I had stuffed in my file cart and took cover behind the fire door in the hallway. I didn't get to see his face as the coffee solidified and released a concentrated hydrogen gas that blew him and his office back to the days of disco, but I'm sure he was surprised. I'd make a joke about strong coffee, but you know how Bob feels about my jokes.

Why would I blow him up, you might ask? Doesn't seem very subtle, but it's all about the profile. This guy is essentially an arms dealer, so his enemies are fond of bombs, specifically exotic explosive devices. Feds will assume they planted a device, which will appear to be very sophisticated and worthy of his enemies' time, money, and expertise. Ballistics will never find fragments of my cup—a hardened polymer that dissolves into the same type of melted plastic you find from a variety of objects at ANY fire investigation. So the end result is a crime scene that points a smoking gun at a very specific class of perps.

Unfortunately the explosion didn't take out his security detail, and those guys were tough as nails. Within a few seconds of the blast, they stumbled into the hallway, ears bleeding, and opened up on me with two TEC-9 submachine guns. The Kevlar poncho saved my ass, but it felt like I was inside a laundry bag getting beat up by a bunch of gorillas with sledgehammers. They emptied their clips and bounced me down the hallway until I smashed through a quarter-inch glass conference room window. I'll never forget the looks on the faces of the poor bastards cowering under the conference table as I pulled a flash grenade from my suit jacket pocket and chucked it into the room. It's a nonlethal stun grenade that uses a bright flash of light and a loud bang to knock anyone within ten feet of it unconscious. I dove back into the hallway as it detonated. Meeting adjourned.

I had to go through all of this rigmarole because no one could know that I was ever there. Bob's instructions were very specific: target eliminated with a covertly planted device so that the identity of the bomber would only be a matter of speculation. So I was not in a position to get into a gun battle with the security guys, who were now reloading in the hallway. I knew I had to make a move before they got those second clips in, so I whipped out The Pig. It's a little invention of mine, kind of like a Taser, but instead of using wires to deliver a high-voltage shock, it uses barbed darts and thin surgical tubing to pump drugs, poisons, and other nefarious liquids into the target. I can dial up all kinds of exotic, untraceable cocktails with The Pig. I just need to get close enough to deploy it. And since these guys were fifteen feet down the hall . . .

I took off at a full sprint. The first one chucked his TEC and went for the Beretta on his hip. Dumb. By the time he had it out, I was fully airborne, smashing my size twelve, nondescript, brown wing tip directly into his chest. As he went down, I deployed The Pig into his armpit. Side note: forget the neck, Dexter. The medical examiner will see that a mile away. ALWAYS choose a hairy injection point. You could jab a horse needle in there and lazy-ass autopsy drones will never go bushwhacking for clues. He's out before he hits the floor, but his buddy now has the TEC locked and ready to rip right in my face. I bench-press his buddy into him just in time for him to pull the trigger. The barrel is buried in the guy's ass, causing the blowback to reverse in the chamber. The TEC-9 explodes in his face, and he goes down.

Now I had a mess to tend to and I had about thirty seconds before the fire crews would come crashing into the hallway. I bagged both TEC-9s in my Kevlar poncho and quickly removed the shrapnel from the security guys' faces. Then I dragged them both into the target's burning office so they would get good and charred and fit right into the scenario. Scooping up the shell casings was a major pain in the ass but I bagged them all, got into the stairwell, and jumped through the door on the floor below just before the fire crew went stomping past.

Yes, that is a lot of extra work *after* the target is already dead, but remember that we don't just whack people pell-mell and drop our guns at the scene like you see in some of the shittier movies about our profession. It's all about finesse and keeping the politics under control. Next day, the *New York Times* reported a terrorist bombing. That's when the job is truly complete, when the paper of record prints your target's epitaph on the front page and shovels coal into the formidable engines of the Bullshit Express.

Back to Bendini, Lambert & Locke and asshole lawyer guy. I didn't have the time to whip up as good a concoction for him. First off, El Injerto is no longer available, due to rebel activity in that region. You can get it black market, but it's up to 1,500 euros a pound, and that kind of price gouging is reserved for rappers who think eating contraband whale at a sushi restaurant is cool. I have a backup pound of Diablo Gold Coast from Colombia—Juan Valdez, baby.

Not only is this an amazing coffee, but it's also inexpensive. Only twenty-two bucks a pound. Yeah, I know you can buy a pound of that free-trade Starbucks dreck for eight bucks a pop, but you might as well brew up a pile of hobo whiskers and call it a day.

So, I grind up the Diablo, pour some boiling Fiji water into a French press, and brew it black and strong. It's inky and oily and *smells* like the victors of the Spanish American war *looked*. He takes one sip and raises an eyebrow. Now, some people say they like black coffee because they think it makes them manly, like saying you like cigars, even though they taste like rolled turds, no matter how expensive they are. But this guy is a true connoisseur of black coffee. Thank God, because if he hadn't been, he might have been coughing up blood by now. He takes another sip, like a lion sucking marrow from the leg of a twitching gazelle.

"Intern maggot?"

"Yes, sir."

"If you are not at my desk at oh-seven hundred every single fucking day of the week with this coffee, I will personally see to it that the only job you ever get in the state of New York is the monkey shit shovel boy at the Bronx Zoo. Is that perfectly clear?"

"Yes, sir."

"What's your name?"

"John."

"See you tomorrow, James."

That afternoon, the admin who brought me up to the Barracks comes to tell me I'm being assigned to a different department—asshole lawyer's department: Wills and Trusts. When I ask her if this means I can move out of my dank ass dungeon office, she just laughs and tells me not to push my dumb luck.

If you've ever wondered why death is so fucking complicated—not for the dead guy but for the family he left behind—it is because even the most expensive law firms love to charge exorbitant fees to handle their Wills and Trusts but hate to do the actual work. They know that when you are dead, you aren't going to do shit to them and neither is your blubbering, grief-stricken family. So they don't care about fucking things up royally. My assignment was to update as many wills and trust documents as possible, based on the reams of legal addendum notes that someone bothered to type up after client meetings but never bothered to actually execute in the Wills and Trusts. You wouldn't believe how many of the beneficiaries in these older wills were people who were already deceased. That'd be a kicker at the reading, right? Welcome to probate hell. Your golden goose just took it in the ass.

I gather up a truckload of the ancient file boxes that have been left to rot, sneak them out through the service entrance in a laundry cart, and take them back to HR, Inc. Now, with this type of shit, Bob is a fucking rock star. He has a team all ready for me, and these guys work 'round the clock popping dexies as they tackle the mind-numbing task of updating these documents. Bob may not be the best with providing intel—and never forget that is by choice—but he sure as hell is the king of field support. And with the paper-pushing cage match they had going over at the firm, I needed it more than with any other gig.

Needless to say, when I show up thirty-six hours later with no fewer than two hundred files updated and looking tip-top, I make an impression on Hartman *and* asshole lawyer guy. Normally, I am not into making impressions, but this gig, and probably my life, depend on me winning one of the three slots. So, through the weekend and over the next few days, I keep impressing them with the work. Hundreds of delinquent files that had been collecting dust and roach wings are now viable, and the partners can bill for the work! I am making them some money now, and with their base rate of $750/hour, I am making them *a lot of fucking money*.

9

THE KEYS TO THE KINGDOM

I am sitting in my cube, admiring the work Bob and his crack team have done for me that day, when none other than Bendini, one of the partners, walks up with asshole lawyer guy. Of course, asshole lawyer guy is playing the part of congenial business guy so that he can suck up to his boss. Bendini ignores him and gently places his hand on my shoulder. He is probably in his early sixties and looks like what I always imagined Geppetto, Pinocchio's puppet maker "father," had looked like. He is thin and fit, but his skin has some serious city miles on it. He wears a thick, old-timey mustache that is always in need of a trim. His watery blue eyes are shockingly kind, and I find myself depressed that I never had a real grandfather. This is the way he is looking at me, like a benevolent grandfather. He offers his hand. I stand and shake it.

"What's your name, son?"

"John."

"My son's name is John."

Fuck. Memory hook.

"It's a good name."

You can hear asshole lawyer guy's eyes rolling a mile away.

"John, I'm having a hard time believing you're just an intern."

Double fuck. I know he doesn't know why I'm there, but he's complimenting me the way you compliment someone you believe is an undiscovered talent or star.

"I enjoy working here."

"Well, you are doing a standout job. We've billed into six figures since you've been in Wills and Trusts."

These guys love money more than their own children.

"My father was in Wills and Trusts."

"He must have been a force to be reckoned with in your . . . hometown."

Hometown was well seasoned with snooty condescension. I'm not from the actual hometown he was referring to, but I felt offended and then congratulated myself for owning it.

"Thank you for saying so."

"I came over to congratulate you on securing one of our three intern positions."

Yes. Hell yes. There are three days left in the competition and I am already in. This will put me on many shit lists and radar screens, but FUCK IT, this is my last gig. They are never going to see me again. Now more than ever I am tempted to try to have a little bit of fun on this assignment, even though I know that's a bad idea. You can't assign fun to the murder of another human being. It just doesn't work that way. I am telling you this because I don't want you to ever get cocky. Ego is your worst enemy, and people will stroke it when you blow them away with your work ethic. But you have to let it go because it can start to cloud your judgment.

"Thank you, sir. I'm honored."

"You're welcome. A man of few words. Good."

I just smile. I would be an idiot to speak after what he just said.

"I'll see you around the floor."

They both walk off, asshole lawyer yipping in Bendini's ear like an annoying lapdog. Bendini looks back at me as they walk. It's the look of a man who just found a diamond in the rough.

10

TURNING TRICKS FOR THE GOLDEN TICKET

After turning in my four hundreth viable file, Alice walks into my cube. She makes herself comfortable on my small desk, which improves my entire cube decor exponentially.

"Well, this is certainly an improvement on your previous assignment."

"I've been looking for you."

"Really?"

"Yeah, I believe I owe you some beers and wings, counselor."

She just got the associate position, beating out the Yalie douche. Now she'll have infinitely more access than she did as an intern.

"Damn right you do. But we'll have plenty of time for that, now that we're working together."

"Excuse me?"

"That's right. Evidently you've raised more than a few eyebrows around here with your hard work *and* new revenue stream."

"And you're here to make sure I don't fuck it up."

"No. I'm just here to help you turn over more volume. Greed is an insatiable mistress. Plus, I've been working for Bendini for most of my internship, and he thinks we'd make a great team."

"Is that so?"

"Of course, you'll still have to work in this Roach Motel, and I'll have a cool junior associate's office. Oh, and I'll kind of be your boss slash slave driver. Technically."

"I wouldn't have it any other way."

"Good answer."

This is working out better than I expected.

As we begin work going through a fresh batch of files, I can't believe my luck. I need intel and access, and Alice is my golden ticket. She is one of Bendini's favorites, so I can use her to move closer to the center of his circle and eventually get a closer look at *all* of the partners. The only problem is, it's all I can do to keep from constantly looking at *her*. This is dangerous territory. Alice is pretty, but pretty I can handle. It's the raw sexuality that, like some exotic oil, seeps out of the invisible cracks in her conventionally beautiful facade that worries me. Oh, and let's not forget that she is brilliant, interesting, and has the kind of dark, twisted sense of humor I like. I just have to work through it. Sleeping with office colleagues tends to make you a D-list watercooler celebrity. Suddenly all of your co-workers become that hair-plugged creep and his merry band of star fuckers on TMZ, making cracks about your office love affair over caramel macchiatos.

———

Rule #5: Don't shit where you eat.

Bob has a saying about office romances: "If you fuck their brains out, you might as well blow their brains out." To this day, I can't prove it, but I'm sure Bob whacked a girl I was seeing on Job #17—"Eva." She had nothing whatsoever to do with my assignment. She did work in the same office, but in a separate division twenty-eight floors above where I was working. And we never even saw each other at work, so it wasn't like our little tryst was an egregious security breach. I met her at a coffee shop down the street—a rare gem that served real Turkish coffee. It wasn't until after our second date that we even realized we worked in the same building. But Bob found out about it because his mission in life is to crawl up your ass and watch your every move in an effort to, as he says, "minimize human error." I think he does it to live vicariously through us, because he sold his youth to some cigar-chewing war dog on Parris Island.

Basically, like Bob, you are not allowed to be human. And dealing with Bob's controlling bullshit is, without question, the most difficult part of this job. I would rather shoot my way out of a pitch-dark subbasement with one exit and a pellet gun than have to deal with that anymore. I remember the conversation we had about Eva. He said he was concerned that I was "distracted." I reminded him of the sixteen flawless assignments preceding that one. He said I was getting cocky. I reminded him that I was twenty years old and needed something other than my AR-15 to cuddle at night. He said, "Get a pro, like everyone else." And he handed me a slip of paper with a phone number.

That was the last time we spoke about Eva. He had not told me flat out to stop seeing her, so I did the stupid thing and ignored what I now understand was a warning. Two weeks later, after the assignment was finished, I tried to call her several times. Eventually I went to her apartment. The smell hit me when I walked up to her door. I know that smell. It's sweet and sickening. A bottle fly—a huge, lazy black sucker that will travel hundreds of miles to dine exclusively on rotting flesh—buzzed past my ear and crawled under the door.

I stared at that door for a long time, imagining what Eva looked like in there, bloated with her face twisted in some final expression of agony and terror. And I thought long and hard about killing Bob. But when I walked out into the street, I felt like I was surrounded by buildings that seemed to be closing in on me, mocking me with their power, reminding me that they could crush me like an ant. At that moment I realized how insignificant I was, how utterly vulnerable and exposed. I would never kill Bob, but he had the power to erase me and what little identity or existence I had managed to carve out after all these years.

So I called the number on the slip of paper.

I know what you're thinking. Sex with prostitutes is not only disgusting, but it's a sign of failure, an overt confession that you no longer have the sand to attract even the most desperate of potential mates. And you're right. But not in the way you think. The truth is that when your whole world is already a total fabrication and you're a liar to everyone you meet, intimacy with an emotional cripple who has no feeling from the waist down is a primordial kick in the nuts. Fucking for real gives you hope that you can love someone, or be loved, on any level. Faking it will empty you like a gutted fish. As soon as I learned this, I burned the slip of paper.

The truth is that I am a killer. What I do is evil. And the fact that I brought a normal person into my carnival of madness is unforgivable. If I could apologize to Eva, I would. I can blame Bob all I want, but I am the one who opened that door. And by doing so, I killed her.

———

Rule #6: Don't kid yourself.

I see assassins in movies all the time saying the people they kill have it coming. That's Hollywood's way of attempting to make people like us "relatable" and "sympathetic." Look at *Grosse Pointe Blank*. John Cusack actually says that to Minnie Driver.

"If I show up at your door, chances are you did something to bring me there."

That may be true and it often is. Look at the partner I am trying to zero in on at Bendini, Lambert & Locke. He is selling out the names of people who, for better or worse, are helping the police bring in people even more evil than me—people who truly erode the foundation of society and destroy every form of innocence. Without question, that fucker has it coming. Problem is, God almighty is not going to strike him down with a lightning bolt. Unlike Job—who never did a damn thing wrong—this guy will not be attacked by a swarm of flesh-eating locusts on Central Park South. I will take his life, most likely in a brutal way that will damage me further and damage the people who have to clean up the mess. There is nothing good or noble or even cool about that. We are not antiheroes with a silver lining. And we are sure as hell not relatable or sympathetic.

So don't kid yourself. If you're going to do this, you can't ever try to justify it. You are the bad guy, and that is your role. Without you, there is no benchmark for judging good guys. We are the yin. Civilians are the yang. If you keep your role pure and undiluted by everyone else's reality, then you will survive to the ripe old retirement age of twenty-five. Don't ever forget that purity might save you from a bullet, but it won't save your soul. Only a lightning strike can do that.

———

I spend the next week and a half working closely with Alice, gathering what intel I can. She is fairly liberal with office gossip but seems oddly cautious about revealing anything business-related. I am convinced it's because she is threatened by me and wants to protect the associate job she just landed. So I decide to try to work the gossip angle, goading her to let me in on her secrets, convincing her that I give a shit. However, since we are fairly busy at work, and there are eyes and ears everywhere, I'm just not getting anywhere at the office.

Because Alice has been somewhat persistent about seeing me socially, I decide to agree to have a drink with her and try to work something from that angle. If I get her juiced up, maybe she'll open up more or even take me back to her place where I can more easily have access to her laptop. Due to the aforementioned issues in my past, I decide to run this by Bob first.

"Do what you have to do, John," Bob says impatiently. "We need movement. The Feds lost three more witnesses last week."

"Are *they* the client, Bob?"

"You know I don't discuss clients with operators. But I will say that this client is especially annoyed by delays. Hence my sense of urgency."

"Of course."

"Work the girl. She sounds promising."

"When you say work the girl . . ."

"I mean whatever means necessary, John. You say she wants to see you socially. Do it. If she wants to fuck you, do it so well you get asked to do it again."

"But you've always said . . ."

"Maybe you're not hearing me, John. By any means necessary. Do we understand each other?"

"Yes, Bob."

"And get a surveillance package going on her. I shouldn't have to tell you that at this point in your career."

"Roger that."

On Friday morning, I see Alice and tell her I'd like to grab a drink with her. She is excited, and her excitement gives me an all too familiar feeling that I need to shake. From time to time, you are going to develop an affinity for an asset. That's natural. You just need to constantly remind yourself that business is business and those types of feelings have no place in *this* particular business.

11

MR. GOODY TWO-SHOES IS AN ASSHOLE

After work, I wait to meet Alice outside a bar in the East Village. I'm assuming she wants to drink in hipster paradise because chances are nil that she will run into anyone from the office. The bar is one of those downstairs speakeasy-type places where it always feels like it's three in the morning. As I wait for her among the tattooed bike messengers and website designers talking about sustainable farming and tantric sex, I think to myself that Alice is a woman with diverse interests and tastes. Normally, this would be a major turn-on for me. In this case, however, it makes her unpredictable, so I tell myself that I should approach this evening with the same caution and respect shown by a snake charmer removing the lid on his basket. I will let her be in control. And even though Bob has given me carte blanche to take one for the team, I am going to call that Plan Z. I don't need any more distractions, albeit highly pleasurable ones, standing in the way of my objective. Since I can't allow myself to lose my edge to booze, I take a truckload of dopamine stimulants and speed. As long as I don't keel over from an aneurism, this will keep me razor sharp.

When Alice arrives, a few things become crystal clear. Number one: she is really into me because she's changed into a tight-fitting dress that would never fly at Bendini. Number two: she must live nearby, because there is no other way she would have had time to change. And number three: judging by the trail nod she just gave the bartender, she is no stranger to this particular saloon. So I am in for it tonight. Her normal sexiness has been ratcheted up several notches from smoldering to inferno and her bed is probably a short stumble down the street.

"Let's do a shot!" This is the first thing she says when she sits down.

"Nice to see you too."

She has that look in her eye. The gunfighter's squint. She is already thinking several steps ahead. I have noticed that when women decide they're going to sleep with someone, their whole demeanor changes. It is as if they feel they can relax, let go, and reveal whatever they want about themselves—no matter how upsetting it might be to their male counterpart—because they know that men drool and shake like starved wild dogs at the mere scent of potential sex and all will be forgotten when the clothes come off. But even though she is exhibiting the same bravado that tends to infect men when they are about to get laid, her desire to drink heavily betrays her vulnerability. She needs liquid courage. Now I am really in trouble because I know that her feelings for me are genuine. If they weren't, then we would already be back at her place.

"Maybe we should start with a beer." Just call me Buzz Kill.

"Waiter!" She is not acknowledging my resistance.

The waiter, looking very put out, walks up.

"Can I help you?"

"Do you have Don Julio Añejo?" She winks at me.

"Yes."

"Please bring Mr. Goody Two-shoes and I a shot each with beer backs."

"Okay."

He shuffles away. At least I have his terminal laziness on my side.

"Tequila?" I raise an eyebrow.

"Mexican Scotch." She smiles.

"Well, at least it's not Jäger," I joke.

"Lord no. You would not like me on Jäger," she says dramatically.

"Why is that?"

"Because I can't keep my clothes on."

"Waiter!" I yell.

We both laugh, but I'm thinking the faster I can get her wasted, the easier it will be to snoop her apartment while she sleeps it off.

"You're funny. Seriously, I would do a striptease on the bar."

The waiter comes back, fully annoyed now.

"Yes?"

"Two shots of Jägermeister," I say.

"So, cancel the Tequila?" he drones.

"Absolutely not. We can handle both," Alice blurts.

The waiter smiles sarcastically and walks away.

"He thinks we're tourists." I laugh.

"So you're basically saying you want to see me naked," she says, her voice like a purr.

"No, I want to see you do a striptease on the bar. Put it on You-Tube. Get a movie deal. That's all it takes these days anyway."

"With what I'm wearing under this dress, you'd get a million hits in the first hour."

"Now that's all I'm thinking about."

"Why do you think I said it, dummy?"

She puts on lipstick. Strong move.

The waiter breaks the awkward silence by making it back to the table much faster than I expected. He silently drops the shots and beers and shuffles away.

She raises both shot glasses.

"To interns."

"I'm not drinking to that."

"Okay, let's drink to you seeing me naked."

"You're killing me."

We drink. She hits them both at the same time. Tequila *and* Jäger. Fucking awful.

"Congrats again on the promotion. How is the Yalie douche handling it?"

"He was passed out drunk in his Jag. Totally devastated."

"He's probably never lost at anything."

"I'm sure it doesn't help that I'm a chick. His dad's going to give him fifty swats with a dirty old fraternity paddle."

"His dad is a big CEO. This is going to be very embarrassing."

"It will be on the bee-stung lips of every skin job in Rye."

"Proud of you, Alice. You deserve it."

"Thank you, good sir. You haven't done too shabby yourself. You took out those other intern plebes like a trained assassin."

I laugh, mostly about how I was literally considering killing them all to get the intern spot.

"Yeah, well none of those tools know how to work. They think they're going to just get it all handed to them, like everything else. Money and privilege cuts their balls off. Makes them passive," I spit, realizing those fuckers genuinely put a bad taste in my mouth.

"Go on. You're on a roll," she says, enjoying my working-class tirade.

"They're like male lions. Great-looking. Always getting the best-dressed award at the kill. But they rarely kill anything themselves. Lioness does most of the killing."

"Duh. Men are ALWAYS taking credit for the brilliant shit women do. Even in the jungle. It's bullshit."

"Not me. I'm like the jackal. I fight for every scrap, like it's my last."

"If I were to kiss you right now, would it taste like blood?"

"Alice. We work together. Hasn't anyone ever told you not to shit where you—"

She kisses me. It tastes like brown sugar and sex. I'm fucked.

"I live nearby," she coaxes.

"Of course you do."

"I have an Xbox."

"Enticing."

"And cats."

"Stop it. I'm going crazy with lust."

I agree to go home with her. This makes her very happy but she orders another round of courage for good measure. I could use a strong drink myself. The tequila has latched onto the speed in my head, and they are crashing around my psyche like Tom and Jerry. So we drink some more. And the verbal foreplay flows like a full-bodied Barolo—darkly playful and mind-numbingly strong. By the time we are ready to leave, my arms are full of tiny red crescent moons where she's been digging her nails into my skin every time she wants to make a point and, in my estimation, hold on to this moment for dear life.

I know what you're thinking. The whole idea of James Bond pumping Pussy Galore for information is as much bullshit as the name Pussy Galore. If anything, a woman is more likely to lie to you the more she is invested in trying to land you as a boyfriend, spouse, sugar daddy, or whatever. Plus, the LAST thing a woman wants to talk about while basking in the caramel-colored light of multiple orgasms is work.

"Was it as good for you as it was for me? Light me a cigarette and oh, out of curiosity, what are the Russian missile launch codes?"

The good thing is that I'm not planning to ask her anything about work. Since she's had time to go home, she undoubtedly took her laptop with her to do work over the weekend (she never stops), and it's just sitting there, waiting to tell me what I want to know.

When we get to her place and she starts to undress me the moment the front door closes, what I thought was a steely resolve begins to quickly disintegrate. After several minutes of deep-sea tongue exploration and rough trade groping, I am saved by the bell when she excuses herself to go to the bathroom to do whatever women do in the bathroom when they know they are about to have sex. Like Robert Johnson, I am now standing at a crossroads with the devil on one side and desolation on the other. Not only do I want to close this proverbial deal with Alice, but also I can feel that part of me actually needs this. This is a rare opportunity to mix business with pleasure, and to deny it goes against every fiber of my being. For a split second, I decide to give in to the dark side and go for it. Then I hear the water running in the bathroom, and the sound reminds me of when I couldn't stop washing my hands after my first kill. That's when I remember I already made my deal with the devil.

So I move quickly to the kitchen to fix us a drink. I pour her a vodka martini with an Ambien chaser. She comes out of the bathroom, downs it, and proceeds to devour me like a female mantis. But she's snoring before I can finish undoing her impossibly complicated bra fastener. I can disassemble, clean, reassemble, and load an MP9 Tactical Machine Pistol in total darkness in about twenty-seven seconds. I have never once successfully unfastened any woman's bra.

While she dozes, I go to work snooping her place. I find her laptop in her workbag and fire it up. The password screen appears, and I slip my thumb drive into the USB port. I have some password hack programs that I bought from Russian gangbangers for a king's ransom, and they are pretty damned effective. However, Alice's laptop has an unusual amount of security encryption protecting her log-in screen, even for an attorney. After three and a half hours of hammering her system, I'm still not in. I'm beginning to get a bit anxious because I have only about an hour left on the Ambien I gave her.

While I wait, I move to Plan B and install a small, wireless transmitter on her laptop motherboard. This device will track every data event that happens on her laptop through her processor. The transmitter is virtually impossible to detect, unless someone knows exactly what to look for. The only problem is it sends me a raw data dump that takes time to sift through. But this proves to be a sound move, because my encryption breakers are still not into her hard drive when I hear her stir. I quickly shut down her laptop and put it back in her bag.

"Did I pass out?" She is groggy, trying to focus.

"Yep."

"Did we . . . ?"

"Of course not."

"Such a gentleman. Wow, my head feels like it's going to explode."

"I guess Tequila and Jäger might be a good recipe for an incendiary device."

She laughs, then holds her head in agony. I might have overdone it with the Ambien. My bad.

"Look at me. I'm a real classy date."

"I had fun."

"Me too. The parts when I was conscious anyway. What time is it?"

"About three-thirty."

"Holy shit. Do you mind if we have hot sex another time? I think I might need to barf in the not so distant future, and I don't know you well enough to ask you to hold my hair back."

"Rain check."

She kisses me and I am on my merry way.

12

THE MOTHERFUCKER

After leaving Alice's place, I go home and take a very cold shower—yes it does work—and drift off to sleep, kicking myself for squandering a free pass to knock boots with a woman whose beauty and intellect are matched by what I am guessing is a profoundly depraved sexual appetite. But I feel better about it the next morning when I open a packet of data downloaded from my transmitter. I'm in luck. It looks like Alice answered a few e-mails after I left. I pour myself some coffee and click on a message in her in-box. An encrypted e-mail program begins to load. Then I see the logo in the upper right-hand corner of the screen:

Motherfucker.

- Special Agent. Organized Crime Unit.

Motherfucker!

- Cover name: Alice

Cheeky little monkey. Alice is just about the best cover name there is, if you're into that whole literary thing. And if you're into the whole rap thing, you could say *playa been played.* In addition to operating under my nose without a scent, she's been assigned to Bendini, Lambert & Locke to find out which partner has been selling witness protection names to the street. After being there more than a year, she has a suspect: Bendini.

Invariably, every job throws you a curveball. Sometimes, like this one, it doesn't break and hits you square in the jaw. I like to call it The Motherfucker. And you learn to take it on the chin, so much so that when you *don't* take it on the chin, you get very superstitious. Everyone knows that this work attracts bad luck like flies on shit. Bad luck likes the taste of your blood, sweat, and failure. It's the universe telling you, "Hey, asshole, I see what you're doing. And if you think I'm going to make things easy for you, think again." It comes with the territory, so put a six-pack on ice for The Motherfucker because you're going to become BFFs. And now it's time for me to suffer one of the biggest Motherfuckers of my career: Alice, the curveball.

It's not a curveball because Alice is a fed and I didn't know about it. Undercover people are undercover for a reason—because they're good at it. I'm not psychic. I may have eyes in the back of my head, but they don't have X-ray vision. All of the bullshit TV shows and movies that portray people like us as omniscient are written by gutless nerds who never even got into a grade school scrap. I don't care how long you're out here on the razor's edge, sooner or later you're going to get cut, and there isn't a damn thing you can do about it. So the revelation that Alice is a junior G-man is only part of what makes this a Motherfucker.

The fact that she is pursuing the same case as me, for different reasons, obviously pushes the Motherfucker needle into the red. What blows the cylinders is her pursuit of a social relationship with me. This is a Motherfucker because I am staring at the abyss of questions that is Alice, and it's impossible to tell just how deep the rabbit hole goes.

I get paid to be paranoid, so of course I'm into triple golden time with Alice now. Bob has mentioned to me from time to time that he suspected the FBI might have infiltrated our ranks. Since this is my last job, of course I have to suck on that thought now. Thanks, Bob! Fuck it. I have to keep my head clear. Alice is here because, like me, she's the best at what she does. Which makes sense because this Bendini thing is a big fucking deal. Of course the feds are involved. Selling names on a witness protection list is like bailing out banks *and* paying a record bonus to the fucking executives that made the banks fail. These are the kinds of crimes that make careers. And think about it from the FBI perspective. Word gets out that snitches ain't safe and you can say good-bye to snitches forever. What would a bunch of dudes in wing tips with fifty-year-old haircuts do without snitches? Those guys couldn't blend into a JCPenney long enough to take down a ring of mattress tag cutters.

So they're bringing out the big guns. Rightfully so. They needed to take a page out of the CIA comic book and whisker themselves up a proper mole. And here she is—an eating, drinking, fucking chameleon who's going to burrow into the oak paneling of Bendini, Lambert & Locke until she brings the house down. And she has the hots for me, the guy looking to blow the house up.

The question is, what the fuck am I going to do about it?

The first step in dealing with The Motherfucker is to find a quiet place to allow your well-hung brain to operate on the problem. My brain, as usual, is a kung fu movie with two rival styles beating the shit out of each other in a long, bloody turf war: my style and Bob's style. Bob would say kill her. Get her out of the way. She could potentially blow up the entire assignment and maybe even HR, Inc. If you're a reactionary control freak who used to suck up to meathead drill instructors by bouncing quarters off your bed, then that kind of dull-edged, superficial thinking is the tits.

But if you're a predator, that kind of thinking is 100 percent counterproductive. First of all, she just became an even bigger asset than she was before. Not only is she going to be one of Bendini's associates—giving her the kind of access I could have never gotten no matter how many dicks I sucked in Wills and Trusts—let's not forget she is also *investigating* him with all the resources of the U.S. government behind her. She's going to gather intel on him so fast it will make my head spin. She's like a cheat in an RPG that jumps you ten levels of play. She's a fucking Easter egg. I get closer to her; she gets me closer to Bendini. Fast track. She's going to open doors for me, and if it turns out Bendini really is our guy, I'm going to slam his head in one of them.

My plan becomes twofold. First, I need to know everything she knows and when she knows it. Like Bob suggested, I need to set up a 24/7 revolving tail with wiretaps and a total infestation of surveillance bugs. But since having Bob find out that Alice is a federal agent will sort of butt fuck my plan before it ever gets off the ground, I have to lie to him about Alice's importance in the game and scramble the surveillance on my own.

Second, it's time to break Rule #5: Don't shit where you eat. I need to get as close as I can to Alice. Access. Trust. It's not just about having sex and sharing a toothbrush. Believe me, you will be trained in the art of doing the nasty, and it will become one of your greatest assets in the field. When people get addicted to fucking, it's like any other addiction. Their IQ goes down a few notches. They should just call it "having stupid" because that is what it makes you.

But we're talking about a seasoned federal agent on a deep-cover assignment. Love is the only thing that will truly inspire trust and deliver the access I need. Even federal agents become blind as bats when it comes to love. It's primordial, and people pursue it with greater fervor than even basic sustenance. When they are deep in it, even the most intelligent, vigilant people get careless. If I'm going to pull this off, I need to get Alice's guard down by starting a real romance with her. Or at least what seems like one.

This is not going to be easy—mainly because I'm potentially dealing with two separate women here. There is Alice, the cover name character invented by the FBI. Then there is the FBI agent *playing the part* of Alice in her deep-cover assignment. That person could be anyone. Sound familiar? Am I in any way similar to my cover persona? The bottom line is that we're both driving the Bullshit Express, and I'm wondering how far we can go before we run off the rails.

The only way to ensure success is to deploy the one thing that just about every woman wants: romance. Sure, Alice is working deep cover on the biggest case of her life with ramifications that could shake society to its very foundations. But that doesn't mean a girl has to stop putting meat in the bear trap to bag her soul mate, does it? Romance, versus casual sex, is the only reason Alice would endeavor to shit where *she* eats. Problem is, to say I am capable of romance is like saying the spider is capable of spending a weekend in Cabo with the fly and enjoying a couple's massage. I have no love in me. I don't know what it is because it has *never* been given to me in any way, so I literally have to invent that emotion within myself. I'm sure you can relate, as we are all at a distinct disadvantage when it comes to weaponizing romance.

This is where film literacy comes in, boys and girls. Remember what I said before about using movie characters (not Tom Cruise) to model behavior and help you better assimilate yourself into normal society? Everything you ever wanted to know about how to feign love and manipulate an asset is just a download away. I recommend you ease your way into it with the following movies, which are like the Cliffs Notes of the genre: *When Harry Met Sally, Sleepless in*

Seattle, Pretty Woman, Eternal Sunshine of the Spotless Mind (okay, that one's for me). They will tell you everything you need to know. If you are a guy, you have to embrace all things that go against your nature: thoughtfulness, sentimentality, caring, listening, and purchasing expensive gifts. If you are a girl, you have to embrace all things that come naturally to you: emotional cannibalism, psychological manipulation, and insatiable greed. Back to animals. Men = confused and desperate for pussy. Women = powerful because they have the pussy. The quest for love is shockingly similar to tracking a kill.

For Alice, I am going to take a few steps off the beaten path. I am positive she has seen the movies I mentioned above—probably several times. So, for the sake of authenticity, I will need to pull from something a little more obscure. Keep in mind, Alice is already interested. The difficult part is believability. After all, she is a federal agent and her bullshit detector is not to be underestimated. In other words, if I do my usual *fuck them and then be too disgusted to be in the same room with them* routine, she will bolt. I need her to *feel* that I love her. However, my love must feel reluctant, playing on the most popular subgenre within the romantic comedy genre—unrequited love. If Alice believes I love her but, for whatever reason, I am trying to deny myself that love, she will breach for me like a shark breaches for a bucket full of chum.

For that kind of angst, I believe a foreign film is in order. I can guarantee you she doesn't tolerate subtitles, so there is no real danger of her recognizing my method. One story that comes to mind is *Cyrano de Bergerac*, starring Gérard Depardieu. It's actually the perfect scenario. Cyrano deeply loves Roxanne (Anne Brochet) but is so filled with self-loathing because of his hideous appearance (me, turned inside out) that he hides his love for her. In fact, he sacrifices his own desires to assist the handsome Christian in his quest to win her love.

I realize that I don't have time to take it that far. However, I will convince Alice that I have feelings for her but refuse to act on them because I am protecting her from the ugliness in my soul, etc. Of course, I will have to sell the whole package, but this will be a lot easier for me because my reluctance to love will be absolutely real. Maintaining the charade once it starts working on her will be the hard part but, with any luck, I'll confirm that Bendini is the target and he'll be dead before any of this becomes a problem.

Tonight I'm going to trade in my body armor for a well-tailored black suit. Well, there might still be some body armor, but I'll definitely be molting out of my brownish gray wallflower uniform. I'll take Alice to an amazing dinner at some out-of-the-way French fusion place run by a brilliant, yet disgruntled chef who refuses to accept reservations or menu substitutions. Despite the line around the block, I'll have a table and the chef will have prepared a meal that is never on the menu. I will crack jokes, make eye contact, and maybe even try a bit of hand touching. Of course, these are all movie moves, but too obscure to be recognizable. And when we go back to her place, I'll give her the James Bond shagging of her life (Sean Connery style), and stick around for some—gulp—cuddling. And when she falls asleep on my arm, I'll try not to chew it off and slink home (Coyote style). Hey, baby steps.

ALL INFORMATION HEREIN IS CLASSIFIED
SURVEILLANCE TRANSCRIPT: AUDIO RECORDING—
INFRARED LASER MIC (150M)

Location: Alice (censored) Residence/Bedroom, East Village,
   Manhattan
Subjects: John Lago and Alice (censored).

Alice: Let's go again.

Lago: Are you trying to kill me?

Alice: No, I'm just trying to fuck you. Again.

Lago: I'm that good?

Alice: Let's just say I've never been with someone with your
         extensive training.

Lago: You make me sound like an electrician.

Alice: Now you're getting me hot.

Lago: I think I need to sleep.

Alice: OH NO. If we aren't going to fuck, we're going to talk.

Lago: So, if I fuck you, I'm saying I don't want to talk to you.
         And if I talk to you, I'm saying I don't want to fuck
         you.

Alice :   Pretty much.

Lago: You're going to be an excellent lawyer.

Alice: So, we're talking?

Lago: Only because my dick is permanently stuck to your leg.

Alice: What are you doing?

Lago: Cuddling?

Alice: Page one of the girl manual. Always cuddle after lovemaking.

Lago: Sorry.

Alice: It's okay. My idea of cuddling involves a Japanese sex swing.

Lago: I guess there is no manual for you.

Alice: You are correct, sir. So, we're talking?

Lago: At least until I regain consciousness.

Alice: Where are you from? And I know it's not Peoria because I'm actually from there.

Lago: You're shitting me.

Alice: Nope. Can't you tell by my ample Midwest curves?

Lago: Not going to answer that.

Alice: Then answer the first question.

Lago: Let's talk about it tomorrow. I'm exhausted.

Alice: So, we're fucking?

Lago: All right. Fine. I hope you like a good buzzkill. I was an orphan from the time I was an infant, and my first memories are from when I was eighteen months old. I was living with a foster family in New Jersey.

Alice: Didn't they tell you where you were born?

Lago: They died in a car accident before I started to speak. When I was older, I asked social services for information. All they had were some partial birth records. Basically just the hospital in New Jersey where I was born.

Alice: So you have no idea who your parents were . . . at all?

Lago: I know nothing about my father. . . .

Alice: What about your mother?

Lago: Are you sure you want to know this?

Alice: Yes. Come on. I can handle it.

Lago: Okay. My mother's drug dealer shot her when she was pregnant with me. The bullet grazed my chest when it went through. That's how I got my first battle scar.

Alice: This one here?

Lago: Yeah.

Alice: Oh my God. It could have broken your little heart.

Lago: Yeah, my lucky day, I guess. She died instantly and they delivered me six weeks early.

Alice: Oh my God. I'm so sorry.

Lago: Me too.

Alice: That is insane. Thank you for telling me.

Lago: Really? Why? What's so great about damaged goods?

Alice: You're not damaged goods. But now I know why you have that . . . look.

Lago: What look?

Alice: Most people, if they are exhausted, drunk, bored, or preoccupied, show it in their eyes. They drift, pulling their attention from one thing to another. But not you. You have eyes like a bird of prey. A hawk or something. It's like you are always waiting for a mouse or gopher to cross your field of vision so when it happens, you'll be ready to strike.

Lago:	I think I look like that because I feel more like the mouse or gopher waiting for the hawk.
Alice:	Paranoia. Makes sense.
Lago:	Yeah. In foster homes, you learn pretty quickly to watch your own back. I remember when I was five and some dirty old granddad came into my room in the middle of the night, reeking of whiskey. My hackles went up. Even if I didn't know the specifics, I knew he was there to hurt me. So I hurt him.
Alice:	At five? How?
Lago:	Baseball bat. Under my bed. Wasn't much of a player, but I always kept it handy. Made me feel somewhat safe. That night I understood why.
Alice:	What happened?
Lago:	I nearly killed him. Hit him so hard on the side of the head it broke his orbital bone and he lost an eye. Did my first tour in the junior psych ward for that one.
Alice:	I could barely pour cereal into a bowl at five.
Lago:	Your animal self takes over. You can feel it. Even though you're small, you can feel its power. The shrinks called it rage, but I knew it was more than that. The anger was more like the fuel I could dump on the fire to make it explode when I needed it to.
Alice:	But what about being a kid?
Lago:	Next life. I'm thirsty. Want a glass of water?
Alice:	Sounds lovely. But we're not done yet. Not by a long shot.
Lago:	Why am I not surprised?

—END TRANSCRIPT—

13

THE STAGGER STEP

It's early Sunday morning and I just left Alice's apartment. Yes, we conjugated our office romance. No, I'm not going to reveal any details. This isn't *Penthouse Letters*, although you would probably want to buy that issue if I were a contributor. Just suffice to say I have planted the seed (terrible pun I know) that will germinate into my plan. A little postcoital confessional did the trick. I told her a sob story about my dark past, and she took the hook like a good little fish. The nice thing was that I didn't have to lie about it. It was weird telling the truth for once. I felt vulnerable doing it, but it was also kind of exhilarating. And when I heard myself saying it, *I* even felt sorry for me. Up yours, Cyrano. I don't need a circus nose to get a sympathy fuck. I have a hideous soul and that kind of ugliness is far more tragic than physical abnormalities.

I trudge up the steps to my apartment (never, *ever* take the elevator), about to settle into the Sunday *Times*, followed by an Ambien-induced coma that will rival deep-space travel cryo sleep—like in *2001: A Space Odyssey*. Actually, that would have been the perfect gig for me. I could spend years in a stone quiet spaceship with a glib computer named Hal. Hal would have trusted me a lot more than Dave because I wouldn't be such a tight ass like Dave was. As long as we played chess and I could space walk whenever I wanted, we would have been cool. I unlock all seven locks on what is now the pod bay door to my ship.

I need protein before I sleep. Alice depleted me like a litter of hungry wolf pups sucks the life out of their mother. I open the fridge and am puzzled by the odd smell of aftershave that suddenly hits my nose. I don't wear aftershave, and if I did it would not be the noxious drugstore shit I smell. But then it all makes sense when a baseball bat hits me in the side and breaks two of my ribs like dry kindling twigs.

———

Rule #7: Get your shit together.

In fighter pilot training, they talk about having ice water in your veins. This is not just a bunch of nut-grabbing dude speak. Controlling the nerves wrapped around your panic button is critical to survival in combat. They call it Performance IQ. It is a proven fact that anxiety of any kind will actually lower your Performance IQ (make you more stupid), and if you really think about it, what other IQ is more important? Success is all about delivering *in the moment.* Anyone can be a star in practice. But how many people can nail it at game time, in the fourth quarter, in the final seconds, when it counts? Very few. You have to fight the animal brain that wants to flee. Fight *or* flight is bullshit. Flight is the default. Fight only happens when flight is not an option. Because *fight* requires a sharp, committed mind that can think ten steps ahead. The advanced level of this is being able to launch a rational, effective counterattack when you're injured. Broken ribs tend to turn your brain to mush and motivate you to curl up into a ball and sob. Then your opponent will *really* give you something to cry about.

So when the second swing comes, I'm ready. I duck as the Louisville Slugger whips through the air above my head. When I come up, I double punch Babe Ruth in the sternum, knocking him about five feet back into my cool glass table. It shatters, of course. Fuck! That was my Tony Montana cocaine table. I've never had any strippers dance on it but I was *planning* to. And now, it's . . . (Performance IQ kicks in) . . . *hundreds of razor sharp, deadly weapons glittering in the morning light.* Hmm.

You're going to laugh at this, but I grab two oven mitts hanging next to my stove and snatch up a couple of thick glass daggers courtesy of my former kickass coffee table. People grab glass shards with their bare hands all the time in movies and use them as weapons, right? Yes, in movies. But in real life that is like trying to fight with a knife that has points on both ends. You will not only shred your hand, but you will also certainly cut the flexor tendons that work like that little rubber band in a windup balsa airplane. Snap those and your hand becomes a limp, useless flipper that can't even pick up a penny. Babe Ruth gets up quickly, trusty bat in hand, and I see his face.

Motherfucker.

It's Hartman, the intern drill sergeant at Bendini, Lambert & Locke. I guess when he said he was going to skull fuck me, he wasn't kidding.

"What the fuck are you doing in my apartment?"

His sweat-soaked head is covered in tiny cuts oozing blood. I can even see one small shard stuck in his pasty scalp.

"Taking out the trash."

"That sounds like a line from a shitload of really bad movies."

He takes a swing and I sidestep him, bullfighter style, and punch a hole in his gut, just below the sternum. The key to "edge fighting" is to open up a large blood vessel, like the aorta or inferior vena cava, with the smallest puncture wound possible. That way, it's almost impossible to stop the bleeding without opening the wound more and suturing the vessel and that, for obvious reasons, is not a viable option.

I can tell I have not hit anything of value on Hartman because he doesn't do the stagger step. A sudden drop in blood pressure, due to a sudden loss of blood, followed by the body releasing a truckload of fight-or-flight adrenaline causes the stagger step. The legs buckle slightly, kind of like when a drunk takes that first step off the bar at closing time. Unfortunately, Hartman seems unfazed by the four-inch puncture wound that probably trashed half his spleen. That is the sign of a professional with fighter pilot experience. In other words, the only person I would expect to react the same way is me. Now my head is swimming with scenarios. Who the fuck is Hartman, *really*?

"Who the fuck are you?" I inquire.

"The real question is, asshole, who the fuck are you?"

"I'm just the intern." I grin.

"I guess your girlfriend will tell me if I take off enough of her skin."

"Don't you fucking—"

Whack. He shoots the end of the bat straight at me so the end of the barrel hits me square in the diaphragm, just above my navel. I lose my air instantly. It was a nice move. First he hit me with a statement he knew would catch me off guard. Clearly, if I don't kill him, he's going to go kill Alice. So in the nanosecond it took me to process that fact, he took his shot. And he knew exactly where to hit me so I would be briefly incapacitated. This motherfucker is good. *Whack!* Lower leg. Down I go. I land on my side and feel a sharp pain in my leg. Nice. I just impaled myself with my own weapon. Not part of the edge-fighting playbook. Then he goes for the kill swing, aiming for my temple—the weakest part of the skull and home of the middle meningeal artery, a vessel just itching to burst and cause a fatal brain bleed. Pure instinct makes me roll quickly to the side so he misses and smashes the barrel into the floor. Like Jeter's Louisville Slugger, the bat snaps in half at the label. I promptly grab a piece and impale his foot with the jagged end.

"Motherfucker!"

My sentiments exactly.

Any injury to the top of the foot is excruciating. Hartman may be well trained and all that, but even *he* is momentarily focused on the agony that is now shooting up his lower leg into his groin.

I roll, looking for a weapon and feel the sharp pain in my hip again. I reach down, find the thick piece of glass embedded in my hip muscle, and yank it out quickly. Hartman is coming down on me, bringing the fight to the floor—where all fights end up—and I punch the piece of glass into the space between his ribs, pulling it out quickly. I hear the telltale hiss of the sucking chest wound, or tension pneumothorax, and know that I have punctured his right lung. This is a tough one, even for a fighter pilot. The lung quickly collapses and the heart goes apeshit trying to compensate for the sudden loss of half the oxygenated blood in the panic-stricken body. Stagger step, anyone?

He sticks his finger in the hole. Nice. It might save his life if I weren't going to kill him anyway. But kudos to him for knowing the right triage move. I wrench his free arm behind his back, flip him onto his chest, and land on his back full force with my knee. He loses a few teeth on my hardwood floor and lies there moaning. It's the moan of defeat but defeat with honor. I don't begrudge him the opportunity to bitch about the pain I just inflicted.

"I'm going to ask you one more time. Who are you?" I say quietly.

"Or what? You're going to kill me?"

He starts laughing, sputtering blood on the floor. Then I start laughing. We're both dying laughing because fighter pilots don't talk when they're caught behind enemy lines. I shouldn't have even asked but push it anyway just for fun.

"Who do you work for?"

An explosion of laughter from both of us, followed by horrific coughing.

"Stop, you're killing me," he bellows.

Now I almost want to let him live. Clearly, he's not the tough-talking dipshit G.I. Joe wannabe he was pretending to be at Bendini. He's a professional. And all professionals deserve respect.

"Fine. Then how did you make me?"

"That's for me to know and you to find out."

"What are you, seven years old?"

"You're in over your head, you know? Way fucking over."

"Thanks for the advice."

He thinks us kibitzing for a moment is distracting me from seeing him take his finger out of his sucking chest wound and reach for a holdout .22 strapped to his ankle.

"Here, let me get that for you," I say politely.

I grab the gun, throw a pillow over his back, and fire two rounds into the pillow. Love those .22s. Very quiet and efficient. And when I see that he was using ammo similar to mine, I'm glad I didn't shoot him in the head. That would have been very disrespectful, like something a Chinese prison camp executioner would do. Plus, I'm not cleaning up Humpty Dumpty's broken egg all over my cherry-wood floors. So my relaxing Sunday turned into a brutal first aid session for myself, and an eight-hour ordeal of, you guessed it, putting Hartman's faceless, fingerless corpse into six trash bags and dissolving them in a vat of sulfuric acid in some nameless New Jersey chemical plant.

14

YOU HAVE NO ONE TO BLAME BUT YOURSELF

By around nine o'clock that night, I'm sitting in a truck stop diner outside Trenton, drinking coffee and pondering my next move. Going back to my apartment is out. Guys like Hartman don't work alone. When people with money want someone dead, they stay true to that commitment until it happens or they end up dead themselves. Speaking of which, I can't wait to bring the hammer down on the asshole who tried to put a button on me. He is going to have a serious headache when I get through with him and he'll probably end up hot tubbing in the acid bath without the benefit of being dead.

But that will have to wait. For now, Bob needs to bring me in. I call the office.

"What is it, John?"

"I need to come in."

"How soon can you get here?"

"Thirty minutes."

He hangs up. I steal a motorcycle some dumbass left at the gas pump while he went inside to buy a bag of Corn Nuts. As I ride, I'm thinking of scenarios to explain this fine mess. First scenario—Bendini is definitely our target and Hartman is the muscle protecting Bendini and his interests. In that case, I am supremely fucked, because Hartman may be dead, but Bendini isn't, and if he wants me greased, he'll just send some more mechanics. But, of course, that is the least of my worries in this scenario because if I'm blown, then Bob might just decide on forced early retirement.

Second scenario—Bendini is our guy and Hartman works for one of his customers. Customer places a plumber at the firm to make sure nothing clogs the information pipeline. Guy sees me and somehow knows I'm a pro, so he goes to whack me to protect his customer's interests.

In scenario number one, I am a dead man because my internship at the firm is over and Bob tends to tie up all loose ends associated with unfinished business. In scenario number two, I am in the clear with Bendini but need to watch my back even more than usual. I guess there is always the third scenario—Bob wants me dead.

When I arrive at the office, Bob stokes the flames of my paranoia by stationing half a dozen heavily armed goons in his reception area. After we go over the gory details of the Hartman thing, he finally acknowledges my distrust of him based on the goon squad presence.

"John, if I wanted you dead, I'd kill you myself."

"Anything less would be an insult."

"I don't have any intel yet, so you'll have to stay here until I can figure out what the deal is."

He turns to go, but he isn't finished.

"I'm curious, John. How the hell do you think he made you?"

"No idea."

"Sometimes even the best can slip."

"I follow your protocols to the letter. Always have."

He looks me in the eye, searching for a "tell" associated with lying.

"Please, Bob, you trained me to lie perfectly."

"My gut tells me you're not being honest, John. Not completely."

"Maybe you need to eat something."

"There's the attitude again."

"You want to blame me for this? Go ahead."

"Okay. First of all, you *couldn't have* followed my protocols to the letter or they wouldn't have tracked you without you knowing it. Second, you shared the same office with another professional for weeks and you never even suspected him. Finally, you failed to get *any* intel from him before you shut him down. So tell me, who the hell else should I blame?"

"I see your point," I acquiesce.

I act like I've been humbled by Bob's diatribe because I desperately need some sleep. Vanity and pride are Bob's weaknesses, and when you feign submission to what he believes is his superior intellect, you trigger both. It makes him soften his edge a bit and revert to his mentor persona, the one that has been "nurturing" me since I was recruited.

"Use my shower. I'll have someone bring in food."

"I'm not hungry."

"You'll eat it anyway."

"Okay."

"Let me see your wound dressings."

I take off my shirt and pants and show him—big gash on my hip that I stitched myself. Several minor cuts with butterfly bandages, etc.

"Not satisfied with the hip laceration. Starting to look inflamed. We'll get that recleaned and stapled. And I'm going to put you on Clindamycin for infection. Just to be on the safe side."

"Thanks, Bob."

If he had a heart it would melt.

"Get some rest. We'll work this out."

The warm and fuzzy feeling I got from Bob in that moment went away quickly when, after I showered and had to endure the reopening, cleaning, and stapling of my wound, he locked me in one of the empty offices and left the storm troopers outside all night. He told me they were there for my own protection, but I knew why they were there. Cleanup crew. If I'm blown at Bendini, *I* get swept back under the rug where Bob found me.

15

MY HEAD IS GOING TO EXPLODE

As I mentally climb the walls of my well-appointed office prison, I decide to fully mind fuck myself with all the questions and implications that have come out of me having to whack my intern supervisor in my own apartment. Now that things are clearly heating up over at the firm, what with Hartman trying to turn my head in-side out and all, my assignment has just become exponentially more complicated. There will be a fire under my ass like never before, and I'll get burned if I don't move quickly and avoid all complica-tions. The more I run through everything in my mind, the more I realize that there is one thing I need to do if I want to make it out of here alive:

I have to kill Alice.

I'm sure that sounds cold to some of you. Work on that. To those who have been thinking I should have done it when I first found out she was a fed, you get extra credit. Her presence is only going to make things ten times more dangerous for me now, and I'm too close to retiring to fuck things up and end up getting smoked or, worse yet, eating shit in prison for a dozen consecutive life terms.

The story will come out about Hartman being found shot dead by his homosexual lover (Bob's cliché du jour, not mine), and Alice will smell a rat because there is a conspicuous lack of a body to verify the story. That whole habeas corpus thing is kind of important to

FBI agents. I told Bob the party line should simply be that Hartman disappeared. Disappearance raises questions, but none of them can be answered without a fucking body. Throw an actual narrative (currently unverifiable) into the mix and you've got people like Alice trying to connect the bullet holes to draw a picture of who pulled the trigger and then tried to cover his tracks with a story that would have been summarily rejected in the *Murder, She Wrote* writing room. *Elementary, my dear Watson, he was drilled by Colonel Mustard with his own gun in the IKEA living room.*

My head is going to explode. How did things ever get this fucked-up? Maybe Bob is right. Maybe I am slipping. Then I remember the scene in *Blade Runner* when Roy Batty shoves a nail into his hand to make sure he can still feel and that he still has life. Sometimes pain can bring about clarity and remind us we're still breathing. I take a letter opener off Bob's desk and shove it into my stapled wound. I want to scream so badly that I have to hold my breath. Every part of me wants to run from this feeling, to avoid it at all costs. Just like I want to run from having to kill Alice because I know that, even though it will save my ass, it will ultimately destroy me. But the pain centers me and makes me forget about the outside world. It reminds me that I am alone and always have been. It forces me to focus on what I have to do, what I was born to do.

———

Rule #8: Jump.

Along with an innate survival instinct—which is more specifically an animal thing—we are born with a strong emotional attachment to life, which is specifically a human thing. This is something you will need to cut from yourself like a surgeon cuts out a tumor.

When I first met Bob, as I said I was twelve years old. I was incarcerated at the Tracy juvenile detention center in Northern California, one of the worst in the country. I was serving time there for killing my foster parents in San Francisco. I cycled into their home when I was eight years old after their biological son had died at seven of some disease they never disclosed.

Seemed like a nice place. My impression was that they were a couple of sad old hippies who just needed a warm body to fill the void. They got a reptile instead. But they didn't seem to care about my complete emotional disconnection. That was because they were not at all what they seemed. They were running one of the biggest heroin smuggling operations on the West Coast. Which is why, as an homage to one of my favorite films, I will call them Mickey and Mallory. Their deceased son had been their mule, running balloons all over the city. Imagine sending a seven-year-old into the Tenderloin to deliver half a kilo in balloons to a flophouse full of toothless whores and gangbangers. He didn't die of a disease. He took a bullet when the narcs raided the flophouse. Mickey and Mallory, remaining true to their chickenshit souls, never claimed the body, and their own flesh and blood was buried a John Doe, along with all the other nameless human refuse, in a potter's field.

When I later became their indentured servant and replacement mule, I heard that story from one of the gangbangers I was supplying. His street name was Indio, Spanish for "Indian." Nice guy. He was nice to *me* anyway. The seven teardrop tattoos coming from the corners of both of his eyes indicated he did not really play well with others. He used to give me money for food on the side because he knew my "parents" wouldn't and they counted every cent I brought back from my "errands."

Mickey and Mallory weren't the sharpest tools in the shed though. First of all, they started cutting the heroin with a lot of things other than heroin to boost profits—even though I know they brought in about $25,000 a week in cash. Ah, greed. The fact that it is the undoing of just about every criminal is one thing that *is* very accurate in the movies. And far be it from Mickey and Mallory to do anything other than immerse themselves in this cliché.

Indio was the first to tell me that he knew what Mickey and Mallory were doing and that their days were numbered. He had two "customers" croak in two weeks because of some toxic shit Mickey and Mallory cut into the H. Most greedy dealers were at least smart enough to use something nontoxic because, as Indio used to say, "dead don't pay." Also, if word gets out that you're selling the death trip, the dealer down the block just got a whole new revenue stream.

I saw this as an opportunity. These fucking assholes were using and abusing me, and even though I was eight years old, I was *over* taking shit from anyone ever again. All of the pent-up frustration and rage that had been building in me since my cognitive abilities were mature enough to process just how fucked-up my life had become was now coming to a head. Combine that with my hatred of Mickey and Mallory—mostly because of what those evil motherfuckers did to their own son—and my mind was like a blacksmith, hammering hot metal into the tip of the spear that I would shove right up their asses.

I was going to kill them.

Homicide prior to working with HR, Inc. is common among us, and I am most certainly not the first of our breed to grease my foster monsters. You know who you are. Hell, for some of you, I'm practically telling your story right now. Let's just call whacking these losers our gateway drug. It was for me. I had a hard-on for it when I first started planning the whole thing. In fact, apropos of our current work, I was going to make it look like one of the dealers they had been fucking over did the deed.

So I spoke to Indio. Granted, this was not a very secure thing to do. First rule of murder: don't tell anyone. Second rule: do it alone. Hey, I was eight years old, so don't judge. And it turned out to be a very sound tactical move anyway. Indio was very supportive. We made a deal. He would give me access to weapons and offer any support I needed in exchange for access to Mickey and Mallory's heroin stash and whatever else he wanted to lay hands on after they were gone. We shook on it. He even taught me the secret handshake of his set—the Twelfth Street Vatos. From that point on, I was family.

We got started right away. Indio is actually the first person who taught me to never wait to execute a plan, because when your head gets going, throwing out a bunch of fucking second thoughts, you'll kill the whole plan. Anyway, he gave me the perfect revenge profile. He fully described to me his competition: Hollow Pete, a Crip out of Oakland. Indio had heard Pete talking shit on his corner about how he was gonna peel back Mickey and Mallory's caps for cutting his shit with, well, shit. So Pete provided the publicly displayed motive for killing them. Now all I had to do was the actual killing. Indio told me Pete had a signature killing style and the police would quickly link Pete to the murders if we used it. To hold my hand, Indio assigned his boy Diablito (little devil), a five-foot-three psychopath with a full-face tattoo of Jesus wearing a crown of thorns. I shit you not, when he closed his eyes, Jesus's eyes had been tattooed to the lids with their signature look of despair and longing.

We decided to pull it off on a Friday night because that was when Mickey and Mallory liked to do a lot of acid and fuck on their 1970s-era waterbed. They would be in there for hours, sloshing around and making zoo noises while I sat out in the living room, watching TV and eating my *dinner*—handfuls of dry cereal right out of the box. I started to get nervous when midnight rolled around and there was no sign of Diablito. Then the pager Indio had given me buzzed in my pocket and I quietly unlocked the front door. Diablito walked in. He looked like the devil himself, dressed all in black with black gloves. For a brief moment, I panicked and thought that he was just going to kill us all and take the drugs. That would be the easiest thing to do. But he saw the fear in my eyes and smiled. He gave me the Vatos shake and winked, giving me a look at his face when one eye is Diablito and one eye is Jesus. Ever heard of duality? Look it up.

"*Tranquilo, mi hermanito . . .*" he whispered.

He crept to the bedroom while I stood there, paralyzed with a box of Lucky Charms in my claw of a hand. Then I heard Mickey . . .

"What the fuck?"

He didn't yell or anything. They must have thought Diablito was part of their acid trip. After all, he looked like a sawed-off *Jesus Gangbanger Christ*. What happened after that is kind of a blur. I remember standing there a long time hearing muffled grunts and the ripping off of large strips of duct tape. After what seemed like an eternity, standing there frozen in fear with a late-night infomercial about Zamfir, master of the pan flute, as a sound track, Diablito emerged from the bedroom. He was smiling like one of Santa's elves, kind of skipping around on his heels with glee. He had blood spattered on his shirt and face, and that made his mirth all the more disturbing.

"They are ready for you, *hermanito*."

He led me into their bedroom, a place I was normally forbidden to enter. They were both duct taped to chairs, sitting back to back. Their mouths were stuffed with bloody socks and then duct taped shut. Mickey had a gash across the top of his forehead—probably the source of blood all over Diablito. Mallory seemed only half sane, her eyes wildly searching the ceiling like some mental patient waiting for the aliens to return whatever they found in her asshole the last time they were here.

On the floor next to the bed was a massive suitcase completely FULL of heroin kilos. Diablito saw me looking at it and did a little dance around it. He looked like a psychotic Mexican leprechaun.

"You see this, *hermanito*? This is the future! With this, we will OWN this fucking town and every junkie in it. And it's all because of you. Twelfth Street Vatos will tattoo you on their arms and talk about you over forties in the morning gloom, staring at the dead bodies of their enemies."

Then he spat in the faces of Mickey and Mallory.

"And for you, *hermanito*, I give you these two gringo hippie pieces of shit. They made you their bitch, their fucking slave, kid. Running shit for them at eight years old? You fucking kidding me? I didn't break my fucking cherry 'til I was fourteen. I was playing soccer when I was eight, eating chili mangos and running into the summer night until I was out of breath . . . innocent. But you, your innocence was taken by these animals. And, on top of it all, they killed their own flesh and blood. Blood we must avenge with theirs."

Diablito was crying now, and the tears were collecting the blood on his face and turning red. Crimson drops dotted his shirt and the floor. He embraced me, and for the first time, I felt what I believed might be love. It made me miss everything I never had.

It was in that moment I decided I would find my real parents someday. I would find them just so I would know who I was. I looked at Mickey and Mallory and thought about their dead son and envied him. For better or worse, *he* knew where he came from. He may have been raised by these animals, but there were no questions for him, questions that plague orphans and compel us to search for answers, even if knowing them may destroy us.

"And now, for the pain they have put you through, and the pain all them motherfuckers put you through, you gonna get to experience the best fucking feeling life has to offer . . . revenge. It's better than sex, bro!"

He motioned to Mickey and Mallory. They looked at me like dumb, scared animals in the stun gun line at the slaughterhouse.

"What do I do?" I heard my child's voice say from another galaxy.

"Hollow Pete likes to bag 'em. He's a cheap ass and hates to waste bullets. Pretty cold thing to do, but these assholes got it coming."

He handed me two thick plastic bags and a roll of duct tape. I just stood there, feeling as if the weight of this moment was going to crush my small body like an insect. That was my first experience with duality. I completely understood the situation, yet it simultaneously felt utterly confusing to me. I knew that killing them meant justice, freedom, and a shitload of catharsis for everything they had done to me. Even *half* of what they had done was reason enough. But despite my bloodlust and lack of empathy, there was still a morsel of innocence deep inside me that wanted to run from there as fast as my legs could carry me.

You've heard of attempted suicide survivors who've jumped off bridges and had second thoughts about dying as they plummeted to the water below? This was me. I jumped. I was falling. But I wasn't having second thoughts because I didn't want to go through with it and kill them. I was having them because *I did*. To this day, I have never felt so compelled to do anything. And that scared the shit out of me. I wanted their blood on my hands, yet somehow I knew that it would be my blood too. What was left of the child that still liked to watch Rocky and Bullwinkle, run after the ice cream truck, and yearn for a normal life would be dead. And I would be his killer.

So I did what any eight-year-old would do when faced with an earth-shattering moral dilemma: I froze like a deer in the headlights. As I stood there with the hair on the back of my neck standing up and every muscle tense to the point of exploding, Diablito tried to talk me off the ledge.

"*Hermanito.* Maybe you're not ready, bro. Go in the other room. I'll take care of this."

He tried to take back the bags and duct tape. Then, like the man falling from the bridge, I hit the water at 120 miles an hour.

"No."

"Think you can handle it?"

"Yes."

"Go ahead. I got your back."

As I walked up to them, I felt the black rage surge behind my eyes. Mickey looked at me, frozen with dumb animal fear, and I raised the bag. As I covered his head, I conjured up all of the bad memories of the things he did to me. And that was like pouring gas on a fire. Next thing I knew, I was wrapping duct tape tightly around his neck. Then I was doing the same to Mallory. As they struggled to breathe, suffocating in agony, Diablito touched my shoulder.

"*Vámonos*," he whispered.

"No. Wait."

I wanted to be sure they were dead. So I watched their final breaths and watched their bodies go limp. Somewhere in the distance, I heard a little kid crying. For a long time I thought it was someone in one of the other apartments, but now I know it was me. I was that far from truly feeling anything anymore.

Then I turned to Diablito and nodded that I was ready. And we left. A couple of weeks later, the police picked me up coming out of the flophouse hotel I was hiding in. One of the neighbors had seen Diablito and me leave the apartment the night of the murders. Since I lived there, they compared the fingerprints on the few toys I had stolen and hidden under my bed to the ones on the plastic bags. It was an open-and-shut, but the police and DA wouldn't accept the fact that an eight-year-old had done such a heinous thing. They wanted to blame it all on Diablito and offered to drop the charges on me from murder one to second degree manslaughter if I gave him up. But I'm proud to say I never dimed on him. Not because of some honor code, but because I wanted to take full responsibility for my actions. It was the only thing I felt I had ever done that had made my mark on the world, and there was no way I was going to give it up. So they sent me up to juvie and threw away the key.

I was there three and a half years until Bob came to visit me on my twelfth birthday. Our conversation was short and sweet. Bob was going to become my guardian and enter me into a special program for "gifted children." Or I could stay there until I turned eighteen and they transferred me to Folsom Prison, where I would, more than likely, remain for the rest of my life. When Bob explained to me what I would be doing, it didn't faze me in the least. Because I was uncomfortably numb. I had no emotional attachment to life. That's why I'm here today and Alice is a not-so-gentle reminder that being attached to anyone is the death of purity for people like us. We are in our own dark Eden where the snake is not selling the Tree of Knowledge. He is selling love, and if you take a bite of that apple, you will go the way of Abel when this is clearly the land of Cain.

———

That night I dream about Eva. I walk into her room. It's dark but I can hear her giggling on her bed. She's telling me to take my clothes off and join her. I do. I am smiling, happy to see that she is really alive. I tell her I thought she was dead and she giggles again.

"Get in bed, silly."

I get in. She holds my hands, still giggling. I hear the sound of a police car siren outside. As it comes to a screeching halt in front of Eva's building, its police lights shower the room with bright colors—like a trippy bubble gum machine. I go to kiss her and the lights sweep across her face. She is a rotting corpse. She giggles when she sees my look of horror.

"Don't you want to kiss me, John?"

Her eyes are completely black. She comes at me and I am trying to scream but nothing comes out of my mouth.

"Your mother says hello."

I wake up. It's 5:00 A.M. Bob is sitting in a chair across from me.

"You looked like one of those dogs dreaming that you're chasing something. Your hands were moving like paws digging in the earth. What was the nightmare?"

"Same old same old. Rotting corpses torturing me from the grave."

"Anyone I know?"

That question is so loaded, if it were a gun, it would have blown off half my skull. I look at him and keep my gaze measured but the bile of hatred rises up in my throat and makes me cough.

"You worry too much." He smiles.

"What's the word on Hartman?"

"I have some good news and some good news. The good news is that we've confirmed Mr. Bendini is our mark. The other good news is that it appears Hartman wasn't working directly for Bendini."

"Customer?"

"Looks that way."

"How you like the intel?"

"I'm buying it. Got it from a great source—Hartman's real homosexual lover."

"I thought that was just part of your cover story."

"It was. Just dumb luck that it's true. Guy told us Hartman's connected with a mob family upstate. They paid a guy off to get him placed there, then whacked the guy after Hartman was hired. I guess they wanted to babysit their golden goose and didn't have much confidence in Bendini's people."

"Explains the fact that he's a pro."

"Yeah. I guess he was some military contractor type before this. Shooting ragheads that get too close to oil wells and whatnot. Dumbass probably didn't know what hit him when he met you."

"Bendini's paranoia has to be at an all-time high," I muse, relieved that the fucking Mickey Spillane bullshit is over and I can concentrate on my real job.

"That's why we had to take care of this very well."

"What're you selling the street?"

"Murder-suicide," Bob says with pride. "Married closet homo

whacks Hartman because he's scared. Hartman has been threatening to out him so he can work the guy for money, et cetera."

"But when he sees Hartman dead it's too much for him. So he swallows the gun because swallowing is what got him into this mess in the first place. Two dead cowboys roll down *Brokeback Mountain*. Cops can't wait to get 'em off the books," I say absently. "Sounds pretty clean."

"Squeaky. Bendini will buy it. Too weird not to."

"So how you think he made me?" I call attention to the elephant in the room.

"He was a pro. Takes one to know one."

"What now?" I inquire very gently.

"What now is we're prepping your execution scenario as we speak. You'll be able to take care of business in a couple of days. You up for a wild west show?"

"My spurs are jingling and jangling."

———

When I walk out into the morning sun, the glow of my reprieve is quickly snuffed out by the realization of what I have to do about Alice. I don't want to do it, but this is insect culture, and one of us will eventually have to be eaten to restore order. She may not be suspicious of Hartman's death, but sooner or later something will throw my scent her way and Bob will end up killing us both. So later that day I call Alice and tell her I want to have dinner with her on Friday night. Just the two of us. I tell her I've been missing her and I really need some alone time with her. I can almost feel the heat from her blushing cheeks. I can hear the excitement in her voice. She's in love with me and she thinks I'm in love with her. She trusts me. And I'm going to take her life.

United States Department of Justice
Federal Bureau of Investigation

Washington, D.C. 20535

ALL INFORMATION HEREIN IS CLASSIFIED
SURVEILLANCE TRANSCRIPT: AUDIO RECORDING—
INFRARED LASER MIC (150M)

Location: Alice (censored) Residence/Bedroom, East Village,
　　Manhattan
Subjects: John Lago and Alice (censored).

*KNOCK ON THE FRONT DOOR. SOUND OF ALICE UNLOCKING
DOOR AND OPENING IT, DOOR CHAIN CATCHES.*

Alice:　　Who is it?!

Lago:　　John.

Alice:　　What's the password?"

LAGO IS OUT OF BREATH, VOICE SOUNDS AGITATED.

Lago:　　Just let me in, okay?

Alice:　　Not until you turn that frown upside down.

SOUND OF DOOR BEING FORCED OPEN AND CHAIN SNAPPING.

Alice:　　John, what the hell are you doing!?

SEVERAL UNIDENTIFIED PEOPLE YELL, "SURPRISE!"

Lago:　　What the fuck?!

Alice:　　Happy birthday you crazy motherfucker!

Lago:　　How did you know it was my . . .

*ALICE'S RESPONSE UNINTELLIGIBLE. VOICES AROUND HER
GET LOUDER. THEY ARE WISHING LAGO A HAPPY BIRTHDAY.*

Alice: Human Resources.

Lago: What did you say?

Alice: Human Resources gave me your birth date!

Lago: I think I need a drink.

Alice: Mr. Grumpy Pants is ready to be a birthday boy!
          Someone get this man an adult beverage before he
          kills us all!

KATE, A FEMALE PARTY GUEST, APPROACHES LAGO.

Kate: Hey, you want a hit of this?

Lago: Sure.

LAGO COUGHS FOR SEVERAL SECONDS.

Lago: Whoa. Thank you.

Kate: It's Indica.

Lago: I can tell by the sledgehammer effect.

Kate: Are you okay? That was quite an entrance.

Lago: Tough day at the office.

Kate: So, what do you do?

Lago: Aren't you a lawyer too?

Kate: No, my husband's a lawyer at the firm. Kate.

Lago: John.

Kate: You're not a lawyer, are you?

Lago: Why do you ask it like that?

Kate: No offense. It's just that you don't look like a lawyer.

Lago: What do I look like?

Kate: Forget it. I don't want to say something I'll regret. My
          husband says I'm always doing that. I'm an artist and I

can't keep my mouth shut about my observations. It's kind of compulsive really.

Lago: I want to hear it. I won't make you regret it.

Kate: See, that does not sound like a lawyer to me. Lawyers don't have balls. Well, here goes. I think you are a dangerous man.

LAGO LAUGHS.

Lago: I'm an intern at the firm. How's that for dangerous?

Kate: Wait. You're an intern, so forgive me for asking, but do you get paid or do you work for free?

Lago: I do it for the love of the game.

Kate: Holy shit. You work for free.

Lago: For now, yes.

Kate: That is dangerous in Manhattan.

Lago: Yeah, I'm murdering my savings.

TWO-HOUR LAPSE IN RECORDING. RF INTERFERENCE.
SUBJECTS LAGO AND ALICE HAVE RELOCATED TO ROOFTOP.

Alice: You're so quiet.

Lago: Must be the weed. Got me thinking too much. I hate that.

Alice: What're you thinking about?

Lago: I had a good time tonight but I feel . . . weird.

Alice: I'm sorry I surprised you. Some people hate that.

Lago: No, it's not that. The funny thing is that I had completely forgotten it was my birthday.

Alice: How does someone forget their own birthday?

Lago: Growing up it was never special. No one has ever done something like this for me.

Alice: No one ever threw you a birthday party?

Lago: No.

Alice: Seriously?

Lago: Yeah.

Alice: That's awful. You poor thing.

Lago: I'm not looking for pity. I just want you to understand that this whole thing with you is . . . difficult.

Alice: I know. You looked like you wanted to strangle me when you came to the door.

Lago: Sorry . . . again. I didn't mean to break the chain like that.

Alice: What was up with you?

Lago: I was really . . . angry.

Alice: Was it something at work?

Lago: Yeah. Pressure's getting to me, I guess. Just a shitty day.

Alice: But it turned out great.

Lago: Yeah.

LONG PAUSE.

Alice: Hey, do you want your birthday present now?

Lago: Sure.

Alice: Okay but first you have to answer a question. Cool?

Lago: I guess . . .

Alice: Good. If you could find your father, would you?

Lago: What does that have to do with—?

Alice: Just answer the question. You'll see in a minute.

Lago: I want to find him more than anything. If it's to beat the fuck out of him for being an asshole and abandoning me, fine. If it's to get to know him because he's a decent guy, great. But even if it were just to know ABOUT him, I would accept that too. I just need to know where I come from. For better or worse. Then maybe I can just let it go and move on.

Alice: I'm going to help you find him.

Lago: How?

Alice: I have a contact at the Mormon Church. They're experts at helping adopted kids track down their biological parents. It's kind of a religious mandate for them. They think it's important for people to be connected to their blood in whatever way possible. Her name is Dorothy and she wants to meet you.

Lago: Wow.

Alice: Good present, right?

Lago: Really good. Thank you, Alice.

Alice: Good. I'll set it up. Now let's get back to the party. I think it's time for the spanking machine.

Lago: Why are you so good to me, Alice?

Alice: You don't know?

Lago: No.

Alice: Because I love you, dumbass.

—END TRANSCRIPT—

16

ASAHFP

Saturday morning. Sitting in my new apartment. It's a shit hole. Bob's revenge for me losing my cover on the last one. Just got home from Alice's house. *I did not kill her.* I was fully prepared to do it. There are some unsolved murder cases in her neighborhood—mostly young women. I was going to follow the pattern: strangulation, rosary in the victim's mouth, some Old Testament verse about harlots written in lipstick on the wall. Fairly contrived, but then again, we're talking about a serial killer—God's own sexually transmitted disease. There's nothing more despicable than an overgrown pervert mental patient fuck face who kills people for no real reason.

In fact, it was in thinking about the whole serial killer thing that I decided not to do it. In the end, Alice is not my target and I am not in the business of killing people other than my target. Bob has no problem with that, collateral damage and all. I do. Always have. Alice may be a federal agent, but she's still just a bystander and she isn't pointing a gun at me yet. Don't get me wrong. I'm probably taking the biggest risk of my career and potentially my life by allowing her to continue to breathe. I guess it goes to show you that even a reptile like me has to have standards.

Plus, I now have an endgame, and she can't possibly interfere with it. Actually, I have her to thank for it. On my way to her apartment, I was thinking about one of my favorite movies, *Scarface*, and it occurred to me that I could whack Bendini much in the same way Tony Montana gets whacked in the end of that movie—a cartel-style, balls-out assault.

So, after she was asleep, courtesy of Ambien and a couple gallons of champagne, I loaded up a new and improved Russian Mafia password crack program and took a long look at the case files on her laptop. Mostly, I was looking for routine surveillance reports from Bendini's home. Thanks to the FBI, I now have detailed schematics of his home and grounds, along with comprehensive data on his security systems and security patrol staff. I even know how many guard dogs he has and what breeds. If I knew any more about how Bendini moves, I would have to be Bendini himself. Knowing all of this, I can hit him cartel style and still stay within Bob's program.

I ran it by Bob and he gave me his blessing. In fact, he loves the idea, because his clients are starting to get extremely cranky with him. And when those types of clients get cranky, you run the risk of getting whacked yourself. So I'm calling it operation ASAHFP—As Soon As Humanly Fucking Possible—and I'm already deep into preparations. It feels good to prep this hit because I need to clear my head and keep my eyes on the prize. This shit will all be a distant memory when I'm down in Brazil getting a new face—preferably one that looks a lot like 1968 Clint Eastwood if I find the right surgeon. But first I need to find a way to take out a dozen armed security guards—most of whom are former Navy SEALs and Special Forces operators, get past what is certain to be a bank-style security system, and whack the motherfucker before the sun comes up. Details.

United States Department of Justice
Federal Bureau of Investigation

Washington, D.C. 20535

ALL INFORMATION HEREIN IS CLASSIFIED
SURVEILLANCE TRANSCRIPT: AUDIO RECORDING—
MOBILE PARABOLIC REFLECTOR MIC

Location: Laurel Place Restaurant, Cobble Hill, Brooklyn
Subjects: John Lago, Alice (censored), and Dorothy (censored).

Lago: Nice to meet you, Dorothy.

Dorothy: Pleasure to meet you, John. I've heard a lot about you.

Lago: All bad, right, Dorothy?

Dorothy: You two make such a handsome couple. Maybe you should think about . . . you know . . . marriage. Start a family of your own?

Lago: Don't they say lawyers shouldn't breed?

Dorothy: Oh, John, you're a real hoot.

Alice: Yeah, John, a hoot.

Lago: I'm here all week. Try the veal.

Dorothy: Okay, well let's talk about what I found when I researched your genealogy, John.

Lago: I apologize in advance for exposing you to such misery.

Dorothy: Not to worry. We're all loved equally by the Lord, no matter what our past holds. Speaking of which . . .

SOUND OF PAPERS SHUFFLING.

Dorothy: I don't want to get your hopes up, but I was able to follow a potential lead based on your partial birth records. Obviously, your mother died before she was able to name you. So you would have been listed as John Doe. And, since we know that you were born prematurely, you would have been placed in the neonatal intensive care unit for several weeks. So I searched for babies born around the time you were born that fit these criteria. Luckily, there was only one male child born prematurely and orphaned at that time. I presumed that was you, so I used that information to find the person I believe might have been your mother.

Lago: Holy shit.

Dorothy: Do you want to know her name?

Lago: I'm not, uh, I'm not sure.

Alice: John, you wanted to know where you came from. She's part of that.

Lago: Okay.

Dorothy: Her name was Penny (censored).

Lago: A bad penny always turns up.

LAGO LAUGHS.

Lago: Sorry.

Dorothy: She was only twenty-three. Poor thing was already clinically dead when they delivered you by emergency C-section. I'm getting the police report to see if her assailant—

Lago: If my father killed her?

Alice: Easy, John.

Dorothy: That is one possibility, John, so I am pursuing it. I can stop if you wish.

Lago: No. Go ahead. I want to know.

Dorothy: Okay. I do have some good news. Presuming I'm
           correct about all of this, when you were in the NICU,
           you were there with four other babies. From the time
           you were admitted to the time you were discharged,
           forty-seven people visited the unit. One of them might
           have come to visit you.

Alice: Oh my God, John. One of them could have been your
           father.

Lago: Interesting. Safe to say that if he did come to visit, he
           probably wasn't the one that shot my mother. Whoever
           wanted her dead wanted me dead too.

Dorothy: I would say that is a reasonable assessment.

Alice: Do you have the actual names?

Dorothy: Right here in my hot little hand. I have it narrowed
           down to forty or so strong possibilities. Of course, even
           if your father did visit, he might have used a false name
           to protect himself. So let's not count our chickens just
           yet. Anyway, if these don't work out, we can gather
           some more information and refine the search.

Alice: John, this is so exciting.

Dorothy: Now there's no guarantee one of them is his father.

Alice: I know but, if one of them is . . . Thank you, Dorothy.

LAGO IS BREATHING FAST, SHALLOW.

Alice: John, are you okay?

Lago: I'm fine. Just a little overwhelmed.

Dorothy: John, do you know anything at all about your father?
           Anything that might help us narrow down the list?

Lago: Nothing. According to one of my social workers, my
           mother had a photo in her purse of her holding hands
           with a man. But the photo was covered in blood and
           they couldn't make out who was with her.

Alice: Do you have the photo?

Dorothy: Yes, the photo could be helpful.

Lago: I'm sorry. This is . . . I need some air.

Alice: Wait, John. Don't leave.

PAUSE. SOUND OF ENTRY DOOR CLOSING.

—END TRANSCRIPT—

17

OKAY, NOW I AM FUCKING PISSED

I just finished work and I'm up in Scarsdale, casing Bendini's house. Actually, it's more of a compound that sits on nearly thirty-five acres in one of the wealthiest areas on the eastern seaboard. Yeah, he's a rich lawyer, but give me a fucking break. This is stupid money. As I sit waiting in a small school parking lot on a hill above Bendini's house, my night vision specs reveal approximately twenty armed guards patrolling the grounds. I think back to the *Scarface* plan, and Bendini's place is perfect for it. The grounds are too expansive for such a comparatively small security detail to cover it all. As long as I make it to the house without getting devoured by the man-eating dogs he has patrolling the grounds, I can create a big enough distraction to pave the way for me to creep in and have my way with Bendini. After that, I'll kill him. Bob's right. Ha, ha. My jokes do suck.

A quiet walk around the perimeter of the house yields many disturbing revelations. In addition to the bodyguards roaming around, he does have many dogs, three iron fences—one with electrified razor wire, cameras up the wazoo—that's Dr. Seuss's word for "asshole"—and motion sensors covering every square inch of the property. If a housefly farts, the system will know it. But I like these little Rubik's Cube problems. Makes the job interesting. Never underestimate the power of legit black ops to take your mind off your troubles.

And don't be afraid to tackle the biggest security systems. It doesn't matter how much money someone puts into it, there is *always* a way in. Human beings are not capable of setting up a system with zero errors. They would have to be aliens with superior intelligence or Norwegians to pull that off. And Norwegians don't even lock the doors to their own houses, so they're out. Armed with a shitload of night vision photos and copies of Alice's case files, I set up shop in a nearby diner and start to work out some ideas. That's when I feel the gun in my back.

"I'm gonna sit next to you and you're gonna act like you're really fucking happy to see me. Got it?"

"Yes."

He sits. Goombah. Pockmarked mug. I could cave his fucking pizza face in with one palm strike and watch his brains ooze out his eye sockets if I wanted to, but I'm interested in what he has to say.

"What you got there?"

He's referring to my photos and schematics on the table.

"Do I know you?"

"Don't be a fucking smart-ass. You want the back of my hand?"

I'm trying very hard not to laugh.

"Okay, sir, calm down. I don't want any trouble."

"That's more like it, you fucking pussy."

I want to feel his spine as I pull it out of the base of his skull.

"What's this all about?" I inquire innocently.

"I'll tell you what this is all about."

I see the other guy's reflection flash in the chrome of the shake machine and—WHACK!—he hits me in the head with the butt of his pistol. The weight feels like a .357 snub. I go all Lebowski, sprawled out on the linoleum, dreaming of broads and bowling pins.

When I wake up, I feel like I've spent a week in a Mexican whorehouse. My mouth tastes like blood and fish guts. There is a miniature donkey in my skull, kicking my eyeballs like piñatas. And for some reason my nuts are red-hot on fire. When they pull the greasy gasoline rag off my eyes, I see why. Goombahs have been Tazing my cash and prizes to get me to wake up.

Okay, now I am fucking pissed.

For some reason, I can take a beating anywhere else but in my junk. When I was in juvie, a kid kicked me in the nuts and I shanked him with a number 2 pencil. My sensitivity about my twig and berries probably stems from the innumerable molestation and full-blown rape attempts perpetrated by sweating, mouth-breathing foster fathers, uncles, grandpas, older brothers, and other trolls that the state put in charge of giving me a good Christian upbringing. You'll note I said "attempts." Many of those fine stewards of wayward youth ended up having to suck their government meat loaf through a straw. Anyway, I digress.

"Oh, *now* the motherfucker is awake."

I'm duct-taped to a wooden chair in a room full of greasy meatballs wearing suits covered in luxury logos, like those poodle carriers you see babysitter mistresses toting around places like Beverly Hills and the Upper East Side. And the shoes! Who knew Gucci made ostrich loafers with a four-inch heel and a silver toe cap with an etching of the Virgin Mary? I missed that one at Fashion Week. I thought these Atlantic City dinosaurs had faded into pop culture lore, like Pet Rocks and dental dams.

"Here's the deal, fucko. We're gonna ask you questions. You're gonna give us answers. If we like your answers, we'll be nice. If we don't like your answers, we'll fuck you up like you never been fucked up before in your life."

The rat-faced owner of the borrowed mobster dialogue gets in my mug and gives me a hard look.

"*Capisce?*"

I can't help but laugh at "*Capisce.*" He backhands me and his pinky ring chips one of my teeth.

"Is there anything else fucking funny that you would like to share with the rest of us?"

"No, sir."

"Good. Now we understand each other."

Another pork chop gets into my face. More pockmarks. Garlic and espresso breath. Guy smells like the inside of a rotting log.

"Why you so interested in Frank Bendini?"

"I don't know what you're talking about."

Thump! This time I get a punch to the sternum. I was expecting the face, so I am momentarily paralyzed by the series of sickening palpitations that result from my heart taking a punch in the face.

"As you can see, asshole, I was not fond of that answer."

"Is this guy stupid or what?!" another one yells.

I make a quick assessment of the room. It appears we are in the unfinished basement of what is undoubtedly a nondescript, working-class Jersey home typical of a gangster who is trying to move up but isn't quite Tony Soprano yet. There are six of them, including the one in my face. There may be seven. I can't tell if someone is standing in the shadows staring at me or if that's Mama Luigi's plastic Jesus lawn jockey that only comes out for the holidays. It's weird. I thought for sure I saw someone in there, but when I blinked he was gone.

Whack! I take a tasseled loafer to the shin. Fuck that smarts.

"Are we boring you?"

Raucous laughter. These assholes think they're so fucking funny.

"No, sir."

"Good. Then tell me what the fuck you're doing casing Bendini's place. Since you ain't a fucking eggplant, I'm guessing you weren't there to steal his cuff links."

This brings the house down. I'm no longer amused.

"Casing? I don't understand what—"

A loud buzzing sound, and my nuts are quivering and on fire. I scream in spite of myself. And I am immediately sorry I did, because showing pain to these guys is like showing Slim Jims to a fat kid. The more you scream, the more they get a hard-on for making you scream.

"Okay. We've been nice long enough."

They show me a rusty rose pruner.

"From now on, we take a finger for every wrong answer. You keep fucking with us and you'll be finger-banging your sister with a stump."

"I'm trying to help you."

"Shh."

He presses a fat finger that smells like ass against my lips.

"We know you're on the make, dickhead. It's our job to know these things. We found a lot of interesting shit in your car. We're guessing you're looking to whack the guy."

He pats me on the shoulder and puts my thumb between the blades of the rose pruner.

"You know, losing a finger sucks. But losing a thumb . . . you go back to being a monkey again."

They laugh.

"Shut the fuck up!" he yells.

"So you guys work for Mr. Bendini I take it?"

They laugh their asses off. I'll take that as a yes.

"Yeah, dumbass. We called him. Told him we caught a fucking rat. Said he was gonna drive over here to have a look. Which means you're screwed 'cause he ain't as nice as us."

Shit shit shit. Can you hear the ticking clock? Time to blow this lame-ass party before I blow my cover and the whole fucking gig. But let's have a little fun first.

"I'll tell you what I know but you got to give me a cigarette."

One of them lights a cigarette and shoves it between my lips.

"You guys ever see *True Romance*?"

"Great fucking movie." A chorus of agreement.

How these morons ever got control of anything in this country is beyond me.

"Remember the scene with Christopher Walken and Dennis Hopper? The one where Hopper smokes a Chesterfield and tells Walken where Sicilians *really* come from?"

Now I'm the only one laughing.

"Yeah, Hopper took a fucking bullet in the head after he said it."

"I know. But it was so classic. He knew he was dead, so he just decided he was going to go out with a bang, insulting the shit out of one of the biggest mobsters in the city."

"What's your point, dickhead?"

"My point is this. You're not even Sicilians. What you come from is much lower on the food chain. You're the fucking grease spot that trickled down your mama's ass and stained the gingham tablecloth."

"You wanna run your mouth? Let me open it for ya."

Fat face comes at my mouth with the rose pruners. But I'm already thinking two steps ahead as I fall back hard on the chair, splintering it. I am free of the chair except for the two jagged pieces of the chair arms that are still firmly duct taped to both of my wrists. I think *it's my lucky day* as I shove the sharp stake strapped to my right wrist under fat face's double chin, skewering his tongue and ripping through his soft palate into his brain. He jerks around on the floor like a bluefish that just got the hammer, bright red blood jetting in arterial spray from his mouth.

Hands go to jackets for guns but I already have fat face's gun and I use it to treat Slow Draw 1 and 2 to a bullet in the balls. They hit the ground, clutching what is left of their junk. Judging by the .45 hand cannon I lifted from fat face, there isn't much to clutch. One of them lunges at me, and I finish him by breaking the other jagged chair arm duct taped to my left wrist off in his eye socket. Another fish on deck! Fire up the grill!

And then there were two. One is smart. Takes cover first, then goes for his weapon. The other is trying to flick the safety off his Glock.

"Allow me," I say as I kick the gun out of his hand, catch it, and put two pills through his open mouth.

"Did you say something?" I say with my hand to my ear.

He gurgles and falls hard on his face. His teeth float out on the pool of blood that gushes out of his new suck hole.

Oh yeah, the guy that took cover. He's standing behind a water heater. I switch to the .45 and blow a hole in the canister, showering him with scalding water that turns his face and neck into an angry red blister. As he staggers out, I side kick him in the neck, crushing three of his cervical vertebrae, and dropping him like a sack of shit.

"I think I'll take that Chesterfield now."

I pick up my lit cigarette and take a long drag on it.

"Enjoying yourself?"

Shit. Someone *was* in the dark. He steps out. Looks like a boss. He has the drop on me. Love that phrase. 1950s western style. Got the barrel of a Desert Eagle trained on my chest. Finally, a man with pistol training. But I don't like my odds if I get hit by one of those bowling balls in the chamber.

"Let me guess. Don't try anything funny?"

"Smart-ass. You know how long it's gonna take me to replace all these dead greaseballs?"

I laugh. I like this guy. But he's going to shoot me.

"Gun like that has a lot of kick."

"Not to worry. I can squeeze off two rounds and pattern them in the same hole. It just takes practice."

"Impressive."

"Not as impressive as what you just did."

"Actually, I'm a little off today."

He laughs. When someone laughs, they expel a shitload of air. Plus, he is a chain-smoker, as evidenced by his raspy voice. The air goes out, and for a few seconds, the body is slightly relaxed. This calms everything down. This is why snipers shoot on exhale. Steadies the hand. When he's finished laughing, he will suck in a huge breath. This will expand his chest and make it difficult for him to shoot straight.

He inhales. I exhale.

I fire the .45 from my waist level so the only thing his brain has to react to is the motion below his sight line. If I had tried to raise it, I would be dead. The round hits him square in the Zegna belt buckle, splitting it and blowing a hole in his abdomen. Gut shot. Best I could do. I sit down hard on the floor when he fires. This is risky because he could hit me in the head. But trying a side move would be futile because when it leaves the barrel, a .50 caliber round is as big as a baby Portobello, and even an indirect hit in my chest spells catastrophic blood loss and tissue damage that the best trauma surgeon can't fix on a good day.

As I am falling, the lead mushroom from his gun whines past my right ear and puts a six-inch hole in the drywall behind me. When my butt hits concrete, my teeth make a loud *clack* and my .45 makes a loud *bang*. This time I have it raised and I fire my kill shot. I instantly see a smoking hole in his throat and I can tell by the way he collapses to the ground like a marionette on severed strings that *my* lead mushroom severed his spinal cord, closing him down like last call. He slumps in a crooked heap against an avocado green washing machine and stares at me with dime-size pupils.

"Why didn't you just kill me when I was shooting your boys? You could have easily taken me out while I was distracted," I say to his corpse.

I know the answer: Lack of humility.

Rule #9: God opposes the proud, but gives grace to the humble.

To survive and be successful in this job, you don't have to be that smart. You don't have to be that tough, or tenacious, or have that killer instinct. Above all, you must be humble. When you are humble, you are like a sponge, taking in the world and letting it fill you with the knowledge of what is real. Pride and arrogance are a dry sponge. You learn nothing. You think you know everything when it's not even possible to know everything. And then *you're* the dumbass with the surprised look on your face when someone puts a bullet in you.

If you ever ask a kung fu master who has been training for three decades how much he knows, he will always say, "A lot less than when I started." That's because when he started, he was a know-it-all, his master beat the shit out of him in ways he never dreamed possible, and then he knew that he was nothing but a blind, slow, ignorant slob. And the more he learned, the more he realized that there is too much to learn in anyone's lifetime. And you mother-fuckers only have about ten years to perfect your craft *while* you are doing it. So, be the blank slate or you will have a blank stare on your face like Jimmy "hand cannon" Goombah over there, shitting his gabardine slacks.

18

WE'LL ALWAYS HAVE PARIS

That night, as I nurse my wounds and swallow a drugstore of Vicodin, I decide that what Bob doesn't know about my little field trip tonight won't hurt him and I get into the business of formulating my endgame for Bendini. I'll use the fact that my face looks like raw hamburger to my advantage. So I call the office and let Bendini's assistant know that I was in a nasty car accident. This is the perfect excuse, because lawyers despise it when someone dents their fancy cars. They consider it an affront, an intentional act to destroy the only sliver of personality they have in this world. They figure if they are bald, fat, ugly, hairy, smelly, and suffer from acute micro phallus, as long as they drive a 7 series, 911, or Jag (even though it's basically a Ford), they "still got it." So if you mess with the only thing they truly love anymore, they will go all jihad on your ass.

As predicted, Bendini himself calls the next morning to check on me and encourage me to right the universe by gutting the jackass that hit me—even though most homeless people live in nicer cars than my Honda. He also plays into my hands when he inquires about a very important case I've been working on that he was expecting to review today. It's a massive estate mess that some associate fucked up royally before he was summarily shit-canned. If I can unfuck it, the firm will make nearly a million dollars in uncollected commissions and fees. Bendini's been waiting for it because he probably wants to hide the money from his partners and launder it through some offshore banana boat account so he can buy more condos, white slaves, Cuban cigars, whatever. Of course Bob's people finished it a week ago and I've been keeping that little ace in the hole for a rainy day—which is now.

I roll the dice and tell him I am happy to bring it to his house that night. He agrees, and as the white men say when they are attempting to play basketball at health clubs all over the country, "It's on." So I spend the day gearing up at HR, Inc., avoiding Bob so I don't have to come up with some world-class bullshit to explain my face. Our weapons guys load a couple of duffel bags with a small arsenal of weapons and explosives that are typical drug cartel fare. You're going to love these fuckers. They are very creative, and no request is too difficult. Once I had them make me an armor-piercing RPG launcher out of what looked like a tennis ball can. Worked like a charm, and I just tossed the launcher into the garbage after I blew the target's bulletproof limo to kingdom come.

After gearing up and devising an infiltration strategy based on my photos and schematics of Bendini's property, Bob asks me to meet him in his office. When I arrive, I am relieved, and somewhat suspicious, that Bob is in good spirits. After we review the Bendini plan, Bob attempts to make me an offer I can't refuse.

"So this is it," he says, waxing nostalgic.

"Yeah. Hard to believe I'm out of here after tonight."

"Any interest in being reassigned?"

"No. Want to try my hand at something else. Mix it up a bit."

"What could you do that could possibly measure up?"

"That's just it, Bob. I'm ready to have a normal life. I don't want my new thing to measure up to this. If it did, I might as well just do *this*."

He smiles like he knows something I don't.

"Sell life insurance. It's easy, very boring, and recession proof."

"Not to mention ironic."

"You're needed in *this* capacity, John."

"Bob, I understand that there is no limit to the number of people *other people* want dead. But I have limits. Right now, I feel like I can transition into something else without carrying too much baggage into the new thing. If I don't quit now, I'll never quit."

Bob knows I'm basically saying I don't want to be like him.

"I thought about quitting once. Even walked away from the job for three weeks."

"You're lucky to be alive, Bob."

"Yeah, but they knew I'd be back. It's what I know. It's all I know."

"How do you think I'll do out there, Bob? Outside HR and the life?"

"I've never bullshitted you, John, so I won't start now. I don't think you'll last five minutes in that fucking anthill down there. Your mind is not wired or programmed to do anything else."

"Of course, that's what I'm afraid of, Bob. But I have to try."

"Why? What's the point? Do this a little while longer. Retire at forty."

"And then what? Live alone on my tropical island? Shoot myself at forty-one because my head is full of things I want to blow out and examine on the wall?"

"Is that what you think I'm going to do? I'm forty-three."

"No, Bob. This is all normal to you. And I'm envious of that. The work comes naturally to me, but it will never feel normal to kill people. I know it's a service that has always existed and will always exist. And I know the people we kill are human garbage. I'm not all that concerned about what we're taking from them. I'm more concerned about what *they're* taking from me. Does that make sense?"

"Not to me. But to each his own. All I ask is that you at least think about something that I want to offer you."

Bob hands me a dossier packet.

"Another target? My birthday was last week."

"No. It's a new placement. Paris. Best fucking city in the world. Incredible setup. Apartment. Country house. Cars. Access to a jet when you need it. You'd get one, maybe two assignments a year. Granted, they are more complicated on the planning side, but nothing you can't handle. Please look it over as a personal favor to me. I won't be offended if you say no. Bewildered, but not offended."

He gives me a real smile. Holy shit, I don't think I've ever seen that before. The reason I know is, because he looks like a different person all of a sudden. Like when a guy has a beard forever and shaves it off. You might pass him on the street and not recognize him.

"John, I know I've been a hard-ass. But, pardon the cliché, I did it for your own good. I knew you would last. Talent is talent, and you've got so much of it, it kind of pisses me off sometimes. But I want you to know that I consider us friends, even if you don't."

"I consider us friends."

I lie because "friends" is too weird a name for my relationship with Bob. I feel a connection with him, but I can't define it.

"Here's another cliché, but sometimes I even feel a little like you're the son I never had. A lot of kids come through here, but you remind me most of myself when I was your age."

"You must have been a real asshole."

"Goddamnit, John. Cut the smart-ass routine. I'm trying to be something other than your boss for once. I play the Sergeant Slaughter role, but that's just to keep you aboveground."

"My apologies, Bob."

"I just wanted to say that before you leave HR. That's all, John. For whatever it's worth."

"I'll miss you too, Bob. And I'll think about your offer."

"I appreciate it, John. Let's have a drink."

He pulls a bottle from his desk drawer. I recognize it immediately. Glen Garioch, 1958, forty-six-year-old *bourbon* made in, of all places, Scotland—a glaring contradiction, just like me. Also very rare. Something like three hundred bottles were released. One of my targets of about five years ago had twenty-five of them—at around $3,000 a pop. Ironically, he felt the same way about me that Bob just proclaimed. The difference was that the day he poured me a glass of the Garioch was the day I killed him. As we sipped it, he told me his own son was a terrible fuck-up, hemorrhaging money on cocaine, strippers, and destroyed sports cars. He joked about cutting the kid out of his will and putting me there in his place. We were alone in his office. I told him the reason his son was such an asshole was because his father was spoiling the shit out of him. Guys like that never become men, they stay boys forever. He asked me what to do. I told him the best thing that could happen to his son was to lose his father at a young age.

Then I shot and beheaded him. He worked for Homeland Security and was using his security clearance to run drugs and guns up from South and Central America—unwelcome competition for the cartels. So, as far as anyone knows, they killed him and left his head on the scales in the executive health club locker room.

As I sip the same whiskey with Bob, I almost mention this, but think better of it. That's the kind of story that will ruin the moment and send Bob into a tailspin trying to figure out if I am delivering a thinly veiled threat. Instead we toast to our successes and have a few drinks. When I leave, I see Bob putting his whiskey away, and I know that he will never take that bottle out for anyone other than himself again.

Two hours later, my paranoia is up to DEFCON 1. I'm convinced that Bob's Paris offer was actually a test. Bob knows that I am *very* decisive. So even though I took his reassignment packet with me, I have no intention of accepting, and he knows it. And his offer was as juicy as they come. Who wouldn't want to be set up in Paris with money to burn, killer homes, and a fucking jet? Someone who definitely wants out, that's who. So, unless I accept his offer, I have to assume that Bob will send a team to bag me as soon as I bag Bendini. If I'm not going to remain in the game, then I will probably be viewed as a loose end that needs to be . . . you guessed it, a faceless, fingerless corpse divided into six trash bags and dissolved in a vat of sulphuric acid in some nameless New Jersey chemical plant. Makes sense right?

I guess I never really thought about it that much because I never thought I would be alive to find out. But I am, and now I'm pissed that, on top of the Bendini hit, I'm going to have to plan an even more complicated exit strategy. I can almost hear Bob now, phoning up his death squad with the same emotionless tone he would use to order a pizza. The whiskey confessional was just Bob getting things off his chest because he knows I am a dead man and he wants to be able to sleep at night. I've never felt so fucking alone. In the past, I've always had Bob and the HR team. They've been my family. Not anymore. Sometime tonight they could become my worst enemies. *Duality*. Have you looked it up yet? If not, what are you waiting for?

19

MAN BITES DOG

The last time I stole a car was three years ago, and I did it to get my ass away from the security detail trying to put as many bullets in me as they possibly could. It was a Ford something or other. Not cool but easy to steal. Tonight I am looking for something with a little style—and a big-ass engine. It also has to be roomy enough to transport my small arsenal. Sports cars suck for that. They don't even give you enough room for a set of golf clubs. Then I see it. The *perfect* ride. Cadillac CTS-V Coupe. Six-hundred horsepower V8. Manual transmission for some serious g-forces on takeoff. Race tires and suspension. Recaro seats that hold you tight as a monkey's fist in the corners. This one is black. Looks like the Batmobile. I saw the owner pull up in it in front of a restaurant. Valet took it into the back of a dark parking lot. Easy pickings. The owner was a douche bag, by the way. One of those fifty-something guys who tries to dress like he's nineteen. Thinks he looks hip with love handles hanging over his skinny jeans.

Stealing a car is fairly simple because there are cars that simply can't be stolen and there are cars that practically beg you to steal them. Cadillac is a little in between. Totally doable. Problem is, getting in the door is a bitch on wheels. But this is my last gig, and I will need some horses to get me the hell out of Dodge if they send a posse. Plus, this car will be less suspicious in Scarsdale, where everyone has a license to print money.

So I slim jim the door and hit the security system transformer above the pedals with a Taser. While I'm down there, I cut the ignition wires, but no, I'm not going to miraculously touch them together to start the car. That worked up until the mid 1990s and then pretty much every car rolled off the line with a kill switch that can only be deactivated by, you guessed it, cutting the ignition cables. One kill switch, killed. To start her up, I need to tell the computer that I have the keyless entry chip. I do that with a wireless transmitter similar to the one OnStar uses. It throws a few thousand common signals up against the wall to see what sticks. After about fifteen seconds, the car sees a signal it likes and starts up. The engine sounds and smells like victory.

The drive up to Scarsdale puts me into an introspective mood. Living in Manhattan, I don't get to drive much, and I really miss the insular nature of it. Cars, especially ones with beautifully appointed cockpits like this one, create a kind of silence that allows your thoughts to come out of hiding. My plan to whack Bendini is firmly ingrained in my mind so I allow myself to drift off to other topics.

Like Alice for instance. The music on the radio starts tugging at my emotional shreds, and I realize I'm actually disappointed I'll never see her again. We had a few laughs. What will she think when Bendini is murdered? Will she somehow have a feeling that I did it? If she suspects me, will she come after me? Part of me hopes that she does. Maybe she and I can be like George Clooney and Jennifer Lopez in *Out of Sight*. She's the street-tough federal agent that falls in love with the smooth criminal. Maybe her father is a cop like Dennis Farina in that film. He'll help her to work it out without ever really telling her to do anything illegal because sometimes love is more important than duty or the rule of law or whatever the message was that Elmore Leonard was trying to send. Or maybe she'll just go to the ends of the earth to bring me in. Either way, it would be nice to see her again, even if it's in my riflescope.

Speaking of the devil, Alice sends me a text message while I'm driving. Wants to know if I can "come over for a booty call." Damn girl, I wish I could. I text back "Working. Can't break away." She replies "pussy." I can see her lying on her bed in that awful pink robe she kept since college, thinking of outrageous things to text me, like calling me a pussy. Fuck, I'm going to miss her. I text "good night xxoo" and see the lights of Scarsdale in the distance.

———

Rule #10: Speed.

One thing I learned very early on is that being a predator means having the heightened senses of a predator. As humans, we don't have them anymore. Television, processed food, toxic water and air, and the apathy that comes with an automated, emotionally disconnected society have dulled our edge to that of a Denny's butter knife. Now, in order to get it back, we need pharmaceuticals. *Speed* to be exact. Let's be clear about something. Speed is not just a drug that gets you all jittery and makes you clench your teeth until they break. Amphetamine, also known as a(lpha) + m(ethyl) + ph(en) + et(hyl) + -amine, is a stimulant of the central nervous system—the nervous system of things you control like motor movement—and the sympathetic nervous system—the nervous system of things you don't control, like heart rate. This stimulation triggers the release of norepinephrine (energy), dopamine (cognition), and serotonin (mood) from presynaptic neurons. In some ways, it is a *reminder* of your former glory as a dirty cave dweller intoxicated by violence and the taste of blood. That is why it's addictive. It's fight and flight in one convenient pill and I just took five.

The grounds at Bendini's estate back up against a few thousand acres of Forest Service land. I make my way through the forest primeval in full black ops gear. When I reach the eight-foot wall topped with razor wire at the perimeter of Bendini's house, I do not think of it as an obstacle, but a way in. Up the wall, Kevlar poncho over the razor wire, on the other side, in less than thirty seconds. I land noiselessly on the ground and crouch, unmoving. I am the predator, smelling the breeze for signs of fresh meat.

A guard dog trots along the wall, quickly approaching. Interesting. Akita Inu—the Japanese version of the Akita and one of four breeds closest to the wolf. Like the wolf, and like me, these dogs hunt silently. Barking gives away your position. Barking is what a stupid dog that does not know how to hunt does. He has scented me and now he's running full speed in my direction. With his black fur (rare for this breed), he is almost impossible to see. But I can see his white teeth and the whites of his eyes as he bears down and prepares to unload all of his power on my throat. For a split second, I entertain the thought of counterattacking with my knife. You know, give the son of a bitch a sporting chance. But I think better of it when I see his full silhouette against the hazy moonlight. He is easily 120 pounds. His massive paws are tearing six-inch divots out of the earth as his sprint clocks in at almost 30 mph. Remember The Pig? I pull it and dial in a strong nighty night cocktail. I don't kill dogs. This guy is definitely not a "defenseless animal," but he's also just doing the job he's been bred to do for hundreds of years. I wait until he actually leaps at me to jump to the side. It's kind of hard to switch directions in midair, but he tries, whipping his head back and snapping the air a foot from my face.

I fire The Pig into his belly. He yelps and hits the ground like a sack of potatoes. After a few seconds of drunken staggering, he curls up and passes out like the family dog in front of the fireplace.

There will be more, so I sprint through the forest to the edge of the lawn that skirts the house, planting *black cats*—multistaged explosives loaded with 9-mm rounds—in the trees all around the house. When you set them off, it sounds like you're being ambushed by the entire Bolivian Army and guards start dropping like flies as they get hit with the random trajectory bullets. Black cats are the very definition of diversion, and I plant enough of them around the house to really light it up. I hear more dogs coming through the trees, so I sprint, fueled by a high-octane mix of speed and adrenaline. I don't stop to breathe until I am over the wall and back to the Caddy. Then I collapse, my chest heaving and my heart about to explode out of my chest.

I finally catch my breath and look at my watch. Fifteen minutes late for my prearranged meeting with Bendini. He will be extremely annoyed by now and, by the time I get my shit together and make it to his front door, he may even refuse to see me. I head back to the car to quickly change my clothes, and drive through the front gate. Next thing I know, I'm knocking at Bendini's door, briefcase in hand. Two corn-fed security monsters, sweating through their pinstripe suits, answer the door.

"Can I help you?" One of them half grunts.

"John Lago. I work for Mr. Bendini."

"Look into the camera."

He points to a security camera above the door. I look up at it.

The guard touches his ear, listening.

"Okay, you're good."

"What happened to your face?" The other guard is a fucking Boy Scout. I can tell he doesn't like me but he doesn't know why. He wrinkles his nose, waiting for me to answer.

"Paper cut."

"Funny. Let me look in your briefcase, Dane Cook."

Shit. I need to learn to keep my smart-ass mouth shut.

"John!"

Bendini comes down the stairs. He is genuinely happy to see me. This pisses off the Boy Scout.

"Hey, you goons, let him in. He works for me."

He might as well have told them to sit, roll over, and play dead. Their faces tighten with anger and they let me pass. Bendini slaps an arm over my shoulders and walks me down the hall to his study. The security guys follow us. Bendini sees me looking at them and smiles and waves me on. When we get to the study, they lock the door from the inside. *Damn.* This guy *does not* fool around. I wonder if these cheese dicks sleep in the same bed with him too.

"You're late. And you look like shit. Is that what the animal that hit your car did to you?"

"Yeah. He really creamed my car. Insurance guy says I'm lucky I didn't get hurt worse than this."

"Damn right. Cars are death traps. Just make sure you take that asshole to the cleaners."

"Oh yeah. He'll be lucky if he can finance a scooter after I'm through with him."

"That's the spirit. Well, let's see what you have on the Foster estate."

"May I use your restroom? Long drive."

"Of course. Lars, show him the way."

Lars the Jersey goon points a fat hand to the hallway and leads me to a door. Inside the cavernous, Louis Quatorze gold-plated restroom, I pull the detonator duct taped to my inner thigh and hit the sequence. My charges outside start popping like the hellfire brigade. It sounds like a hailstorm as the bullets strike the outside of the house. I hear voices pitch up into freak-out panic defense mode. Good, they aren't as cold as their swagger suggests. I throw on some ultra-thin leather cop gloves—stylish and crime scene–friendly, and pull a short barrel .45 (mobster special) and a Glock (security geek special) from the false bottom in my briefcase.

Lars knocks heavily on the door. I peek out with an "I'm peeing my pants in fear" face.

"What's going on? Are we in danger?"

Lars sees the Oscar-worthy panic in my face and goes into Boy Scout troop leader mode.

"Get into the tub and stay there."

More charges go off and he flinches. I almost hit him in the arm and say "two for flinching," but there's no time for boyhood shenanigans. Instead I put a 9-mm pill from the Glock in his forehead and pull him into the bathroom with me. Now I'll go whack Bendini and his pals with the .45 and come back here to put it in Lars's dead hand. Lars goes down in the books as the killer—as long as I make Bendini dead within the next ten minutes (the medical examiner's margin of error in determining time of death)—and I trip the fuck out of here and off to freedom.

Then I feel my pocket vibrating and I almost jump out of my skin. I know who it is immediately because when I'm on a job, I carry only my HR phone, and only one person has that number: Bob. My whole career I've never had to answer this phone . . . until now. I pull it out. I have twenty missed calls from Bob. *What the fuck?* Bendini must have a cell tower block on the grounds—countermeasure for FBI mobile phone recon software. By now Bob is fucking furious.

"Bob," I whisper.

"John?"

"Yeah."

"Abort."

"Fuck."

I would say "Why?" or "What the fuck?" but that would be stupid. If Bob's aborting, it's for a very good reason.

"I've been calling for the last hour. Where the fuck have you been?"

There's a knock on the door again. I hang up, kill the lights, and grab Lars's corpse, prying the Glock out of his meathook. Motherfucker's heavy. The door slams open and I'm holding Lars up in a standing position. I heave him at whoever is there and he fires his gun. A bullet blows through Lars's neck and slams into the tile wall.

I am now splattered with blood, viscera, and most likely some very exotic cooties. The shooter turns on the lights and sees me. Sees his buddy Lars.

"Friendly fire," I say and shoot him with Lars's Glock. He falls. I drop Lars in a reasonable landing position to sell the fact that his panicked coworker and he shot each other by accident, at least until the crime scene supernerds arrive. I know it's getting confusing but now I have to make this shit up as I go along! Then I shove the .45 into my pants and run to get Bendini. His study is full of windows and he is a fucking fish in a barrel right now. He gets popped and Bob will never believe it wasn't my fault. *I will get popped too.* I find him under his desk, a thin stream of blood trickling down his face.

"Mr. Bendini. Are you okay?"

"John! My God. What happened to you?!"

"Let's get out of here. You're a sitting duck with these windows!"

I drag him out of there, laughing on the inside as I, Pinocchio, heroically save Geppetto from *my bullets* as they whip through the windows and punch holes in several hideous English fox hunt paintings. Why do all bourgeois people think that the pinnacle of wealth is the crusty fucking English aristocracy?

Two thugs run up and grab us. They hustle us to a panic room like Secret Service agents on a bum rush to save the president. Once inside, all the noise goes away and we can see what's up on the security cameras. The grounds are littered with dead guards.

"Holy shit!" the other guards proclaim.

I make myself puke in the trash can for good measure. I'm viewed with pity and disgust by the guards. A perfect reaction to what they believe is a pencil-neck intern paralyzed by fear.

A goon runs into the panic room.

"Lars and Victor shot each other. By accident."

Thank you, Mr. Goon, for that stirring testimonial. You're my top salesman this month. You win a trip to Maui.

"I was there," I say with a vomit-smeared grimace. "It was horrible."

Bendini shakes his head.

"Amateurs."

I almost laugh out loud but pretend to cough instead.

After a few beats of incredulous silence, all of my charges are finally spent and everyone breathes a sigh of relief. A cavalry of police sirens are heard rapidly approaching the house. Bendini goes to put his arm around me but thinks better of it when he sees bits of Lars's brain and skull on my shoulder. Instead, he awkwardly pats me on the back.

"Sorry about this, son. As you can see, I have some . . . enemies."

"It's okay, Mr. Bendini. I'm just glad you're all right."

"Thanks to you, John."

He scowls at the security men.

"Which is more than I can say for the rest of you high-priced Neanderthals."

They all mumble "Sorry sir" and take on the collective expression of a pack of whipped puppies.

"I owe you one, kid," Bendini says to me in his grandpa voice. Maybe he'll give me a pocketknife and some penny candy.

"Don't mention it, sir."

"Speaking of that, John. I would appreciate it if we could keep this all on the QT at the office. My colleagues tend to get nervous at the mention of all-out gun battles taking place at a partner's home. Not good for business. You understand."

"I understand completely, sir. This incident doesn't leave this room."

"You're going to go far in this business, John. You need to understand that too."

I'm beginning to think I'll be working at Bendini, Lambert & Locke long enough to prove him right.

ALL INFORMATION HEREIN IS CLASSIFIED
SURVEILLANCE TRANSCRIPT: AUDIO RECORDING—
OPTICAL CONTACT MIC

Location: AKA Bar, East Village, Manhattan
Subjects: John Lago and Alice (censored).

Lago: Hey, booty call.

Alice: What the hell happened to you?

Lago: Mugged. ATM machine.

Alice: Jesus, you're lucky they didn't kill you.

Lago: You should see the other guy.

Alice: I guess you missed the memo about just handing
           your shit over to muggers because absolutely nothing
           you have in your cheap-ass Velcro wallet is worth
           dying for.

Lago: We got to go back to the old west. Fucking frontier
           justice. Set up a gallows in Times Square. Everyone's
           strapped and ready to throw down if you look at 'em
           wrong.

Alice: You are a hick.

Lago: No, I'm Clint Eastwood, ma'am.

Alice: Clint Eastwood doesn't drink margaritas.

Lago: I'm not much of a drinker . . . (strange accent)
            Whiskey bartender. The bottle.

Bartender: That's not on the menu, cowboy.

Lago: Why do people insist on calling me that?

Bartender: We good here?

Alice: Yeah. Thanks.

Lago: Saddle up, lady. We're riding off into the sunset. Or
            at least to a bar run by foreigners so we can do as we
            please.

Alice: Enough with the *Gunsmoke* shit. You're killing me.

Lago: Dyin' ain't much of a livin', boy.

LONG PAUSE.

Lago: Tell me you know that line.

Alice: Doesn't ring a bell.

Lago: You've gotta be fucking kidding me. That's one of
            Clint's most famous lines. It's from one of his most
            famous films. *Outlaw Josey Wales.*

Alice: Not really into westerns.

LAGO MAKES A SPITTING, RASPBERRY SOUND.

Alice: Let's go. You're wasted.

Lago: I'm not an animal. I'm a human being!

Alice: *Elephant Man.*

Lago: Thank Christ, she finally got one.

LAGO LAUGHS.

Alice: I'm into romantic comedies, you dick. You probably
            don't know shit about those.

Lago: Is that a challenge? Do you really want me to do the
            deli orgasm scene from *When Harry Met Sally*?

Alice: For the love of God, no.

Lago: Take a shot. Try to stump me.

Alice: Okay. You said you couldn't be with someone who didn't believe in you. Well, I believed in you. You just didn't believe in me.

Lago: *Pretty in Pink.*

Alice: Jesus.

Lago: Jesus loves that movie too. Next.

Alice: Winter must be cold for those with no warm memories.

Lago: *An Affair to Remember.* Total classic.

Alice: Are you crying?

Lago: Yes and no. Try harder.

Alice: Love means never having to say you're sorry.

Lago: That's a low blow.

Alice: You are crying. Let's go home.

Lago: Bartender! Another round!

Bartender: Doubtful!

Alice: This isn't fun for me.

Lago: Who said anything about having fun? Continue.

Alice: Far from this world of brutal lies is a land for lovers who despise violence, weeping for the lost and lonely. A land for lovers, for lovers only.

LONG SILENCE. LAGO MUMBLES TO HIMSELF.

Alice: Ha! Stumped you. *Cyrano de Bergerac*! Are you okay, John?

Lago: Just leave me alone.

Alice: John—

Lago: I said leave me the fuck alone!

SOUND OF BREAKING GLASS. PATRONS SHOUT INSULTS AT LAGO.

Alice: Fuck you, John. Have a nice life. I'm out of here.

Bartender: Hey, douche, you're cut off and you're leaving NOW.

Lago: Get your fucking hands off me.

SOUND OF GLASS AND WOOD BREAKING, PATRONS SCREAMING.

—END TRANSCRIPT—

20

DRUNK DIALING THE GRIM REAPER

Rule #11: Always do sober what you said you'd do drunk.
That will teach you to keep your mouth shut.

I'm quoting Hemingway because last night I had more drinks in one sitting than I've had my whole life. I tend to avoid alcohol because I have seen it make monsters out of the men who were supposed to be my guardians, and, let's face it, it makes you fat and stupid over time. But in light of the Bendini situation, I decided to drown myself in snake oil like an outlaw on the eve of a showdown he's certain to lose. It was at the pinnacle of my nihilistic rage that Alice showed up, looking for a booty call. I was the world's biggest prick. Not only did I burn that bridge, but I blew it to kingdom come. I feel bad, but it was the only way. Got to just rip off the Band-Aid. When she looks back, she'll hate my guts and there won't be any regret because my name will simply go on a plaque in her mausoleum of fucked-up men who failed her.

But that's not why I'm quoting Hem. After nearly killing the bartender and stomping out through the rubble like some kind of hillbilly Godzilla, I decided it would be an excellent idea to call Bob at 2:00 A.M. I thought it was an even better idea to leave him a message telling him I wanted to be relieved of my duties and that he should go fuck himself—or something to that effect. It is now 5:00 A.M. and I'm facedown on the kitchen floor, hoping it was all just a bad dream. Then my phone rings. Bob wants to meet me at a diner in Battery Park. He hangs up before I can say anything other than, "Yes." He does not sound happy. The picture is complete when a black Town Car that might as well be a hearse pulls up to my building to take me to Battery Park.

When I arrive, Bob has a telltale bulge in his jacket. My guess is he's packing something small and light so as not to alarm me. Wants me to think it's "for snakes and such." But *I am alarmed.* He is also wearing a Kevlar vest. Mind you, it's an Israeli-made undercover police vest—very thin and difficult to see under normal clothes. Also, this diner is located near the water and is fairly obscure. It is surrounded by rail yards and other empty industrial places—great for killing someone and dumping them in the river without a lot of witnesses. And let's not forget the two gentlemen posing as police officers sitting in the police cruiser drinking coffee outside. Nice touch. I know they are professionals because most New York cops are not that fit. Also, hitters have a look. Many of them gobble steroids like PEZ, and they end up with that muscle face you see with juicers. These guys are your garden-variety, ex-military (special forces or whatever), bulging-at-the-seams neck breakers.

I know there are more. If Bob were taking precautions with me, and he clearly is, he wouldn't come with only two for backup. My guess is the kitchen staff, waitress, and maybe even the homeless guy taking a shit in a Folgers can outside are all waiting to bag and tag me like a baboon on *Wild Kingdom.* This is it. This is how it's going down. I'm going to do something I never want you to do: I'm going to confront Bob. As they say on *Jackass,* don't try this at home. It's a hundred times more dangerous than any of your assignments will be, and you would be an idiot—a dead idiot—to try it. The only reason I'm doing it is because I'm fairly certain this is going to end badly and I've decided I'm not going down easy. Why should I?

"John, I wouldn't have expected something like this back when you were fourteen, let alone now." Bob is attempting, unsuccessfully, to contain his anger.

"This is a unique situation, Bob."

"So you got frustrated and now you want to quit?"

"Frustrated doesn't quite capture how I'm feeling about this job. All due respect but to say this is irregular is putting it lightly."

Bob slams his hand on the table, knocking everything to the floor. Now I have to be ready for anything.

"Stop patronizing me with that bullshit tone. We're talking man to man here!" he yells. Bob never yells.

"As long as we're talking man to man, may I say that this assignment has been dog shit from the beginning, and you seem to have your head up your ass? Furthermore, I'm not fucking lifting another finger until you get your shit together. If you don't like it, you know where you can shove it. Does that meet your John Wayne seal of approval?"

"Who do you think you're talking to?"

I laugh in his face.

"Am I embarrassing you in front of the low-rent janitors you hired to field dress me? That fucking ape over there can't even pour a convincing cup of coffee."

I stand and throw my coffee mug at the thug pretending to be a waiter. He ducks and it shatters on the wall behind his head. He glares at me. Bob does nothing, which only makes me want to take this further.

"That's right! I'm talking about you, donkey show! Go ahead and pull that hardware you got behind the counter so I can pop your empty fucking balloon of a head!"

He doesn't move a muscle, waiting for slave master Bob to give him a command.

"Nice work, Bob. You can't even find human beings anymore."

"John, do you want me to kill you? Is that why you're acting like such an asshole?"

I sit back down. Bob's tone surprises me. It's almost conciliatory.

"I want you to do what you came here to do and quit jacking me around," I huff.

Bob waves his hand casually and everyone leaves the diner.

"Okay."

Bob reaches into his jacket. I pull my Glock 18 and point it at his face. He laughs.

"You think I would actually try to pull a weapon from my jacket? Maybe you're the one who's got his head up his ass, John."

Bob takes an envelope from his jacket. Empties photographs onto the table. I glance at them. Surveillance photos of Locke, the third partner on the firm's shingle.

"I've had the other two partners on twenty-four-hour rotations since your assignment began."

Bob's right. I am the asshole. Guilty as charged.

"These were taken less than twelve hours ago. He's selling WPL names to a capo from a Brooklyn mob family."

"You're sure about him?"

"Yes. But now I'm not so sure about you."

I shove the photos at him.

"Then put a fucking bullet in my head and kill him yourself."

"Believe me. I thought about it. My partners strongly suggested it."

"But you told them I deserve another chance. Because no one but me can pull it off."

My arrogance is only amusing to Bob now as he quietly revels in the egg on my face.

"No, John. I have plenty of people who can pull this off. I told the partners you deserve another chance because I owe it you—for years of dedicated service."

"Bullshit."

"I have no reason to bullshit you. You're my most valuable asset. I told them to go fuck themselves and if you screwed the pooch they could retire me as well."

"So what are we doing here, Bob? This is not the kind of place where people dole out second chances."

"We're here because I think we have some heat on us from the feds and I'm having the office fully cleaned."

"What? Any specifics?"

"No, let's just say my Spidey sense is tingling. The point is our whole operation is at risk, and I need my best button man to deliver."

"It's going to be a bitch trading horses at the firm."

"Stay put for now. I don't want you to call attention to yourself."

Bob gets up to leave.

"Hey, Bob, thanks for looking out."

"I want you to do something for me, John. Something you would never have dreamed of doing in all the years I've known you."

"What?"

"I want you to trust me."

"I trust you, Bob."

"I don't need to hear you say it, John. I just need you to believe it."

21

LAWYERS, GUNS, AND MONEY

As soon as I get to the office, I brush up on Locke's CV, and things begin to make sense. He's a criminal defense attorney and he has won 99 percent of his cases. The man is an animal and he eats prosecutors for breakfast. Also, not surprisingly, he abhors the press and has never granted them an interview. He is truly the man in black, lurking behind the scenes, occupying the shadows and keeping the streets full to bursting with USDA prime criminal scum. His client list is encrypted, so I have to rely on reports from hundreds of obscure legal journals to get a handle on who *he* handles. Not surprisingly, a fair number of Mafia types owe him their freedom.

But that's not enough for him. Guys like Locke get greedy and power hungry and all they give a shit about is winning. So he gets his hands on the witness protection list and sells names to clients, friends of clients, the highest bidder, etc. Now he can stack the deck for his clients and keep his win percentage in the stratosphere. This translates to millions for him and for the firm. The icing on the cake is the tidy profit he turns by selling the names. That, my friends, is what we call win-win. And, of course, the firm wants the money to keep flowing in, but they don't want to know where it's coming from, so they don't ask.

I'm beginning to think Locke could give Bob a run for his money. He might be a civilian, but he's dangerous, powerful, and his connections are probably the who's who of organized crime. Waxing

him with a cup of coffee ain't going to happen. I've got to find a
way to ambush the bastard when he's not surrounded by an army of
killers. Bob's right. We're rapidly approaching our expiration date
on this assignment. I need a fast track to Locke and I need to get to
him without arousing any suspicion. I need Alice. She's on Bendini's
team, but as an actual employee, she has much greater access than
me, and I'm not about to try to reel in another asset this late in the
game. Of course, Alice would sooner kick me in the nuts right now
than help me in any way. I need to get back into her good graces. I
wonder what wines go best with a generous helping of crow?

United States Department of Justice
Federal Bureau of Investigation

Washington, D.C. 20535

ALL INFORMATION HEREIN IS CLASSIFIED
SURVEILLANCE TRANSCRIPT: AUDIO RECORDING—
INFRARED LASER MIC (150M)

Location: Alice (censored) Residence/Bedroom, East Village,
    Manhattan
Subjects: John Lago and Alice (censored).

KNOCK ON THE DOOR. SOUND OF ALICE OPENING THE DOOR.

Alice: Look what crawled out of the devil's asshole.

Lago: You have a way with words.

Alice: And you don't. Walk away so I can see your tail
           between your legs.

Lago: I'm sorry.

Alice: You're a sorry excuse.

Lago: You think I'll wither away if you reject me and you'll
           have your petty revenge? How long are you going to
           play tough with someone who's used to suffering?

Alice: I don't know. How long are you going to use your
           suffering as an excuse to be a bastard?

Lago: I'm not using it as an excuse. I'm just not. Shit. I've
           never really been with anyone. I mean, I've had plenty
           of . . . You're just my first—

Alice: Girlfriend? Is that what you're stumbling on? Because most guys got past that in the seventh grade.

Lago: The longest I've ever been with anyone is two weeks, and she's dead. Remember I said it ended badly?

Alice: Now you've gone and made me feel sorry for you. You suck.

Lago: I'm not looking for pity. I'm just trying to tell you what you're dealing with. I'm probably going to make a lot of mistakes, fuck-ups that most guys got out of their system when they were younger.

Alice: And you want me to give you a chance.

LONG PAUSE.

Alice: If you can't even say it, why should I give it to you?

Lago: Give me a chance. Please.

Alice: Okay.

Lago: Just like that? Okay?

Alice: Oh, you're still in the doghouse. In fact, if the doghouse had solitary confinement, you'd be in there.

LONG PAUSE. SOUNDS OF PHYSICAL CONTACT.

Alice: Get your butt in here.

LAGO WALKS IN. SOUND OF DOOR LOCKING.

Alice: I have a present for you. I came to surprise you with it at the bar, but then you got all Kiefer Sutherland on me.

Lago: I like presents. Let me guess. Is it a puppy?

Alice: Smart-ass. Now I don't want to tell you.

Lago: Come on. I'm dying. What's my present?

Alice: Wait here.

PAUSE.

Alice:	Here you go.
Lago:	What's this?
Alice:	Read it. One of those men is probably your father.
Lago:	Come again.
Alice:	Dorothy did her research. Went through all of those hospital visitation records from when you were in the NICU. Weeded out the nonstarters and it all came down to ten names. Ten!
Lago:	Holy shit.
Alice:	All you have to do is call them.
Lago:	I don't know what to say. This is the nicest thing anyone has ever done for me.
Alice:	You know what to say, you dolt.
Lago:	Thank you.
Alice:	Nice try.
Lago:	I love you?
Alice:	Getting warmer.
Lago:	I love you.
Alice:	I believe you.
Lago:	You're not going to say it?
Alice:	Hell no. I'm still pissed at you. Nice flowers, by the way. You get those at a funeral home?

—END TRANSCRIPT—

22

AIN'T LOVE GRAND?

Last night I tore several pages out of the Hugh Grant playbook and went to Alice's house to deploy some world-class groveling. I did just about everything but get down on my knees in the pouring rain, and believe me, if there had been pouring rain, that's exactly what I would have done. I brought her some mediocre flowers to add an extra touch of charm to the performance. Of course I know flowers very well and could have easily gotten her a bouquet of rare saffron crocus, but that is not in keeping with my persona and would have aroused suspicion. Plus, the guys that win the girl in romantic comedies almost always have some kind of pathetic flower to represent the ragged soul that they need a woman to cultivate. Suffice it to say that Alice was moved by my performance and I won my way back into her good graces. And her bed, incidentally.

To really cure the meat, I'm taking her to a fancy lunch that she'll feel outwardly guilty about because of my pay grade, but inwardly ecstatic about because I'm willing to throw down for her, even if my persona would realistically be living at poverty level. Ain't love grand? It is, if I can get her to agree to help me get an in with Locke.

"You're really pouring it on, John. You didn't have to do this."

It's like magic, right?

"I actually want to talk to you about something."

"You're pregnant?"

She grins. "Try to be serious at least until the salads get here."

"Okay. What's up?"

"You may have heard a rumor about our boss recently."

She smiles. Of course she knows about the wild west show that took place out at Bendini's house the other night because I'm sure she has him under 24/7 surveillance.

"Watercooler chatter says he might be teeing off with the wrong foursome," she whispers. "One of them tried to whack him over the weekend."

"I was there," I whisper back.

She's legitimately surprised. Good. She didn't know I was there.

"What the fuck? Why the hell didn't you tell me?"

"I haven't told a soul. I was taking him the Foster files we've been working on. He wanted me to bring them to the house because I was out of the office. When I got there it was like a fucking war zone. The whole thing scared me shitless. But what scared me more was Bendini. He didn't actually say this in so many words, but I feel like he implied, very kindly mind you, that I should keep my mouth shut about this or I might piss off the wrong people."

"Oh my God."

"And now I've told you, so you better keep your trap shut."

She's feigning sympathy, but I can tell she's charged up. This is huge for her case and it's great for me because it will keep her sights trained on Bendini, so there's no chance her investigation will fuck with my new orders to kill Locke. She's dying for details.

"What did Bendini actually say?"

"All he said was that he has enemies. And thanked me for saving his life."

"You saved his life?!"

My eyes dart nervously.

"Keep it down."

"Relax. What do you think this is, *Three Days of the Condor*?"

"That is your first good movie reference since I met you. And yes, like in *Condor* I feel like it's possible that there are eyes and ears everywhere. How do I know that the person who tried to kill Bendini doesn't know who I am and want to whack me now as a witness?"

"You watch way too many movies, John. Jesus."

"What makes you an expert?"

She starts to make a point but pulls back, catching herself. She is getting too comfortable with me.

"I thought about this a lot and I think I would feel more comfortable working for someone else in the firm."

"I don't blame you. Who, though?"

"Litigation interests me quite a bit. Maybe I could see about getting a post with Locke's crew."

"The dragon slayer? Are you a glutton for punishment?"

"I've heard he's the best." Spoken like a true bumpkin.

"He's definitely the best, but his people are miserable. They look like zombies. The joke around the office is that they never take lunch because they'd just eat each other."

"Sounds perfect. Can you get my foot in the door?"

"Maybe. A girl I know from law school works in his department."

This makes me laugh because Alice is trying to get me to climb aboard her own version of the Bullshit Express.

"But you do realize you will piss off Bendini to no end if you do this, right?" she warns.

"Yeah. I just want to get on the right path for my career."

That really sounded like a nervous white yuppie. I am scoring regular guy points like a son of a bitch.

"Makes sense. I'll see what I can do."

23

YOU'VE COME A LONG WAY, DUMPSTER BABY

After lunch, I walk into my windowless closet of an office and it's completely empty. The place was wall-to-wall files when I left it. Now it's just white walls. My computer is gone as well, along with all of my personal stuff. I take a breath and try to process this. I know I'm a total fucking plebe, but this is ridiculous.

While I'm standing there with my dick in my hand, my door shuts and locks behind me. I reach for the knob. There is just a keyhole. Presumably, the person on the other side has the key that was never issued to me. But that is neither here nor there because the person on the other side more than likely is planning to kill me. If you think about it, this room is a perfect death trap. I am on the second floor, which has a handful of these types of offices but mostly serves as a giant storage floor for office furniture and file archives. So it's quiet and I rarely see other people here. Also, there are no escape routes. Unlike the other floors, this floor only has one stairwell access door and one elevator—the service elevator. You literally have to use the fucking service elevator to get to this floor. Which is why they love putting interns here because it's dark, lonely, and reminds you every moment that you're lower than a boiler room roach in the firm's food chain.

I can hear someone outside the door, but he's whispering to another person. They are moving quickly, and I occasionally hear their heavy footfalls on the old wood floors near the elevator. I look around my shit box office. I can easily kick the door down, but that is ill advised, as they will have it covered. Chances are, they sent a scout to make sure I was here and alert the rest of the team to move in. If I'm lucky, I have thirty seconds to move. Door is out. No windows. I know what you're thinking. Ventilation shaft. Well, guess what, *Mission: Impossible*, there's a twelve-inch HVAC duct crammed in the corner on the floor. I doubt I'll be crawling into that to escape CIA headquarters.

Then I notice the tiny space between the bottom of the far wall and the edge of the 1950s-era kitchen carpet. The wall it shares a corner with has the same thing, but it's harder to see because of the quarter inch of filth piled up on the carpet. These are floating walls, and they were thrown together to make this room private. Of course none of it is up to code, and that is my saving grace. I hear more hushed voices outside moving down the hallway. Got to make a move now. I pull my knife and quietly shove it into the drywall on one of the floaters. It goes in easily, as these walls are paper-thin. I cut a large cross in the lower part of the wall to score it. Voices getting closer. I shove the heavy metal desk as hard as I can into the wall. As expected, it disintegrates as the desk smashes corner-first in the middle of my cross. I hear someone shouting, but my adrenaline is roaring in my ears like a freight train. I don't have time to pull my ankle piece and I can't find my knife. Must have fallen out when I picked up the desk. Fuck it. I dive through the ragged hole in the wall and leap to my feet, ready to throw down.

Motherfucker.

It's not a team, waiting to pump a thousand silent 9-mm rounds into me and wheel my body parts out onto Central Park South in a hot dog cart.

It's Alice holding a bottle of champagne and two janitors with all of my stuff.

"What the hell is your problem, you freak?"

"Jesus, I . . . what the hell is going on here?"

"You made associate. I came down to help you move your shit. The boys upstairs are waiting to buy you a drink."

She laughs. The janitors are not amused. I'm amused by the irony, which is now thick enough to qualify for fat camp.

"Sorry. Claustrophobic." I give them a sheepish grin.

She takes my hand.

"Come on, weirdo."

We leave the janitors staring at the drywall explosion. Next thing I know I'm sipping champagne in my new office on the fifth floor— with a *window*.

"Of course, you are still my bitch." Alice smiles.

"Of course."

Bendini walks in and shakes my hand vigorously.

"One million dollars in back fees? Unheard of. You, my boy, are a one-man wrecking crew."

"Thank you, sir."

"Everyone else thought you were some kind of goddamned hick. But I knew. I could see it in your eyes. You have the right stuff, kid. Congratulations!"

"I couldn't be happier, sir. I want you to know that I'll work hard to live up to—"

"Cut the horseshit, son. Let's have a drink."

His troll of an assistant appears out of nowhere with a thick stubby bottle of expensive Scotch and pours us all a glass.

"To this young man's bright future," Bendini toasts.

I know this is *The Intern's Handbook*, but I am no longer an intern. I am a junior associate at one of the biggest law firms in New York. If this weren't the worst possible thing that could happen to me as a contract killer, I would be pretty damn proud of myself. Conceived in a petri dish of despair, birthed from the loins of a brain-dead junkie with a third-grade education, raised by vermin abusers, pedophiles, smack dealers, and all manner of welfare system bloodsuckers, and adopted by a homicidal jarhead. By all rights, I should have been dead long ago or at least institutionalized. And look at me now. You've come a long way, Dumpster baby.

And you know what? I'm going to enjoy it. Now at least before I end up a corpse or a prisoner, I'll have a claim to fame that has nothing to do with being responsible for a majority of the high-profile murders that have taken place in Manhattan in the last decade. I'm legit, yo.

After Bendini leaves, Alice settles beside me at the window. I actually have a decent view of the street and the edge of the park. She taps my glass with hers.

"Blue Horseshoe loves Anacott Steel."

"This is your wake-up call, Buddy," I say with a smile.

"I guess Bendini owed you one."

"Yep."

"Still want to try to lick Locke's tasseled loafers?"

"No, I think I'll be fine here, thanks."

"Enjoy it while it lasts, because I'm going to be gunning for you."

She means what she says, but she's not saying what she means. *Gunning* is a great choice of words. For the first time, I'm kind of glad she thinks I'm a loose cannon that she can't seem to put a finger on. It's making this whole thing more fun all of a sudden. Especially since I'm gleefully chucking the rulebook to the wind. I think it's fun for her as well. I just moved up a notch from someone earning her casual interest to a potential player. I touch her ass, just to see if she's going to close up the candy store. She touches mine back. Good. No sense letting work get in the way of a great lay.

That night I decide to pretend all of this is real and enjoy the fruits of my labor. After shopping for new suits with Alice (on Bob, of course), we have dinner at an expensive restaurant that seems to be perfectly designed to annoy the shit out of me. But I am not annoyed. I am half drunk, somewhat on booze but mostly on power. I have a beautiful woman on my arm. And I can tell that she is fully immersed in her fake self as well. All is right with the world as we slip into the high-thread-count bliss of hotel sex. And as we drift off to sleep, I tell myself to remember this because I'll need a happy memory when it all blows up and leaves a bloody mess.

United States Department of Justice
Federal Bureau of Investigation

Washington, D.C. 20535

ALL INFORMATION HEREIN IS CLASSIFIED
SURVEILLANCE TRANSCRIPT: AUDIO RECORDING—
FIBER OPTIC SCOPE

Location: Flatiron Hotel, Manhattan
Subjects: John Lago and Alice (censored).

PHYSICAL CONTACT. LONG PAUSE. SUBJECTS BREATHING RAPIDLY.

Alice: I love doing it at a hotel. Makes me feel like a call girl. Which was my Plan B if this whole lawyer thing didn't work out.

Lago: How much do I owe you?

Alice: You're funny. I should charge you. You just killed one of my billable hours.

Lago: Do I get a discount as a professional courtesy?

Alice: You can sleep in the wet spot. No extra charge.

Lago: That's more than generous.

Alice: So, are you happy now, you cranky fucker? You got the job, the girl, the swinging dick office.

Lago: Yeah. Didn't think it was possible, but I am, I dare say, happy. For the first time maybe ever.

Alice: And you owe it all to me, of course.

Lago: Of course, darling.

CHAMPAGNE CORK POPS.

Lago: That's minibar champagne! It's going to cost us a
          fortune.

Alice: It's a special occasion. We need to celebrate.

Lago: I thought we were celebrating.

Alice: This is not just about the job and how great in bed I
          am. It's much bigger.

Lago: Oh my God. You're pregnant.

Alice: Hilarious. No, I have a surprise for you.

Lago: What?

Alice: You have to promise not to be mad.

Lago: About a surprise? How is that possible?

Alice: Just promise.

Lago: Okay, I promise.

Alice: It's about your father. I called the people on your list.
          My . . . Dad used to work with the government and I
          asked one of his old colleagues to help. I know you've
          been having a hard time getting through them all. Are
          you mad?

Lago: Of course not. So what did you find out?

Alice: I'm pretty sure I found him.

LONG PAUSE.

Alice: You okay?

Lago: Yeah. I'm just kind of stunned.

Alice: I can imagine. But it's also exciting right?

Lago: Absolutely. What's his name?

Alice: Marcus (censored).

Lago:	Wow. What a great dad name.
Alice:	What were you expecting?
Lago:	With my past I was thinking it would be a one-word bullshit street name like Whippet or Snowball.

ALICE LAUGHS.

Lago:	But Marcus (censored). Damn. That sounds like one of the guys from the office, you know. The squash and gin Mafia.
Alice:	I know. He probably wears an ascot and boat shoes.
Lago:	Thank you. I really appreciate all of your help with this. You've been amazing and I couldn't have done it without you. And I do love you.
Alice:	I love you. Call him.
Lago:	I will.

—END TRANSCRIPT—

24

IN BED WITH THE JONESES

The next two weeks are surreal. I am so inundated with work that I almost forget why I am really there. Or I would rather not remember. At any rate, I am reveling in my new social stratum. The other junior associates, my coworkers, are all highly educated, interesting people. They like me because they think I'm some kind of roughneck genius coming from total obscurity. Bob said it best. They know their own kind—the prep school, Ivy League, summering in Southampton circus. But they want to accept me as a convert. They want to adopt and care for me like a stray puppy. So they invite me to their parties and squash games. They ask my advice about cases and bring me their grandmother's homemade fudge. They tell me I must come skiing with them in Beaver Creek this year and ask me to join their crew club. And I drink it all in. I mainly do this because they may be valuable assets when it comes to gathering intel on Locke. But I also do it because these are really the first friends I've ever had. Growing up, I was lucky if a three-legged alley cat would be friendly to me, let alone the well-bred master builders of Manhattan's power elite.

Alice likes some of them, but they don't all like her. The women are especially reluctant to embrace Alice because she is everything they will never be: quick witted, fiercely independent, physically strong, and beautiful in a way only mutts can be beautiful—a total original without the whole Reese Witherspoon vibe put out by every member of what I like to call the Barbie Cabal.

As I sit in my humble, yet well-appointed office and admire my partial, yet spectacular view, I begin to wish that things could just stay this way forever. Maybe Bob will decide I've earned this and send someone else to kill Locke. After all, I'm hardly the subtle breeze anymore that used to blow into hits as easily as I would blow out of them. It's a nice fantasy. I could just transition into my new career right now. Because of my "killer" instinct, I would kick down the corporate ladder and trample everyone ahead of me. I could take this fucking place over. Being a lawyer is not that different from being an assassin. Both require a predator mentality. Both leave unholy destruction in their path. In fact, I only kill people. Lawyers *destroy* people, like briefcase mercenaries with godlike powers at their disposal. Hey, if lawyers could get someone like O. J. Simpson acquitted, they can fucking walk on water and open the gates of hell. This career is perfect for me in every way.

But I know all of this is just a bullshit pipe dream fueled by wishful thinking. Fantasy is a luxury I can't afford, and that's confirmed when Bob wakes me up by lighting a fire under my ass. He tells me the people that ordered this hit are getting very impatient. In fact, they have demanded results and given us two weeks to execute or they will send someone else *and* they will send a team to retire *us*. This is not the first time we have been pushed to expedite the process. However, this *is* the first time we've been threatened. I promise to ratchet up my efforts and then he kind of reads my mind and tells me that I shouldn't get any ideas about dragging it out so he will get fragged and I can be free to play lawyer the rest of my life. He's kind of joking when he says it, but the thought *had* crossed my mind.

ALL INFORMATION HEREIN IS CLASSIFIED
SURVEILLANCE TRANSCRIPT: AUDIO RECORDING

Location: Wireless phone call intercept—IMSI catcher/Roving bug
Subjects: John Lago and Alice (censored).

Alice: Will you miss me?

Lago: Of course.

Alice: Of course what?

Lago: Wow. Really?

Alice: I need to hear you say it.

Lago: I will miss you.

Alice: I will miss you too.

Lago: Why so formal?

Alice: Because that's how you sound.

Lago: Jesus.

Alice: Don't get pissed.

Lago: I'm not pissed.

Alice: Come on. What's wrong?

Lago: I was, uh, I was looking forward to seeing you. There.
          Happy?

Alice: Now I feel bad because you're being all honest injun and boyfriendy.

Lago: Honest injun? Boyfriendy? Why you gettin' all Miley Cyrusy?

LAUGHTER.

Alice: I was looking forward to it too. Rain check?

Lago: Yes. Definitely.

Alice: Thank you for being so understanding. My aunt really needs me.

Lago: When are you flying out?

Alice: Couple of hours. Funeral is tomorrow afternoon.

LONG PAUSE.

Lago: What's wrong?

Alice: I'm just thinking about how easy it is to just lose someone, you know? I could just blink my eyes and you would be gone too.

Lago: I'm not going anywhere. Well, I'm going to get a steak, but I'll chew it very thoroughly.

Alice: Ha-ha. You know what I'm saying. Everything is so fleeting and impermanent. It's enough to drive you bat shit crazy.

Lago: That's why you can't take anything for granted.

LONG PAUSE. SOUND OF ALICE CRYING.

Lago: I'm sorry. I just feel like life is short and I want to remember it all, good or bad.

Alice: That's a good way to think. But it kind of sucks too. Makes me just want to say fuck it sometimes and take off.

Lago: Take off?

Alice:	Yeah. Get the hell out of this city. Maybe even leave the country. Try to just melt into obscurity somewhere and enjoy the rest of my life.
Lago:	That's not your style. You would go nuts. You love the action.
Alice:	I'm not so sure anymore.
Lago:	For what it's worth, if you did get the fuck out of here, I would get the fuck out of here with you.
Alice:	Thank you, John. You're a good guy.
Lago:	I wish that were true.
Alice:	Why would you say that? Did you cheat on me?
Lago:	Oh my God. Wow.
Alice:	Okay, sorry. But seriously, why would you say that?
Lago:	Do you really want to know?
Alice:	Yes. I really do. I want to make sure I'm not fucking Ted Bundy.
Lago:	If only I had his looks.
Alice:	Come on.
Lago:	Some other time. I'm sure you don't need to hear my litany of sins while you're on your way to a funeral.
Alice:	I'm holding you to that. You owe me a confession.
Lago:	Yes, padre. Just be careful what you wish for.

—END TRANSCRIPT—

25

THE UNTIMELY DEATH OF UNCLE SAM

After a squash match with one of my new office buddies, I get in cab to go meet Alice for dinner, but she calls me and cancels. One of her uncles has died and she has to take a flight to D.C. tonight for the funeral. D.C.? Could that be her *Uncle Sam* per chance? Like me, she probably has to have a sit-down with her superiors to discuss her lack of progress. At least she won't have to listen to threats. Or, at least, not life-threatening threats. I tell her I'm sorry for her loss and make it sound like I mean it. She makes it sound like she is all broken up about her uncle. I don't ask his name out of professional courtesy. I hate it when I hear a lie, and I know this would be a lie, so I spare both of us the agony.

I decide to pay a visit to Alice's apartment and try to ramp up my intel. The mountain of raw data that's been dumping to my computer each day from the device I planted inside her laptop is massive, overwhelming, and will take way too much fucking time to sift through without the help of Bob's drone corps. She left the office and went straight to the airport, so I know her laptop is still at home. She doesn't bring it into the office because the feds probably don't want their data just lying around the biggest, most powerful law firm in Manhattan. This could be my best shot.

I decide to do it by stealth. Her neighbors know me well and they would surely mention having seen me alone in her building while she was gone. She lives in one of those wildly annoying co-ops where everyone feels they have purchased the right to your personal business along with their one-bedroom, half-bath, cold-water walk-up shoe box. Also, I'm not sure if it's paranoia or my jungle cat senses, but after the Bendini shit show I feel like someone is watching me. Mind you, I've been under surveillance before and I actually kind of like the exhibitionist thrill I get from it. But in this case, we could be talking about Bendini's goombahs or Alice's FBI support crew, so I need to take extra precautions to keep them from tracking my movements. Aside from that, stealth is a lot of fun. You get to strap on some cool ninja gear and traverse the city on rooftops—like Batman or Robert De Niro in the second *Godfather*.

So I take a taxi with my gear in a duffel bag over to the YMCA that is four buildings away from Alice's. I am a member, which I highly recommend, because it's like having storage units all over Manhattan. You can rent a private locker at each location and keep it as long as you want. And they only require your YMCA card—which has your fake identity on it, along with a credit card—which is also an untraceable Bob special. No driver's license or passport bullshit to give his forgers the night sweats. I stroll into the Y, looking at no one, and head for my locker.

————

Rule #12: Embrace your inner shadow warrior.

You've heard of ninjas. I'm sure you're laughing to even hear that word. That's because you're a stupid American who thinks everything from foreign cultures can be reduced to a late-night talk show bit. And yes, I am aware of the Chris Farley movie *Beverly Hills Ninja*. There is something that people find funny about ninjutsu, but if you know *anything*, then you know that there is *absolutely nothing funny about it.*

First off, they've been around since the twelfth century. Like us, the functions of the ninja include espionage, sabotage, infiltration, and assassination. In fact, Bob created the entire intern program based on four of the eighteen principles of ninjutsu: Hensōjutsu (disguise and impersonation), Shinobi-iri (silent infiltration), Bōryaku (unorthodox battle tactics), and Intonjutsu (escaping and concealment). You might call these the four pillars of HR, Inc.

One of my most shining moments was an assignment wherein I first executed all of these pillars flawlessly. Ironically, my target was a Japanese businessman named Raiden Sanjuro, and his great-great-grandfather had been a ninja in the service of the emperor. He had practiced ninjutsu as a boy but had dishonored his family by rejecting it and embracing Western culture—something he loved more than his own. Nonetheless, it had been ingrained in his psyche starting in his formative years, making it impossible to forget.

He was operating a very successful manufacturing outsourcing company in Manhattan, but it was actually a front for his real business—a network of industrial espionage cells gathering sensitive data from Silicon Valley to the Hudson Valley and selling it to the Chinese government. The Chinese are the best copycats in the world, and they decided a long time ago that it is better to simply take the intellectual property and achievements of others and perfect the process of reverse engineering, finding cheaper, more efficient ways of mass production and distribution. This way, they pay a fraction of what others pay in research and development, while remaining on the leading edge of technological advances and destroying the creators of the original products by selling those products for pennies on the dollar. Sanjuro was one of China's biggest suppliers of sensitive business data, and they paid him handsomely for his services.

The Chinese are also good at protecting their investments. So this guy had the tightest security detail I have ever seen and will probably ever see again unless I get involved in political assassination. He had a small army of Chinese military commandos—all schooled in the United States for language and cultural integration but trained in China to be hard as fucking coffin nails and not give two shits about whether they lived or died. After all, these guys are brainwashed from birth to think of themselves as organs in the body politic, nothing more. If they die, there are a few billion more waiting to take their place and mother China will never skip a beat.

Sanjuro was my target, but being a white boy made my getting an internship at that company a long shot. Of course, Bob pulled it off. He gave me a bullshit military background loaded with technical expertise. Basically, I was a former drone "pilot" with specializations in SATComm, remote avionics, and geomagnetic global positioning systems. Interesting shit, I must admit. Being a gearhead, I ate it up, and Sanjuro's company ate me up. Hensōjutsu (disguise and impersonation). Check.

I was assigned to work with Zhen, one of Sanjuro's sales execs. But this guy was not your usual booze-guzzling golf bully. He was former Chinese military intelligence and he was the biggest asshole I have ever met in my life. When he wanted something, I was his indentured servant with the rights of an ant colony drone. What impressed him was my absolute willingness to do whatever he asked without question or complaint—something he previously thought Caucasians were completely incapable of comprehending. I was on call round the clock, and there were times that I didn't sleep for twenty-four hours. Like everyone else, Zhen got hooked on the freedom I afforded him by basically doing his job for him, and he eventually gave me far too much latitude. The next thing I knew, I had complete access to Sanjuro.

Shinobi-iri (silent infiltration). Check.

Then came the hit itself. I may have lulled Zhen into complacency, but Sanjuro was another matter completely. He was creative in his paranoia and pursuit of hidden enemies and would very often have me strip-searched for concealed weapons. I silently and pleasantly agreed to everything he asked, but this seemed to make him even more distrusting. He told me I had the scheming eyes of a fox and he did not believe I was who I said I was. Yet he didn't send me packing because I was becoming more valuable to the company with each passing day.

Knowing the vigilance of his security detail, this case required some serious Bōryaku (unorthodox battle tactics) if I was going to pull it off. My best kill scenarios did not yield any acceptable escape and concealment scenarios (Intonjutsu). Sanjuro was the kind of man who had an expansive network of loyalists. He had organized his business to run as smoothly without him as with him. So it was not just about the hit. It was also about taking down the organization *with* the hit. Otherwise, what was the point of doing it at all?

It occurred to me that the answer might be found with Sanjuro's clients, the Chinese. If I could somehow make the hit also poison the well with the Chinese, they would systematically eliminate anyone left in order to kill any connection to them and Sanjuro's organization. Then we would be golden. If the Chinese felt exposed by Sanjuro, they would move swiftly to *adjust the situation*. And as I thought about that, the answer for Sanjuro came to me almost immediately. That level of failure would be devastating for Sanjuro. It would be dishonorable and, even though he had severed his connection with his Japanese ancestry, he still lived by the ninja warrior code: death before dishonor. Thus, the only way for him to save face would be to commit the ritual suicide known as seppuku. Sometimes you can get a shark to eat itself if you fill the water with enough blood.

I hacked Sanjuro's laptop—courtesy of Zhen's lazy ass and Bob's crack nerd squad—and gathered enough files to completely destroy him ten times over. I hid the files in a phantom data packet on San-juro's secure e-mail server. The next time Sanjuro logged in, it was set to send itself to several people who would be very interested in its contents: FBI, CIA, Homeland, the usual suspects. The cover letter with it involved Sanjuro explaining that he wanted protection from the Chinese, immunity from prosecution, etc. Of course, the Chi-nese secret police have people in *all* aspects of our government—as do we in theirs—so it would be a matter of hours before Sanjuro's clients found out about his betrayal. At which point, Sanjuro would commit suicide to balance things out with Buddha, and I would go down in HR history as a fucking genius.

But things didn't quite work out the way I planned. The e-mail did go out and Sanjuro was placed on the Chinese "Ten Most Wanted to Torture and Kill List," but I had overestimated Sanjuro's dedica-tion to Japanese custom. Instead of going all Bushido Blade and evis-cerating himself on his kitchen floor, he grabbed as much money as he could fit into his Louis Vuitton luggage and attempted to flee the country. Bob was not happy. In order to clean up what had become a prodigious mess, I had to take Sanjuro before a helicopter picked him up from the roof of a luxury hotel in Los Angeles. He was holed up in the celebrity overdose suite just below the helipad.

Sanjuro had a dozen thugs protecting him at the hotel, and he was heavily armed. Bob's people intercepted the call for the helicop-ter and hid me in the cargo hold of a chopper that we sent in place of the one Sanjuro ordered. While the pilot bullshitted with two of Sanjuro's security detail on the roof, I slipped out and dropped down into Sanjuro's suite. Ten guys sounds like a lot, I know. However, keep in mind that Zhen was not part of the ten, nor were any of the other Chinese military guards that had been part of Sanjuro's origi-nal detail, on account of their new orders to kill him with extreme prejudice. So he had pulled together a motley crew of muscle—and that's being generous. Knowing this, my biggest concern was Sanjuro himself. But I knew at this point that he was a fucking pussy and would try the escape route first. So as he bolted for the helipad, the chopper pilot was waiting for him with a syringe full of the same black ops knockout juice he used to take out the security guys on the roof—my own recipe, of course.

Meanwhile, inside the suite, the ten thugs came at me in laughably predictable ways. My biggest challenge was to keep them from firing their weapons *before* I killed them. The last thing I needed was hotel security, followed by LAPD, charging up here to heroically stop a gun battle in the $10,000-a-night presidential suite. Also, we needed to cart these fuckers out of there without a trace, so a bloodbath was not an option.

What ensued would have made Sanjuro's great-great-ninja-grandfather proud—of *me* that is. I had been studying their fighting techniques since I started with HR. My whole body was a weapon. Every point from fingers to toes, elbows, knees, chin, brow ridge, heels, everything. And when you are trying to be silent about combat, you tend to rely on the most effective kill strikes. You don't have time to break a chair over someone's head or pick them up and throw them through a plate-glass window. It's a close-quarters dance, and it is eyeball to eyeball.

The first two tried to pull MAC-10 submachine guns—a cheap, unreliable gangbanger special. I shoved the barrel into the eye socket of one and used the strap to snap the neck of the other. This little exchange made me seem vulnerable to the others. They figured they would take me while I was busy killing their buddies. What they didn't know was that is exactly what I wanted them to do.

"Jump in, boys. The water's fine."

The two that jumped on my back ended up falling on each other as I slipped between them and crushed both of their throats with each of my feet in a move they call "hawk seizes mouse." When the other six saw this, I could see that they were regretting getting too close to me, but they also knew retreat was not going to be possible. Two of them stupidly reached for guns. Both got open-hand strikes to the nose and shards of their own facial skeleton in their frontal lobes. Two others actually tried to bolt and got the caveman special—grab the back of the hair and strike the cervical vertebrae for a quick and painless internal decapitation. The last two tried to pull the old high-low on me. One went for my legs while the other tried to tackle me around the head and torso. I grabbed the guy on top by the head and flipped him over my shoulder, simultaneously snapping his neck and using his body as a sledgehammer that I brought down on the bottom guy, crushing his chest and obliterating his heart.

The chopper pilot brought Sanjuro in and set him down on the couch. When he came to, we had already removed the bodies of his security detail and refreshed the room to look pristine. He looked like he thought he was dreaming at first, but when he saw my face, he smiled.

"I am not surprised," he said.

"I am," I said.

"Why?"

"Because *this* . . . this is not the action of an honorable man, running from failure."

He stopped smiling and bowed his head. I might as well have deflowered his sister, the way his whole body slumped in shame.

"But, out of respect for your ancestors, I am prepared to help you do the right thing," I said evenly.

I set a katana down on the coffee table. I had taken it out of his apartment. Judging by the slight fray in the handle wrap and tiny pits in the metal, it was in excellent condition but very old. He wept when he saw it.

"You are a man of honor," he whispered.

He bowed deeply to me and shoved the blade into the space just below his rib cage. He did not have to disembowel himself because the initial puncture severed his superior aorta and that was all she wrote.

Bob was pleased. In the end, I got what I wanted and it was the right outcome, but Bob warned me never to leave anything to chance again. And I never did. Until this assignment, of course.

26

BOYFRIEND-GIRLFRIEND SHIT

Back at the YMCA locker, I don what appears to be a traditional ninja uniform but is actually a black ops hybrid of my own design. The fabric is a microfiber and Kevlar blend. So it's breathable, flexible, and will stop blades, spikes, needles, and even bullets with calibers up to 9 mm. Plus, it looks totally badass. I wear black rock climbing slippers that have sticky stealth rubber soles, and put on form-fitting rubberized gel gloves that stick like glue to any surface but leave no marks whatsoever. As I make my way up the stairs and out onto the roof, I pull on the hood with narrow eye slits and now I'm in full ninja mode.

Then comes the best part—roof hopping. There's a reason why most good action movies and crime TV shows have rooftop chase scenes. First off, they are fun. Stunt men and women *love* doing it. Of course, they have safety lines, but I can guarantee you they wish they didn't. When you leap across a roof between multistory buildings, it is the closest thing you'll ever get to flying. Yeah, you could go skydiving. But you know you have the chute. And flying is about getting from point A to point B. Birds don't generally drop straight down out of the sky and land on the ground unless they are attacking prey. In the end, you're not even jumping that far. It's the *exposure* that makes you feel like Iron Man. As you jump fifteen feet or so, you are clearing more than one hundred vertical feet below you, and it feels like base-jumping the Chrysler building.

The other thing I love about roof hopping, I think as I leap the four blocks to Alice's apartment, *is that I'm afraid of heights.* Other than that, I'm pretty much afraid of nothing. I'm not bragging, that's just reality. When I was a child, I failed to thrive (for obvious reasons) and never developed a healthy sense of fear or apprehension. Also, I was held by my ankles out of a ten-story building by a dealer when I was seven years old, so that might have something to do with it. This is going to sound weird, but I've sought out that fear rush ever since. It's almost as if finally feeling *anything at all* suddenly made me a human being. Until then I had always been convinced I was a robot. I almost never got sick or upset about anything. It's probably primordial, to go back to my favorite topic. My brain saw no room for emotions because they would either (a) hinder my predatory instincts or (b) result in zero gains from the outside world.

So when I'm up here it feeds, for lack of a better word, nostalgia about my youth. Some people get that way when they see a baseball field or smell trout on the grill. I get that feeling from vertigo and the Freudian fantasy of falling to my certain death on the pavement below. Or maybe into a hot dog cart! I love it when that happens in movies! *Wham!* A falling body obliterates a rusty Nathan's cart. The sidewalk is showered by hot dog water, and the wet wieners skitter across the sidewalk like bait fish on the deck of a boat. Classic.

When I land, silently mind you, on Alice's roof, I'm thinking about how cool she would think this is. Maybe sometime we can go roof hopping together, leap a few blocks downtown to grab a bite? Beats dodging strollers, obese tourists, and those people who can't seem to walk a fucking straight line, right? How would I present it to her without arousing suspicion? Or maybe I *should* arouse suspicion. That always seems to arouse *other things.*

I climb the fire escape and coax open the kitchen window. I slip into her apartment like a cat and find her laptop dutifully sitting on the small desk in her room. This time I brought the big guns—

Bulgarian password crack programs that not only annihilate encryption but also, wait for it, maintain enough encryption after forced entry that the computer itself is unable to generate a log-in record. So you never know you were hacked in the first place. Downloaded them for free from a site that will remain unnamed because the one group that you *never* want to piss off is the hacker community. They can truly unravel your life like a cheap sweater and all you can do is sit back and watch.

The crack programs do their magic and in fewer than five minutes I am uploading Alice's entire hard drive onto my cloud server. While that cooks, I start thinking about Alice's secret stash of Pop-Tarts and remember the scene from *Pulp Fiction* when Bruce Willis goes back to his apartment to get his father's watch—the one that had been in Chris Walken's ass in a Vietnamese prison camp. Alice keeps her Pop-Tarts hidden in the back of that annoying corner cupboard with a lazy Susan jammed full of pots and pans she never uses. She doesn't hide them so I can't eat them. She hides them so I don't know she's eating them. Alice has a little bit of extra weight on her ass, which I absolutely *love*. Classic case of a closet carb junkie. I'm doing her a favor by sentencing two Pop-Tarts to death by toaster.

The upload finishes with a satisfying *ping* and I close Alice's laptop, leaving it exactly as I found it. This is followed by a satisfying *pop* from the toaster. I follow the intoxicating aroma of burning high fructose corn syrup and enriched flour through the living room.

As I turn into the kitchen, *I find the barrel of a gun in my face.*

My eyes rack focus from the gun barrel to the pointer of said gun—like a camera in a Hitchcock film—and I see Alice staring back at me.

"Slowly drop to your knees with your hands behind your back."

Fuck fuck fuck fuck, I am thinking and mentally slap myself hard because I know I can't let the fact that it's Alice holding the gun influence me to react in any other way than that of a cornered predator. Then I start to think this is a potentially hot sex scenario and have to slap myself mentally again, this time a bit harder. Which kind of makes it even more of a sex scenario. *Fuck!*

So many questions. What's she doing here? Why did she lie about D.C.? Does she know it's me? *No fucking way.* Even if her people are watching me, those goons couldn't possibly have tracked me across the rooftops on a moonless, cloudy night in a black, completely nonreflective ninja suit! So, she lied. She needed to buy a little time away from me with the bullshit uncle story. Or maybe she just forgot something?

"Are you deaf asshole? Get down now!"

Glock 22. Five-pound trigger. She's about a nanosecond from double tapping my face with a couple of hollow point nines. Looking at her face in this moment, I get a glimpse of the real Alice—whatever her name is—and her raw power sends a chill down my spine. But I need to make a move, pretty much now, or she is going to kill me. I do as she says and drop to my knees. This makes it possible for me to fall to my side and sweep her legs out from under her. As she falls hard, hitting her head and losing her gun, I'm thinking that people in law enforcement are just at too much of a disadvantage. *They have to try to bring you in first.* They can't just shoot you, which is what she should have done if she expected to survive this. Right now she's kicking herself for not shooting me and working out some story with her superiors later. After all, a ninja strapped with all manner of weaponry invading your home is pretty much automatic grounds for lethal self-defense.

But I'm thinking too much because she is now off the ground and on her feet as fast as me. We square off. Her war face is so funny I want to laugh out loud, until she slams her foot in my guts and knocks most of my wind out. I say most because the Kevlar lessens the impact of body blows by distributing force to a wider surface area. It still hurts like hell, but that small advantage allows me to counterattack instead of doubling over and fighting for air. I don't care how tough you are, a shot to the breadbasket puts you into instant survival mode, trying to draw the life-giving breath that just got violently pushed out of you like a burst balloon. Why do you think boxers and MMA fighters do thousands of sit-ups? That muscle armor keeps you from going into the perfect position to receive a knee to the nose that could put your lights out for good.

To counter, I pretend to start to double over and catch her knee in my hands on the upswing. I hook the knee under my arm and do a hard vertical clean and jerk. She flips backward. Her knees land on the kitchen counter and send her torso pitching forward. One of the hands that shoots out to defend her head from hitting the floor makes a *snap* sound. Her finger is broken and she yelps from the pain. I instantly feel terrible and hate myself for it.

I know in that moment I cannot kill her—which would be the best tactical decision I could make for so many reasons—but my purity is dead with her. I can't do it, and now I need to get the fuck out of here without inflicting too much damage. But the one thing standing in the way of that goal is Alice. She uses her good hand to flip herself onto her feet and set her broken finger in one smooth move. She's pissed. Not so pissed that her judgment is affected. Pissed that she allowed things to get this far, a feeling that is clearly new for her.

She puts her hands up. Fucking Keysi Fighting Method. If she's any good, this is going to suck. It employs a 360-degree rotational attack zone and the use of any and all available objects. As I am choosing fight styles in my head to best counter her, she smashes the top off a saltshaker and expertly whips the salt into my eyes. There you have it. I'm completely blind and my eyes are in searing pain. I want to yell out "The old salt in the eyes trick, eh?" but don't have a chance because she is coming at me with everything in the kitchen—Jackie Chan style. She uses a stool to buckle my knees and breaks a heavy pot over my back. I feel her slacks as she goes to finish me with a KitchenAid mixer and use the fabric to literally climb up her body with my gloves. The mixer falls away harmlessly as I get her into an Eagle Claw grappling hold, swiveling her in front of me and encircling her neck with my free arm. To avoid her stomping feet, I leap backward with her in my arms and land on the kitchen counter. I wrap my legs around her chest and pull her in like a sea otter pulls in an oyster it is about to crack.

But I don't crack her. Instead of shutting off her windpipe, I use my legs to constrict her chest cavity—like a boa constrictor. This actually forces blood to her head and heart while making it impossible for her to breathe. She passes out, but only due to increased pressure in the brain transmitted through the veins returning to the chest. This is common in crush injury patients. I do it this way because I don't want her to suffer irreparable brain damage from oxygen deprivation.

If that's not love, I don't know what is.

I check her vitals as I lay her on the floor. Strong heartbeat. Autonomic nervous system has kicked in and she is breathing steadily. She looks and sounds like when we are in bed together and it makes me a little sad. But there is no room for sadness in this business. And there is no room for what I think I am feeling right now. It's what saved Alice's life tonight, and it's what I now know will be the end of me.

As I sit there by the kitchen window, trying to catch my breath, I look back at Alice and *she's gone.* Seconds later, she opens fire. I jump through the serving window that separates the kitchen from her minuscule dining room and slide across the table. I sprint for the bedroom window as she fires expertly through the wall at what she believes is my path. But I am very low to the ground. If I had been standing straight, she would have killed me for sure. As I lunge to dodge bullets, I'm hoping that I remember correctly that there's a Dumpster in the alley below Alice's bathroom window.

I know what you're thinking because you've been reading this handbook and heeding my words about life imitating art:

That only works in the movies.

True. But it *is* an option in real life, just not a very pleasant one. Let's get one thing straight: garbage is not soft. It's like jumping into a Burmese tiger trap full of punji sticks with all the glass bottles, wire hangers, and broken plastic. Hell, a cardboard milk carton feels like a cinder block when you fall on it at terminal velocity. But the air that's in the trash bags is what I'm counting on. Even though I will be shredded by what's in them, that split second wherein I push the air to the edges of the bag and force it to pop creates a measure of stopping power that impedes my rapid progress toward the iron hard Dumpster bottom. Having said all that, I'm not even sure the motherfucker is down there. And in order to keep from getting shot, I will be diving *through* the window, hoping to narrowly miss the fire escape on either side. Basically, I'm going to attempt something similar to what Trinity did in *The Matrix*. Spoiler alert!

I focus, sprint, and leap like Superman, my fists leading the way. No time to turn my body and go feet first. Alice rounds the corner as I am in midair and empties her clip. Bullets zip past with that horrible air-ripping sound that you hear just before it becomes a flesh-ripping or bone-crunching sound. As I smash through the glass, I feel a bullet tear through my shoe and take out a healthy chunk of my heel. Then I somersault like a Mexican cliff diver and point my feet toward the ground.

The only thing below me is a hot dog cart.

27

A MOMENT OF CLARITY

J ust kidding. There is a Dumpster below and it's full. Thank God it isn't garbage day. I feel like I am falling forever, windmilling my arms to maintain orientation and target trajectory. My feet slam into the first few bags and I hear and feel a ton of glass breaking. Why don't motherfuckers in Manhattan recycle! I feel the shards biting at my suit as I plunge into the plastic pillow of edges, filth, and stink. I finally hit bottom and the pain from my wounded heel shoots into my brain like a 10,000-volt electric shock. That, and the smell of hundreds of putrescent baby diapers make me puke immediately. A bullet rips through the bags and ricochets around the garbage can. I look up. Alice is coming down the fire escape, trying to get a good shot. I jump and take off down the alley. By the time she hits pavement I am long gone.

As I nurse my wounds in my apartment, I start going through the data I uploaded from Alice's laptop. I'm ecstatic to see that the FBI still considers Bendini their prime suspect in the stolen witness protection data case. The longer they stay off Locke, the better. I find myself feeling a little disappointed in Alice's detective skills but remember that she doesn't have the resources I have at my disposal. Her people have to gather intel *legally*. Mine by any means necessary. The most interesting thing is that, at one point, her superiors recommended that I be treated as a *person of interest*! Holy shit. Their reasoning was never stated in their e-mail communications.

Eventually she told them she disagreed with their assessment, and then they dropped it. Alice, you little minx. What did I tell you? Love trumps all. Alice was protecting me! Who knows what they would have found if she had agreed to dig into my life.

So now let's talk about the elephant in the room: Alice lied about her so-called uncle and about leaving town. Why would she do that? The scenarios are buzzing in my head like noisome flies when my phone rings—not the Bob phone, but the one assigned to my persona. I look at the display. It's Alice. Shit. Shit. Shit. I send it to voice mail so I have time to think while she figures it was just a bad connection and moves to a better spot to dial again. Her bedroom has the best coverage so she's probably walking there from the kitchen while attempting to clean up with her broken finger before her sweep team arrives to dust for prints and search for other evidence of my presence that they will never find.

The phone rings again. I answer.

"Hey, how's D.C.?"

"I need to see you. Now. Where are you?"

She sounds desperate and afraid.

"Waiting for a table at Morton's. Where are you?"

"Home."

"Alice, what's going on?"

"Just get over here quickly please."

She hangs up.

Fantastic. No idea what's going to happen now. Asking her more questions will just arouse her suspicion. Not showing up will solidify said suspicion. If she confronts me because she believes it was me in her apartment tonight, then she has a team there and they're going to try to take me down. No way she'll confront me about it if she isn't ready to go all OK Corral on me. Bob *is not* going to like this. Not one bit. My concealment of Alice as a federal agent is already enough to get me killed. Potentially blowing the operation by getting into a ruckus with a *team* of federal agents who consider me a prime suspect and who believe I assaulted one of their own is enough to get me burned alive. I have no choice but to go cowboy on this. I will go to her apartment hoping for the best and preparing for the worst.

I attempt to survey the area as I walk up to her building. I don't see the telltale signs of men with lots of guns waiting to pounce. There are no undercover dipshits trying to look natural. There are no black cars or SUVs parked in strange places. Seriously, the feds need to just buy normal cars that look like everyone else's cars. Crown Vics and Tahoes are a dead giveaway. I also wear a tiny scanner in my ear with a supersensitive antenna. I keep switching all around the channels to find their chatter. Those guys never shut the fuck up. I can't tell you how many times I've made the feds because of their incessant radio chatter. It's like listening to a bunch of coked-up auctioneers at a strip club salad bar.

I knock on Alice's door. In my left jacket pocket I'm holding a flash grenade. In my right, a full auto Glock 18 machine pistol with a seventeen-round magazine. That kind of firepower will at least give me a fighting chance to get out of the building. If shit goes down, Alice becomes my human shield, I pop anyone standing between me and the door, and Alice gets a pill under the chin before I get my ass out of there. I've been nervy waiting for a lot of bad things to pop off, but never like this. I can feel the sweat dripping down my sides.

She opens the door and looks at me for a beat. Then she wraps her arms around me and starts to cry.

"What the hell is going on?"

She pulls me into her apartment and stands under the lamp. I see the awful cuts and bruises all over her and I feel like I might puke again. This makes it easier for me to act convincingly surprised to see what has happened to her and I use that to my advantage.

"Oh my God. WHAT HAPPENED?"

"Someone broke in. John, he tried to kill me."

"When? I thought you were leaving tonight."

"A few hours ago. I felt bad about missing dinner with you so I booked a later flight. I was going to change and surprise you. When I came home, he was here."

I hate myself. Even more than usual.

"What happened?" I say as I look at the bullet holes in the wall.

"We fought. I have a gun, so . . ."

"You have a gun?"

"A lot of women have guns in New York, John."

"Sorry. I'm just in shock. Did you call the cops?"

"Yeah, they were here."

That's when I notice the mess left behind by her sweep team— latex gloves, fingerprint dust, paper packets for swabs and whatever. Fucking slobs, those guys.

"What did they say?"

"I filed a report. They'll never catch him. He was wearing a mask, so I couldn't even give them a description."

"A mask? Jesus."

"Can you just hold me? I don't want to talk about it right now."

"Yes. I'm so sorry."

We embrace. It's a very strong embrace. Feels like she's afraid she'll fall and never stop if she lets go.

"Sorry about your steak."

"Forget it. I'm just glad you're all right."

"Let's go to bed."

"Are you sure?"

"Yeah. I'm going to explode if we don't."

She laughs. Her split lip cracks and bleeds. I feel sick again. I kiss her and taste the blood. She starts to undress me. I start to do the same, but then I remember my heel. If I take off my sock I'm finished. She will see the bloody bandage and *she will know.*

If you don't think she knows what she hits with that gun, think again. I found all of her spent targets in a shoebox when I was snooping around one night. She obviously prides herself on her marksmanship. I guarantee you she remembers hitting her assailant in the foot less than three hours ago. Not to mention the fact that I'm covered in bruises and scrapes from my little Dumpster dive.

Then it hits me. All of this is irrelevant anyway. Alice is no longer an asset to me, so keeping up this charade of boyfriend-girlfriend is unnecessary. I've gotten what I needed from her. She doesn't suspect I was the one in her apartment. I'm free and clear with her, and this is no longer about the job, so there's no point in continuing to risk everything with Bob.

Part of what I was feeling when I came over here was a sense of responsibility. I was feeling protective and I wanted to comfort her. These are not feelings associated with an asset. And they are potentially lethal. Not only to me but also to her. Bottle flies. Another gray, bloated corpse goes unnoticed in Gotham until the smell gets to be too much for Mrs. Shavitz on the third floor. The dirty amber film of death over her lifeless eyes. This grim diorama is only going to be filled with more hideous things if I continue with Alice. I think about the assignment and my own welfare and I realize I simply don't give a fuck about myself or HR, Inc. I give a fuck about Alice. My feeling of responsibility for her, the very thing driving me to stay with her tonight, is also the very thing that's going to make me walk out that door. She'll be hurt, but hurt is better than dead.

This is my moment of clarity.

I stop kissing her and pull away. I know exactly what will turn her against me, what will poison the well. Just like I know how to kill people, I know how to kill this.

"What's wrong?" she asks.

"I just . . . don't think this is a good idea. After what happened."

"But I'm the person it happened *to* and I think it *is* a good idea."

"You're not really in a great frame of mind right now."

"What the fuck are you talking about?"

"You think sex will make it all go away, but it won't."

"I don't think sex will make it go away. I think it will make me feel better, safer, comforted, and supported. I know you're a fucking robot, but try to understand things from the human perspective for once."

"Why do you have to attack me when you don't get what you want?" I'm really laying it on thick. "You're like a child having a temper tantrum."

"Yeah because I get what I want. It's called having balls. You should try a pair on for size sometime."

"Maybe I should go."

"Perfect. As soon as you have to feel *anything* the only thing you can think to do is run out the fucking door. Look at me! You get this too, asshole. Not just the fun and games. I'm hurting and scared and I need you right now. Look me in the eye and tell me you're going to walk out that fucking door."

At this point, I am utterly out of my element. I have no idea what to say. I have no idea what to do. All I can do is look at my feet. And I can feel the blood pooling in my sock. I hope it doesn't stop. I just want to bleed out right now and be done with all of this.

She's looking at me, expecting a response.

I can't look at her.

If I do, I don't know what will happen. I know this feeling. It's the same feeling I have when someone is pointing a gun at my head or swinging a knife at my throat. I want to force myself to look up. *But I don't want to see it coming.* A bullet would be welcome compared to this. A knife in the heart would be like a warm blanket by a roaring fire. Then I hear her bedroom door slam and it's all over.

"Alice?" I say quietly, not really attempting to elicit an answer.

And there is no answer. There never will be an answer again. When Alice is done with something or someone, *she is done*. She once told me she left her fiancé after she found out he had been corresponding with his old girlfriend on Facebook. She never spoke to him again and they had been *living* together.

She is all or nothing. And now, I am nothing.

ALL INFORMATION HEREIN IS CLASSIFIED
SURVEILLANCE TRANSCRIPT: AUDIO RECORDING

Location: Wireless phone call intercept—IMSI catcher/Roving bug
Subjects: John Lago and Marcus (censored).

Marcus: Hello?

Lago: Marcus?

Marcus: Who is this? How did you get this number?

Lago: My name is John. I found your number through the Mormon Church. They help adopted people and . . . orphans find their biological parents.

Marcus: Oh Jesus.

LONG PAUSE.

Lago: Marcus? Are you there? Please don't hang up.

Marcus: I'm here, John. What's your date of birth?

Lago: According to my partial birth records, it's February 2, 1989.

Marcus: And where were you born? Under what circumstances?

Lago: New Jersey. My mother was murdered and I was born several weeks premature. Her name was Penny.

Marcus: My God.

Lago: Are you . . . ?

Marcus: Yes, I think so. I had a . . . girlfriend named Penny.
           She became pregnant. We were into some pretty bad
           things, John. I'm so sorry.

LONG PAUSE.

Marcus: John, are you still there?

Lago: Yes. I just. I can't believe it's . . . you.

Marcus: It's pretty shocking for me too. When I woke up today,
           I never thought I'd be speaking to my son.

Lago: Are you glad I called?

Marcus: Yes. Of course. Why do you ask that?

Lago: I don't know. It seems like, since you didn't, uh, want
           me before . . .

Marcus: It wasn't that I didn't want you, John. If I had stuck
           around any longer I would have gone to prison. Like
           I said, your mother and I were into some bad things.
           Drugs. The police thought I shot her.

Lago: Did you?

Marcus: No. I loved her. It was our . . . dealer. It's complicated.

Lago: I know. I read about it in my file. The dealer's name
           isn't mentioned, though.

Marcus: He's dead.

Lago: Too bad. I would have liked to return the favor.

Marcus: Believe me. I would have too. But I wasn't the only
           one. He was killed in prison.

Lago: And you left the country.

Marcus: I had no choice. The drug charges made me an
           accessory to your mother's death. I would have gotten
           twenty-five years.

Lago: That's how old I am.

Marcus: John . . . I can't tell you how sorry—

Lago: You don't have to say that. I have lived with plenty of junkie, uh . . . drug addicts . . . in the foster system. I know what that does to people.

Marcus: But I'm your father. And I put you in harm's way. You should . . . You should hate me.

Lago: I've tried. Believe me. It's hard to explain. I don't feel. I mean, I'm not an emotional person.

Marcus: Why did you want to find me, John?

Lago: I just had to know where I come from. Who I am. For better or worse. I think . . . I may not be around much longer.

Marcus: What?

Lago: I'm also into some . . . bad things. Like father, like son.

Marcus: Drugs?

Lago: No. Something else. I can't talk about it over the phone. There are people that may, uh, want me out of the picture.

LONG PAUSE.

Marcus: You need to come here, son. Whoever they are, they won't find you here. They haven't found me yet.

Lago: I found you.

Marcus: You'll be safe. I promise. Will you come?

Lago: I would . . . I have to think about it.

Marcus: Okay. I can respect that. Just know that you're welcome. Anytime.

Lago: Thank you. I better go now.

Marcus: Okay. You'll call back?

Lago: Yeah. I think so. Good-bye . . . Marcus.

Marcus: Good to talk to you, John.

—END TRANSCRIPT—

28

THE PATH OF MOST RESISTANCE

I get a call from Bob the next morning at 4:00 A.M. He wants to meet before I go into work. For once I'm looking forward to it. After breaking it off with Alice, I need a reboot back at HR, Inc. I need to get my head back into the game and jettison all potential distractions. I'm ready to take the ball and run it into the fucking end zone and I don't give a shit who I run over to get there.

"I think we have a scenario for you."

Bob is looking more optimistic than usual. I can't be certain, but I believe he might have a twinkle in his eye.

"Do tell."

"Every year, the Bendini, Lambert & Locke board has its annual meeting. It's mandatory in the firm's bylaws for all partners to attend. Locke is guaranteed to be there. And it's always off-site."

"I like it so far. Bastard is practically invisible in the office, and it's always good to get the target out of his element."

"According to our intel, it's always some top secret tropical locale. Locke *hates* going because he complains that he does not feel safe."

"Sharp guy."

"Yeah, not his first rodeo."

"So, you're thinking hotel?"

"They don't trust hotels. They always rent a villa or some monstrosity and staff it to the gills with security."

"Okay . . . When do I get the good news?"

"The good news is we aren't going to try to take him when he's fully protected. We're going to take him the one place where he *can't* be fully protected. I'll give you three guesses."

"You're not serious."

"About the three guesses?"

"No, about the location for the hit. I already guessed it. And I just realized why you're so happy today."

"I'm happy because we finally have a solid game plan for you to complete this assignment. Something that should also make you happy."

"Let's not get carried away. You want me to take him on the plane, don't you?"

"It's perfect. Their corporate jet goes out of a municipal airport on Long Island. Security at the airport is a joke. And it's a Gulfstream 650. Plenty of room for you to hide until they're airborne."

"He can only take a fraction of his detail. The best ones, but still."

"Exactly. This is our only window."

"Timeline?"

"Still working it. They change the date often, to avoid patterning. But it will definitely be within the next seven days."

"That's a relief, Bob. You got a sim?"

"The team already has a simulation model ready for you to cycle through."

"Good."

"John, I don't want you to think about anything other than execution."

"Of course. Why do you say that?"

"It's your final assignment. That's all. What you do after it's completed is your business. I won't stand in the way."

"Thanks. Better get to work."

As I walk out of Bob's office, I am relieved and somewhat excited.

There is a light at the end of the tunnel of horrors and I feel like my old self again. I can face the day at the office with no concern of running into Alice and feeling awkward. I am focused. In seven days, I will be free and clear to do whatever the fuck I want. It will all be over. HR, Inc. and Bob will be in my rearview mirror. And Locke will be a dead man.

When I arrive at the office, I simply go about my day doing the work that is assigned to me. I never see Alice. I know she's avoiding me, which is a relief. Bendini visits me a couple of times at my desk and I hand him hundreds of thousands in billable files to keep him from attempting to engage me in small talk. But he still manages to invite me to his niece's wedding in eight weeks. I enthusiastically agree to go to the wedding to get him out of my fucking office. He gives me the Geppetto look and pat on the back, his signature move in our relationship. I smile back, the lying Pinocchio waiting for his nose to grow and drive itself through the old man's heart.

After work I drive to an airplane hangar in Jersey. Bob's team has rented a G650 jet and we go to work on the simulation. He stops by the hangar later and we discuss the kill itself. Since the hit is far more sophisticated than anything a mobster is capable of, we decide to create a revenge profile around a CIA scrub job. Evidently, Locke sold out one of their operatives using witness protection as a cover to infiltrate some domestic terror cell being formed by Al Qaeda snitches that flipped their sheik—or something to that effect. Operative's name hits the street, and he and five other agents buy it in a car bomb. The CIA doesn't take kindly to that sort of shit. So I prep for a ghost op—which is fitting, since calling this a suicide mission is an understatement.

29

TILL DEATH DO US PART

Two days into the planning and Bob is getting restless. His operatives are having a hard time finding out the exact itinerary of the board meeting—something that is kept under very heavy security for obvious reasons. So, once again, gathering intel becomes my job. I explore every possible avenue at the office to find this information but come up empty. Corporate travel doesn't even know the itinerary. A third-party company plans the entire meeting, and they're in D.C. As usual, Bob shows no reluctance to pass the buck.

"What about the girl you've been working?"

"I cut her loose. It was ugly, but clean."

"She may be the only chance we've got. Can you fix it?"

"How do you propose I do that?"

"I see your point. Not your area of expertise, John."

"Exactly. And we're way past flowers and candy here. It would take a fucking miracle for her to even look at me again."

"I'll put a team on it."

I'm a big believer in Murphy's Law, so I wasn't surprised by this turn of events. And Bob's right about Alice. Her access is much better than mine. Bendini has a weakness for beautiful women, and he likes to have her around as much as possible. She'll have to ensure he has the briefs he needs prior to departure so he can review them when he travels. Simple deduction says that her deadline, the night before departure, equals my insertion time. But since Alice and I are not speaking, a casual conversation wherein I could easily extract this information is all but impossible. She's giving me a world-class cold shoulder, and when I see her in the office, she avoids me like a plague-infected rodent.

There are no work-arounds here. After our little mixed martial arts encounter in her apartment, the bureau has undoubtedly beefed up her security. The data signal I had coming out of her laptop is dead. Her apartment is one big firewall now, with no data coming in or out, at least none that I can see. The unpleasant truth is that I have to get her to *speak* to me. This is going to require some serious finesse. Somehow I need to make Alice remember how much she loves me in an authentic way that feels motivated by her, not me. We have to remember that Alice likes to be in control. So if she feels in any way manipulated by me, she'll bolt and my last chance will be FUBAR. So, with HR's "social trainers," people Bob hires to help robots like us seem human, I come up with a master plan.

Phase One: a foot in the door.

For this, the team literally gives me a mannequin's foot with the word *JOHN* written directly on the heel. *I'm a heel.* Get it? I place it just inside her office door when she goes to the restroom. Then I wait in the break room nearby. When she returns, she stops short at the sight of the foot. She stares at it for a few seconds, then picks it up and reads the heel. There is a tiny camera embedded in the foot, so the team and I can judge her reaction, and as a bonus, I have her office wired up with a camera (her own computer camera) and a couple of mics (in her computer speakers) for the next phase. I go back to my office and wait. The team calls. Phase One is a success. We got a very slight grin out of her. They send me a hard copy. I can't believe it. I know that smile. It's the same smile she puts on when she wants to have sex or order Thai food.

Phase Two: "La Cucaracha"

Alice is obsessed with this Mexican dive restaurant a few blocks away, which we have completely wired up with cameras and mics. While Alice eats lunch, *our* mariachi band sashays up to her table and begins to play "La Cucaracha." She is about to tell them to get lost when she hears the new lyrics we wrote for them. The song is now all about how *John is La Cucaracha*. She can't help but laugh out loud. She looks around the restaurant to see if I am there, spying on her. She looks slightly disappointed when I don't pop out. This conveys that I am being respectful of her space and that I am not too eager. It works. That afternoon, I get a text from Alice with a little snippet of the mariachi performance. The only thing she writes is *"hijo de puta"* which means "son of a bitch." By insulting me, especially in Spanish, she is preparing to forgive me. This is her way of opening the dialogue by continuing to express her anger but doing it in a cutesy way. She knows me well enough to know that I would think being called a son of a bitch in Spanish is funny. I'm close.

Phase Three: Diamonds are forever.

I know what you're thinking. Is this motherfucker actually going to ask her to marry him? The answer is yes. When a wolf goes in for the kill, he goes straight for the throat. Predators need guarantees. I need a guarantee. And you better believe that Alice needs a fucking guarantee, because she's a predator too. Nothing but the taste of my blood in her mouth is going to satisfy her.

For the final phase, the team arms me with the most deadly weapon I have ever held in my hand: a two-carat Harry Winston diamond engagement ring. Two carats because a junior associate from Shitsville would have to sell both kidneys to get any more rock for his money. Harry Winston because Alice is obsessed with watching *any* red carpet coverage of any awards show, and the jewels are always from Harry Winston.

On to the presentation. Alice is a big fan of Batman. So the team places a powerful spotlight with a Batman symbol gobo on the terrace of the Getty suite at The Pierre Hotel. *The Bat Signal*. Alice works late, like usual, and goes out onto Bendini's terrace to sneak a cigarette, like usual. When she's out there, we fire up the gobo. The Bat Signal appears in full glory on the surface of the low clouds and it's clear which roof the gobo is occupying. Then I send her a text, my first direct communication in this little operation. All it says is "to the Batcave"—Adam West's go-to line whenever he and Robin, his bitch in tights, would see that Commissioner Gordon (his bitch in pinstripes) was calling for help. A few minutes later, I receive a text from her: "Pow!"

ALL INFORMATION HEREIN IS CLASSIFIED
SURVEILLANCE TRANSCRIPT: AUDIO RECORDING—
INFRARED LASER MIC (300M)

Location: Surrey Hotel/Rooftop, Manhattan
Subjects: John Lago and Alice (censored).

Alice: Holy elaborate apologies, Batman.

Lago: If I'm Batman, does that make you Catwoman or
          Batgirl?

Alice: Everyone wants to be Catwoman. She's like every
          chick that dresses like a slut for Halloween. So
          definitely Batgirl.

Lago: Too bad. Catwoman is hot.

Alice: Yeah, but she's been around the block.

Lago: And Batgirl is more like the girl next door?

Alice: The one you bring home to mom.

Lago: I would bring you home to mom. If I had a mom.

Alice: Charming.

Lago: I'm working on it.

Alice: Work harder, okay?

Lago: Okay.

Alice: What's this?

Lago: Open it.

Alice: Um . . . What the hell is this?

Lago: That's me, growing some balls.

Alice: Really? Let's see.

Lago: See what?

Alice: I think you said something before about saying the things that need to be said.

Lago: Will you marry me?

Alice: Why are you still standing?

Lago: How's this? I think my knee is in pigeon shit too.

Alice: Better. Now try again.

Lago: Will you marry me?

Alice: Why should I?

Lago: Because I love you.

ALICE IS CRYING AND LAUGHING.

Alice: I love you too, you son of a bitch.

Lago: Is that a yes?

Alice: That's a hell yes.

PAUSE. PHYSICAL CONTACT.

Alice: Harry Winston. Nice touch.

Lago: Now you can walk down the red carpet.

Alice: Those other bitches will look like trolls compared to me.

LONG PAUSE. PHYSICAL CONTACT.

Alice: Did you get a room at this place or are we going to fuck al fresco?

Lago: You're standing in it.

Alice: No way.

Lago: Way.

Alice: Who did you have to kill to get a roof terrace on Central Park?

Lago: The front desk clerk. And the manager. And most of the cleaning staff. It was a bloodbath.

Alice: But well worth it, right?

Lago: Absolutely.

Alice: Can't believe I'm getting married.

Lago: That makes two of us.

Alice: I've always wanted a big wedding. Holy shit. How the hell am I going to find time to plan it?

Lago: Might I suggest we elope? We can go to some exotic locale and actually enjoy ourselves. No pressure. No caterers running late or terrible wedding singers. Just you and me.

Alice: My parents would kill me. Then they would kill you.

Lago: Just think about it. We could leave tonight.

Alice: And waste this hotel room? Not on your life.

Lago: Then this weekend.

Alice: You're telling me you want to go away and get married this weekend?

Lago: Yes.

Alice: I don't know if you're a lunatic or just very decisive.

Lago: Can I be both?

Alice: Of course. That's what I love about you. You're a freak. Like me.

LONG PAUSE. PHYSICAL CONTACT.

Alice: Is this for real?

Lago: What do you mean?

Alice: I mean, is this really happening? Are you really into it, or are you just desperate to get me back?

Lago: I'm really into it *and* I'm desperate to get you back.

Alice: Good answer.

Lago: When you shut me out, I felt like I was going to die. I don't ever want to feel that again.

Alice: I'm sorry. That wasn't fair. I just have this tendency to completely write people off when I'm hurt. Bad habit.

Lago: If I hadn't put this all together, do you think you would have ever spoken to me again?

Alice: I doubt it. I'd convinced myself you were just another zombie waste of time in a suit.

Lago: It's a pretty nice suit for a zombie.

BOTH SUBJECTS LAUGH.

Alice: You surprised me tonight.

Lago: Like I said, I grew a pair. And did what felt right.

Alice: See. You've had a heart all along, Tin Man.

Lago: And this whole time I was hoping for a brain.

LONG PAUSE.

Lago: Is this real for you? Are you sure you want to shack up with a creep like me?

Alice: I like creeps. If you had a van and some candy—

Lago: Seriously. I just want you to know what you're getting into.

Alice: What am I getting into? Are you living a double life as a Cuban drug lord or one of those guys with wives all over the country? Oh, maybe a serial killer. That's okay because we can get a house with a big crawl space.

Lago: Can we be serious for a minute?

Alice: If you insist. But if you're going to try to convince me not to marry you, I'm going to throw you over the fucking balcony.

Lago: I don't want to do that. I just. What happened before can't happen again. I'm not perfect and—

Alice: And you're afraid I'll crucify you for your mistakes?

Lago: Yeah.

Alice: I will crucify you. But you have my word I'll never shut you out again.

Lago: And you have my word that I will try to pull my head out of my ass as soon as possible.

Alice: That's good, because when your head is up your ass it makes kissing you a little difficult.

Lago: Feel like trashing a hotel suite Keith Richards style?

Alice: Is it possible we'll get arrested?

Lago: Pretty much guaranteed.

Alice: Then yes.

—END TRANSCRIPT—

30

WONDERLAND REDUX

My evening with Alice was a huge success. The HR team really nailed this, and I couldn't have done it without them. Alice accepted my proposal and I convinced her that I'm head over heels in love with her. We spent the night in a hotel, but she invited me to dinner at her apartment tonight. She jokingly said she would be cooking and that I should taste her food before I really commit to marrying her. When I'm there, I'll clone her keycard so I can access Bendini's office and grab the partners' classified travel itinerary. Then Bob and I can finish our execution planning.

Rule #13: Everything is a weapon.

If you approach this job thinking that the only weapons you have at your disposal are guns, knives, poison, explosives, and all of the usual clichés, then you will be dead before you can collect your first paycheck. Think about the predator. Truly effective predators do not bull their way toward the prey and attempt to take them by brute force every time. They stalk, lure, and even seduce. A pack of coyotes, some of the most effective and misunderstood predators in the wild, use one of the most brilliant luring and stalking methods I have ever seen. As some of you may know, coming from places like California, Arizona, and Colorado, coyotes have figured out that domestic pets are a strong addition to the menu. But with their elaborate shelter—someone's home—they aren't always easy to get. I have seen a pack of coyotes send a female in heat to lure a male, nonneutered dog away from a house, only for the males to tear him to shreds when he heads out into the woods to get laid. That is not just killing; it is the dance of death, a fluid waltz with a climax of blood.

I'm telling you this because, no matter what happens to me, I want you to know my real intentions with Alice. If I fail, Bob will blame her and he will claim that she's the reason I lost my focus. But you've been with me every step of the way and you know that is not the case. I might have done more than necessary to seduce an asset. I might have overstepped with her in many ways. But in the end I know that she has played a major role in what I believe will be my ultimate success with this case. And in the end, even though I will use those things that we all associate with the word *weapon*, I would not be in the position to use them if I had not used the true weapons of a predator—cunning, persistence, and most important, patience.

ALL INFORMATION HEREIN IS CLASSIFIED
SURVEILLANCE TRANSCRIPT: AUDIO RECORDING

Location: Wireless phone call intercept—IMSI catcher/Roving bug
Subjects: John Lago and Marcus (censored).

Marcus: Hello?

Lago: Marcus?

Marcus: Is this John?

Lago: Yes. Can you talk?

Marcus: Of course. I'm glad you called.

Lago: It sounds like someone's there.

Marcus: It's a festival. In the street. I forgot which Saint.

Lago: I didn't call for small talk. I hope that's all right.

Marcus: Fine. I'm not one for small talk either. What's on your mind?

Lago: When my mother died, what was it like?

Marcus: In what way?

Lago: I mean, for you. What was it like for you?

Marcus: It was . . . hard to describe. I thought I would die too. I wanted to die.

Lago: Because you loved her?

Marcus: Very much. We had been together so long, I couldn't imagine life without her. She was the only real family I ever had.

Lago: Were you married?

Marcus: Yes. We had eloped a few years before her death. We ran away to Honduras and got married in this little church outside of town.

Lago: Is that why you went back there?

Marcus: Yes. I mean I had to get out of the country, and this place had some connection to her.

Lago: I love someone.

Marcus: John, that's great. What's her name?

Lago: Not just yet. Okay?

Marcus: Sure. Can you tell me a little about her?

Lago: Yes. She's beautiful.

Marcus: That always helps.

Lago: It certainly doesn't hurt.

Marcus: What's she like?

Lago: She's tough and kind of no bullshit. Like a guy, you know? But she's also very much a woman. Almost too much of a woman, if you know what I mean.

Marcus: I think so. She sounds like a handful.

Lago: She is! You have no idea. Was my mother that way?

Marcus: No. She was very quiet and gentle. Unassuming. I don't think we ever raised our voices to each other once. And those were some hard times.

Lago: I'm having kind of a hard time too.

Marcus: Do you want to talk about it?

Lago: I'll try. I, um, I'm in this line of work . . . it's not very conducive to having a relationship.

Marcus:	How so?
Lago:	It's . . . dangerous.
Marcus:	Can you tell me anything about it? Maybe I can help.
Lago:	I can't tell you about it. Not over the phone. Maybe not ever.

LONG PAUSE.

Marcus:	John, are you there?
Lago:	Yeah. I'm so tired.
Marcus:	You want to talk later?
Lago:	No. I'm running out of time.
Marcus:	Why? John, I might be able to help you.
Lago:	How? You're in Honduras.
Marcus:	I'm a very resourceful person. I couldn't have lasted this long if I wasn't.
Lago:	No one can help me, Marcus. I just need to talk a bit.
Marcus:	Let's talk.
Lago:	If you could've done something to protect my mother, even if it meant that you might die, would you have done it?
Marcus:	Yes. Without a doubt. And since she was pregnant with you, I would have gone to the ends of the earth . . .
Lago:	Are you there, Marcus?
Marcus:	Yeah. It's still just . . . hard to think about all of that.
Lago:	I know the feeling.
Marcus:	Is she in danger? The woman you love?
Lago:	Yes.
Marcus:	Then you need to do what you can to protect her. You are my son, and I don't want you to be in harm's way.

	But I also don't want you to live with what I've had to live with. It's just . . . no way to live.
Lago:	I need to tell her everything. That's the only way.
Marcus:	Then do it. Come clean if that will protect her.
Lago:	She'll probably reject me.
Marcus:	Not if she loves you.
Lago:	You think so?
Marcus:	I know so. I did . . . things that I was afraid to tell your mother. Horrible things that were a part of my . . . addiction. But she took me back. Love is that way. It's something the two people in it can't control. Takes on a life of its own.
Lago:	I'm afraid.
Marcus:	Good. Then you will approach this with the right amount of caution. Fear is a great asset if you use it right.
Lago:	That's an interesting thing to say.
Marcus:	Why?
Lago:	I don't know. I guess I didn't expect you to be so interesting.
Marcus:	Because I'm an old ex-junkie hiding out in Central America?
Lago:	No . . . Yes.
Marcus:	Someday, you'll get to know me, John. And I think I'll surprise you.

—END TRANSCRIPT—

31

THE CLOSEST I EVER CAME TO BEING REAL

Dinner with Alice tonight. I don't know what makes me more nervous, having to dose her and clone her keycard, all the while expecting the feds to come down on her apartment like Blitzkrieg at any moment, or talking about "the wedding." I bring a bottle of Silver Oak cabernet, the right kind of medicine to soften the edges of both potential problems. I push the buzzer on her door. No answer. My guess is she's in the shower, as Alice is compulsively late. It's her way of saying, "I'm important and all you peasants can wait until *I* am ready for *you.*"

Now that I'm her betrothed, she has blessed me with a key to her apartment. As I unlock the seventeen locks on her door (the two hinges could be easily popped by a savvy thief), I half entertain the idea of just grabbing her and taking off tonight. Bob can whack Locke himself, get off his ass for once and earn like the rest of us. I have plenty of money, so I don't need the bonus. And Bob will be so busy taking care of Locke so the "clients" don't take care of him that he won't have time to come after me. At least not right away. By the time he did get around to it, we'd be long gone. I'm sure the real Alice would rather live like a queen in some obscure, tropical locale than hack it out with the FBI for another decade making five figures and watching all the white boys get promoted.

The door swings open and I stride inside, the man of the house.

"Honey, I'm home!" I pronounce in my best 1950s TV Land voice.

No answer. Probably in the bathroom doing lady things. I crack the wine and pour two glasses. As the first mouthful of wine warms my throat, I feel oddly at home. I start thinking about the whole eloping thing again. Alice said she wanted to get the fuck out of here. The wine begins to speak to me with its oaky vapors, convincing me to take Alice away with me tonight and put HR and Bob in my rearview. By the time the glass is finished, I'm anxious to give her the good news.

I walk through the living room and stop short when I see something coming out from under her bedroom door. The apartment is fairly dark, so at first I think it might be just a shadow. Then I switch on the hall light, illuminating the fact that it is a *pool of blood*. I pull my gun and listen for the presence of anyone moving on the other side of that door. My heart sinks when I hear nothing.

I take a step, forcing the issue. Then another. Then I am at her door, my shoe thoroughly drenched. I still hear nothing. I put on gloves and wrap my hand around her bedroom doorknob. It's broken and loose and slips right out of the door, landing with a sickening wet thud on the blood-soaked carpet. I stand there, looking at the door, and tell myself I know what the fuck is in there and I *do not have to see it*. I can leave all of this to the bottle flies and the men in rubber suits. My hand reaches for the doorknob.

"Why am I opening this fucking door?"

Hearing my own voice like that, in a situation that requires absolute silence, is terrifying. My hand is shaking for the first time ever. Every last drop of saliva has vacated my mouth and my head is pounding to the point that I think my eyeballs might burst out of the sockets. I walk into the room. It's pitch-black, but the light from the living room cuts into the room like a razor.

Then I see Alice.

I bite my lip hard enough to draw blood so I can to keep from screaming. Her body is facedown on the carpet in a thick pool of blood. I move closer, despite my instinct to run. Her hands are full of defensive wounds—deep cuts and purple bruises from the fight she put up. Her hair is matted around her skull, soaked in the dark blood that came from the multiple blunt force trauma wounds. Her legs are wildly askew from being broken several times over. Her naked back is covered in stab wounds that look like hundreds of screaming red mouths. Holding back vomit with guttural rasping breaths, I gently move her head with my foot. Her face stares back at me, beaten so badly it is no longer recognizable. It is the purple, swollen mask of merciless bludgeoning with black eight-ball hemorrhage eyes staring through red slits. I have killed many people, but I have never damaged someone this horrifically or put them through this much agony. Whoever did this is a monster and wanted the whole world to know it.

"Why did you let them in?" I ask.

My voice is thin and childlike.

"I thought it was you," I answer for her in a condemned whisper.

"I was going to ask you to go away with me," I say.

The words drip down into the carpet and soak into the blood. I stand there for a long time, staring at the ring on her finger, thinking that Alice was the closest I ever came to being real. The pain of seeing her like this has nowhere to go. It is so foreign to me that it feels like a ghost passing through my heart, stopping it momentarily. I react violently at first, a wave of blinding rage surging into my hands and face. I feel the edge of madness, a black hole pulling me into its center with a force of emotional gravity that I know will crush me. Then, like a safety switch, the numbness sets in and I am immersed in its dark water. I pull the engagement ring from her stiff, swollen finger. My body goes cold and I allow my feelings for Alice to bleed out onto the floor. Our emptiness is now the only thing we share.

I leave her room, my reptilian gaze zeroing in on getting what I came for and erasing all evidence of my presence.

United States Department of Justice
Federal Bureau of Investigation

Washington, D.C. 20535

ALL INFORMATION HEREIN IS CLASSIFIED
SURVEILLANCE TRANSCRIPT: AUDIO RECORDING

Location: Wireless phone call intercept—IMSI catcher/Roving bug
Subjects: John Lago and Marcus (censored).

Marcus: John.

Lago: Did I wake you?

Marcus: It's okay. What's up?

Lago: I'm in a . . . something terrible. I feel sick.

Marcus: John, have you been drinking.

Lago: Sorry.

Marcus: It's okay. I just want to know where your head is at—

Lago: She's dead.

Marcus: Oh my God. What happened?

Lago: So sweet. They . . .

LAGO IS CRYING.

Lago: Her face. I'll never . . . What they did.

Marcus: Tell me.

Lago: Beat her. Her hands . . .

Marcus: What about her hands?

Lago: She fought them. They were like animals. No mercy.

Marcus: Who are they?

Lago: I don't know. Could be anyone. The phone book.

Marcus: You have no idea who they are?

Lago: No. I want to find them. I have something . . . for them.

SCREAMING, UNINTELLIGIBLE RANTING.

Marcus: John. Wait. John? Try to calm down.

SOUND OF BREAKING GLASS AND WOOD.

Marcus: John. Stop! Someone will call the police! Stop!

Lago: The police?

Marcus: People. They'll hear you and call them. You don't want that.

Lago: I'll kill them.

Marcus: John. You're not going to kill anyone. Do you understand?

LONG PAUSE.

Lago: Yes.

Marcus: Tell me about her.

Lago: We were . . . going to get married . . . I see her when I close my eyes. I see what they did. It wasn't her anymore. Wasn't her.

Marcus: I'm so sorry.

Lago: I'm so sorry. I'm so sorry. I'm so sorry.

SOUND OF LAGO RETCHING.

Marcus: John? Are you okay?

Lago: Y . . . yes. I'm sick. So fucking sick.

Marcus: I know. I've been there. It's good to get it out of you. Do you feel a little better?

Lago:	Better. Need to sleep.
Marcus:	No. Don't sleep yet. Stay on the phone. Get some water. Do you have any coffee?
Lago:	Make the best coffee.
Marcus:	Actually. Forget the coffee. I don't want you to hurt yourself.
Lago:	Best coffee.
Marcus:	Water, John. Drink some. Okay?
Lago:	Yes.

WATER RUNNING. LAGO IS DRINKING AND SPUTTERING.

Lago:	Oh God.
Marcus:	Good. Now sit and focus on my voice.
Lago:	Marcus. Thank you.
Marcus:	It's all right. Just listen. I have some important questions.
Lago:	I'll try to answer.
Marcus:	The people that did this, do they know about you?
Lago:	I don't know.
Marcus:	Would they know where to find you? Where you live?
Lago:	Impossible.
Marcus:	Are you sure?
Lago:	Off the grid. It's . . . impossible.
Marcus:	What do you mean "off the grid"?
Lago:	Can't talk about that.
Marcus:	What about work? Do they know where you work?
Lago:	That is . . . possible. That . . . is yes.
Marcus:	Don't go back. Just don't go back.

Lago:	No.
Marcus:	That's right. You can't. They'll wait for you there.
Lago:	They'll wait. That's where I'll find them. I'll wait.
Marcus:	No, John. That is a bad idea. Do *not* go back.
Lago:	I want to . . . I want to show them something.
Marcus:	You can't risk that. I understand what you want to do.
Lago:	I want to . . . Lots of guns.
Marcus:	John. Don't say things like that. You have to focus for me. Please.
Lago:	Focus . . . on . . . you.
Marcus:	John, have you taken anything other than alcohol tonight?
Lago:	Oxys.
Marcus:	When?
Lago:	Don't know. Hour or so.
Marcus:	You probably threw it up. Don't take anything else, okay?
Lago:	Marcus?
Marcus:	Yes, John.
Lago:	Help me.
Marcus:	I'm trying. I'm sorry I'm not there.
Lago:	You left.
Marcus:	I'm sorry.
Lago:	It's okay. I am . . . a predator. I survive.
Marcus:	I know. And we're going to keep it that way, right?
Lago:	Yes.
Marcus:	I want you to come here, John. Where I live.

Lago:	Your house?
Marcus:	Yes. Will you come?
Lago:	I will.
Marcus:	Good.
Lago:	How will I get there?
Marcus:	I'll tell you. Will you remember?
Lago:	I don't know.
Marcus:	Can I call you tomorrow? When you're feeling better?
Lago:	Yes.
Marcus:	How? I need a number.
Lago:	I'll call you.
Marcus:	Is it a landline?
Lago:	Yes. Need to sleep.
Marcus:	We'll talk tomorrow and I'll tell you how to get to me.
Lago:	Okay. Marcus?
Marcus:	Yes?
Lago:	Thank you.
Marcus:	No problem. I'll talk to you . . .

THE LINE GOES DEAD.

—END TRANSCRIPT—

32

ARE YOU OUT OF YOUR FUCKING MIND?

Remember when I was telling you about Intermittent Explosive Disorder—the blinding, uncontrollable rage that turns you into a violent, sometimes homicidal, maniac? It's important to mention, because if you don't learn to control it, you will find that it's quite capable of controlling you. Right now, it's controlling me. I may sound lucid but I can assure you I'm not. It's 5:00 A.M. and I'm walking down the street barefoot. I have blood and broken glass in my hair. The throbbing in my skull is the result of either my raging hangover or head trauma from whatever train wreck I just crawled out of. I am downtown and heading somewhere with a purpose. As I round the corner and see the familiar buildings, I know exactly where I am: two blocks from HR, Inc. I have my Glock 18 in one jacket pocket and a fistful of mags in the other.

I try to think why I'm going to the office, especially in this state. Then I remember. Silly me, I'm going to kill Bob.

"Are you out of your fucking mind?"

That's the question you're asking me right now. The answer is yes. I am out of my fucking mind. And yes, it's because of Alice. I've seen some extremely fucked-up shit in my time, but none of it holds a candle to what happened to her. I'm sure that Bob was well aware of my feelings for her, the very same feelings that are now compelling me to kill him. Since he was aware of how I felt about her, he wasted no time wasting her as soon as she stopped being of use to us. And now I'm pretty goddamned sure he knows she was FBI. Of course, in typical Bob fashion, he attempted to create an execution scenario for Alice that could be assigned to the mob and their love of baseball bats (only equaled by their hatred of the feds). This smacks of his method, and now I'm going to show him my method.

"Put the gun down." He attempts to emotionally disarm me with a tone that's supposed to force me to see the futility of my actions.

"Fuck you."

We're standing in his office. It's too early for any of you to be there. Too bad, because you're going to miss a good show. I point the gun at his face. This makes him very angry.

"Why?"

"Why what, John?" His teeth are set with fury.

"You know what the fuck I'm talking about."

"No, I don't. Put down the gun."

"Or what?"

I smile at him.

"Or I won't ask again."

"You won't have to."

"You're smarter than this, John."

"Am I?"

"Look at yourself."

"Unfortunately, I *am* looking at myself, Bob. I'm a forty-something psychopath who thinks he has the right to delete anyone he sees fit. I'm a master manipulator with a rabid jackal for a soul. I'm you if I don't delete *you* right now."

"Are you finished?"

"No."

"Yes you are."

I am too bleary eyed and emotional (a kiss of death on both cheeks) to see the flash grenade he has placed on top of his files like a paperweight. He artfully hits the floor as it detonates. The concussion blows me off my feet and into the back wall. The flash knocks me out long enough for two of Bob's goons to scoop me up and drag me out of his office. When I come to, I'm in the HR medical unit. Goons are holding me down while Dr. Hatchet and his merry band of ex-stripper nurses prepare needles.

As soon as I can feel my hands again, I plunge one of the needles into the neck of Goon #1. Goon #2 tries to apply a chokehold, which, ironically, exposes his own throat. My elbow cracks his trachea. While he tries desperately to breathe, I plunge the second syringe into his leg. Nighty night, fuck face. Dr. Hatchet runs, leaving his screaming, cowering litter of nurses to fend for themselves.

I take a quick assessment. I am in a building full of killers. I'm half blind and barely able to limp at a geriatric pace. Gun. I search Goon #1 and find my Glock in his jacket pocket. No mags. Fuck. I have seventeen rounds. Not bad, but like I said, I'm in a building full of killers—with much bigger guns. The nice thing is that survival is not my objective. I just need to put a bullet in Bob and then take my medicine like a man. Am I willing to die for Alice? No. I want Bob to die for Alice. As Bob himself would say, my death would only be collateral damage.

I look at the clock. 6:30 A.M. By now all of you are in the training arena and Bob is strutting around like a gamecock, extolling the virtues of his superior fighting skills. I make my way there in an attempt to ambush him before Dr. Hatchet spreads the news of my escape. When I arrive at our training dojo, the place is very dimly lit. In the middle of the room, Bob is with some of you, teaching you blind combat techniques. Everyone is wearing blackout blindfolds and removes them when they hear me come in. Bob leaves his on.

"John."

"Bob."

"Up for a little sparring?"

Two goons walk in with shooters, and I toss my Glock on the ground. I walk over to Bob and his dark circle of death.

"Just to prove to you that you're wrong about this, I'm going to let you have a go at me. Put the guns down!"

The goons silently obey.

"You can take off the blindfold, Bob."

"I'll leave it on. This is what they call a teachable moment."

I teach Bob how to fall on his face as I sweep his legs and send him sprawling to the floor.

"Cheap shot, asshole," says one of the more surly recruits.

When I take the time to glare at the recruit, Bob side kicks me in the nuts while he is still on the floor. I bend over and almost puke from the pain. Bob takes that opportunity to hit me in the jaw with a roundhouse. I go flying and take out three or four recruits. Sorry about that. While I lay there, attempting to put my mind back together piece by piece, Bob begins his training lecture as if all of this was part of today's lesson.

"There is no such thing as a cheap shot in a life-and-death situation," Bob pontificates. "There is only advantage versus disadvantage."

Bob picks me up using an old wrestling move called the fireman's carry and hurls me into a wood rack full of practice weapons. It explodes like an adult-size barrel of pick-up sticks. I can barely see from the blood pouring out of the gash in my scalp.

"Do you think John swept my leg because he caught me off guard? Or, do you think I allowed him to do that, anticipating a comment from one of my *lesser* students—a comment that would briefly distract him so that I could *take advantage*?"

Mumbling from the recruits.

"You did it on purpose," offers one of the female recruits. "He's younger and stronger. You took advantage by distracting him. Then you took advantage after you disabled him with the kick to the nuts.

Then you took advantage of him being dazed from the kick to the jaw."

Bob turns to me.

"One of my *better* students."

Bob gives me the "come hither" hand gesture. I drag myself up and take on the posture of a kung fu style called White Eyebrow. Bob assumes the posture of Monkey Style kung fu.

"White Eyebrow versus Monkey. Who's going to win?" Bob queries.

"White Eyebrow is superior," offers the student who made the smart-ass comment earlier.

I attack. Bob counters with a shocking level of ferocity. I am weak and pukey from booze and what is most likely a raging concussion. The worst thing is he can easily anticipate everything I do. He is beating the shit out of me. His heel striking me behind the ear sends me to the ground. I lie there, half-conscious, and the lecture continues.

"As you can see, John has been trained well. But I'm the one who trained him!"

He switches to jujitsu and tries to get into me for grappling holds. I switch to silat, a Southeast Asian style purely meant for killing or serious injury. Bob didn't teach me this style, so I pummel the shit out of him for a change. All of your collective jaws drop.

I kick him so hard he does a back flip and lands on his chest and face. He lies there, gasping for breath.

"Unfortunately for Bob, I'm using a style he didn't teach me. Bob has made the mistake of assuming I would employ only his training."

I fly in for a spine crushing pile driver and he rolls. I hit the hard floor instead, bashing my kneecap. He rolls across the floor like some kind of animal and gets his arms around my neck. I struggle to escape, but Bob is too fucking good at Gracie, and I find myself in a death hold, completely at his mercy.

"But I didn't make the mistake of assuming you would do the smart thing and take advantage of me by using a weapon. Instead, you did what I thought you would do—tried to finish me in some spectacular movie style, even though your gun is a few feet away. How'd that work out for you?"

33

THE FALLEN ANGEL

I'm awake and in a hospital room. It's a very weird hospital room. Almost too white and pristine. At first I think I'm dead and this is hell. Then I think it's just a dream until an ugly nurse walks in to check my vitals and she smells like a mackerel cannery. I don't dream about women like that. Then I realize that the hospital is weird because it isn't a hospital at all. It's the HR medical unit. I'm the only patient in this hospital. Dr. Hatchet smiles at me with nicotine-stained teeth.

"How we feeling? Still got a case of the assholes?"

"Get the fuck out of here," Bob orders.

Dr. Hatchet exits and Bob walks up.

"Hi, John."

"Hi, Bob."

"How are you feeling?"

"Not bad."

"Good."

He punches me square in the jaw. I am about to lose consciousness when he hits me in the stomach. That wakes me up as I struggle for air.

"Guts over brains. Right, John?"

I gasp in acknowledgment. He grabs my collar. Through my watering eyes, I see that he is furious but also deeply disappointed in me.

"God cast the angel into the pit. He was nowhere near as disappointed as I am in you, John."

I try to answer but still can't breathe.

"If we weren't so deep into this operation, I would burn you now. Today. But that satisfaction is a luxury I cannot afford. I'm well past my deadline with this client and we have one window to pull this off. But you already knew that, didn't you, John?"

"Yes, Bob. I did."

"Good for you. You might think you're pretty smart, but a lot of stupid people do. See, you're just smart enough to completely fuck yourself. And that is what you've done by putting me in this position. You can forget about your future. This business is over for you. I'll make it my life's mission to brand you a loose fucking cannon."

"Works for me, Bob."

He is furious, almost to the point of tears. It's unnerving to see him this way because I never would have guessed he had it in him.

"You're so glib, John. So dismissive of me. Have you forgotten who pulled you out of juvie and saved you from becoming some gangbanger's bitch?"

"No, Bob. I haven't. This was not about—"

"Shut the fuck up. You're a disgrace and you don't even deserve to be in the same room with me or anyone from HR. You may have some accomplishments under your belt, but they mean about as much as a drop of piss in the ocean now."

"I killed a lot of people, Bob. I don't consider those *accomplishments*."

"No. You are an elite assassin, trained by the best in the world to take out the worst. You perform a crucial service to society. Killing is only the means, John. But based on today's actions, I can see that you might as well have set everything I've taught you on fire."

"You shouldn't have killed her, Bob."

He angrily pulls out a gun, chambers a round, and hands it to me.

"If you really believe I killed her then have your revenge."

I hold the gun. It feels like the heaviest thing I've ever had in my hand. I look at Bob. If he did kill her, then *he* is clinically insane, and we all know that is impossible for a calculating sociopath like Bob.

"I may have stepped on a few insects in the past, John, but I'm not about to throw myself into the oven by killing a federal agent just because you're fucking her!"

He picks up his gun and empties the clip into the wall and all of the medical equipment. Glass, smoke, and cotton wool fill the air. He throws the gun across the room. I've never seen him this way. I feel like everything is crumbling around us, a house of cards made of cement slabs, all with suicide kings.

"Don't insult my intelligence again, John."

"I'm sorry, Bob. I've lost control."

"You're goddamned right you've lost control. And it makes me sick to see you this way. John, it makes me a failure."

Cry me a fucking river, I think as I sit silently, wallowing in what I want Bob to think is mental self-flagellation. He softens a bit.

"The good news is that your gross incompetence hasn't killed us. We found your girlfriend's keycard and laptop in one of the bars you got thrown out of. Couldn't crack her laptop so we sent someone into the firm with the keycard last night and acquired the encrypted travel itinerary. You've got twenty-four hours to get your shit together."

"You trust me to get it done?"

"I don't really have a choice. Either you do it and we all ride off into the sunset or it doesn't get done and we all get scrubbed. And it's not just about you and me, John. You fuck this up and *everyone* pays, even the snot-nosed recruits you just embarrassed yourself in front of."

"I'll get it done."

He pauses for a long time, looking at his watch and then me.

"Who did her, Bob? Any idea?"

"Brooklyn family. Old case. Revenge for some meatball she put away. If it's any consolation, I had their whole crew whacked out. Didn't want you wasting time on them too."

"Thanks, Bob."

As he walks out, I see myself in the mirror and remember what he said about the fallen angel. That's me, out to make the world pay with blood and pain. Bob uses this. It's just another hard asset that helps him guarantee his return on investment. It's also the only reason I'm still alive.

34

THE FRIENDLY SKIES

Night is enveloping everything like a dark tide. A bloodred harvest moon is on the rise, signaling the baptism by fire that is imminent. I'm moving through a wet field toward a private airport in eastern New Jersey. I can see the G650 that will carry Locke and his entourage to a secret island compound off the coast of Belize. His partners will travel in different aircraft to the same destination. In the corporate world, they call this "Risk Management." If one plane goes down, they don't lose the entire brain trust. Locke and his entourage have not yet arrived. They are due to depart at 0100. There's a single armed guard posted near the plane and one in the hangar. They're not pros. The dew on the scrub grass is soaking my legs and the inside of my shoes. I don't sweat it because I am thinking that this might be the last time I ever feel such a sensation. This might be the last time I feel anything.

In the past, I've never thought about any of this. I'm thinking of it now because I'm convinced that, in a few hours, I'll be dead. Up to now, I have taken my entire short-ass life for granted. Twenty-five years is a tear in the ocean. It is less than nothing. And I've spent most of it either holding on to the pain of the past or waiting for the future. Until now, there has been no *now* for me. But tonight, I am the wolf. I'm breathing in my world, sensing it through all my capacities. Not just sight, the least reliable of all senses, but smell and touch too. And it's bittersweet. But I refuse to lament anything.

I am a killer. I have ended many lives. Whatever happens to me, I have it coming. That is not newfound morality that makes me more *relatable* to the average Joe. Fuck the average Joe. He is a fucking slob and he is eating, shitting, fucking, and fighting his way through the world's most protracted suicide. This is knowing myself for the first time.

I am wet shoes.

I am cold, damp breath.

I am sweating hands.

I am gravity crushing the grass beneath my boots.

I am Kevlar and metal and lead.

I am laser sighting.

I am death.

And I am coming.

Dark clouds are building in the sky and I am taking that as a sign, a metaphor from the Almighty telling me that I should prepare myself, like a samurai, for ashes and dust. But I embrace it. I'm inside the black and I'm comfortable here.

I move with purpose across the tarmac, using whatever I can to shield me from the guards. They're more interested in their fucking iPhones than doing their jobs. I can see the glow of their phone screens on their faces as they check e-mail, update their Facebook slaveware, dream of living, breathing, and fucking through the anonymity of text and memes. But I'm stalled behind a fuel truck, waiting for an opportunity to approach the aircraft undetected. Then the dark clouds that were warning me of my impending doom a moment earlier bring forth an unexpected gift—rain. As the drops begin to fall, Dumbass 1 jogs from the tarmac into the hangar to wait out the rain with Dumbass 2. Thank you, duality. You have once again shown the beauty of a universe with a split personality.

I crouch and creep under the airplane and climb into the landing gear bay. This is where the op simulation comes in very handy. In total darkness I have to climb into the belly of the plane and feel my way to the back. I use my infrared flashlight to locate the access panels above me. I find the panel that leads to the main passenger cabin and mark it with a black light marker.

Then I cram myself as deep into the back of the belly as possible. If I am anywhere near the landing gear when it retracts back up into the plane, I will be crushed or at least lose one of my limbs. So that I don't asphyxiate, I have a breathing device that will deliver fifteen minutes of life-giving oxygen from roughly 25,000 feet (when air pressure is nil and things get dicey for humans) and 51,000 feet (when humans just straight up die). And let's not forget about hypothermia. At cruising altitude the temperature will drop to minus fifty or sixty degrees Fahrenheit. I know I can withstand this for about ten minutes before I pass out. Of course I have a shitload of speed to keep my mind sharp and pump up the overall performance of my nervous system. I also have Acetazolamide, a drug that hard-core mountaineers take to prevent altitude sickness. It makes the blood more acidic and more efficient at transporting oxygen to my major organs. And I brought along a blister packet of cyanide. I know, old school spy shit. I figure in the unlikely event I am captured and not killed, I will just check out cold war style and leave those assholes to deal with my foaming, twitching corpse.

Sounds fun, right? Actually, what I just described *is* the fun part. The rest of it is a total drag. When we reach cruising altitude, provided I am still alive and conscious, I have to jack open the access panel to the main cabin so I can crawl into the plane. I am hoping to have *some* energy left to kill everyone on board, but you never know, so I have a syringe full of adrenaline to chemically bond with the speed and turn me into an unstoppable monster that feels no pain and has the strength of five orangutans. I have only used this rocket ship speedball once before, and if memory serves, the last time I shot it I tore a man's arm off and beat him to death with it.

I can hear them loading the baggage into the plane. They have also started fueling it, something I thought they had already done before I came aboard. That sucks. Now my whole respiratory system will be irritated and burning from here on out, and that is significant, considering I will barely be able to breathe as it is. I shove my nose into my Kevlar jacket and try to minimize the damage. After what seems like an eternity, I am extremely light-headed (also bad for the whole blood-brain-oxygen combo). But I can hear the heavy vehicles carrying Locke and his entourage enter the tarmac. By the sound of it, he's got a bunch of gung-ho ex-military juicers protecting him because they drive like fucking maniacs up to the plane, screeching to a halt, and banter like a bunch of frat boys all the way into the passenger compartment. *They are fucking heavy too.* The plane sinks down a few inches on its wheels when these sides of beef get settled into the leather.

That means things will definitely get very ugly. Big men who are experienced fighters are a major pain in the ass. They see themselves as gladiators and they will always try to get you to take them on "man to man" if you have the drop on them. I love it when they say *"mano a mano"* and have no idea that means "hand to hand." Learn some basic fucking Spanish. Only half the country speaks it. Anyway, don't fall for their bullshit. They die just like everyone else when you do your job properly. No amount of toughness and teeth gritting is going to help even the biggest oaf to overcome the catastrophic blood loss of a torn aorta. Think of yourself as a slaughterhouse worker. Don't get too close to the livestock and use the right tech to stun them and bleed them out.

The pilots finally button up the plane and start to taxi. I get ready, strapping myself to anything metal with some strips of 5,000-pound webbing. This will keep me from getting sucked out of the landing gear housing if I am knocked unconscious on takeoff. A Gulfstream 650 is basically a rocket ship with cushy leather seats and busty bimbos serving steak sandwiches. It needs fewer than 6,000 feet to take off at a speed of 300+ knots. It has a top speed of Mach .925, and it gets there in a hurry. Until we get into our less aggressive ascent pattern from 10,000 feet and up, I will be pinned to metal and unable to move a fucking muscle.

The pilot's a fucking cowboy because he doesn't even slow down as he taxis and turns to takeoff position. Then he punches the throttle. By the feel of it, he uses about 3,000 of the required 6,000 feet of takeoff runway and we shoot nearly straight up into the sky. Because of the plane's attitude—pointing nearly vertical—I am now at the mercy of some serious G forces. I have no control whatsoever over my body, so you can imagine my dismay when I slide straight down and my legs are hanging out of the landing gear housing, dangling in the wind—the 400 mph wind, that is. In this position, when the landing gear goes up in a matter of seconds, I'll be cut in half.

So, I move my hand like a broken seal flipper and pull my speedball from the chest zip on my Kevlar jacket. It feels like I am attempting to dead lift a Volkswagen as I attempt to move the thing toward me. I manage to pull off the syringe cover with my teeth as I hear the pilot attempting to retract the gear. One of my pieces of webbing is blocking it momentarily, buying me precious seconds. I jab the syringe into my neck and plunge it. Almost immediately, I am jacked to the gills on gack. I claw my way back into the landing gear housing as the servomotors chew their way through my webbing. When I get my feet inside, it's much easier to maneuver, which is good, because the webbing that was hindering the landing gear servomotor just snapped. The sudden release of the gear causes it to whip up into the housing, knocking me back into my hiding hole with the force of a freight train. The last thing I see is my hand just before my face smashes into it.

35

MANO A MANO

When I wake up, I'm hypothermic and gasping for air because we're almost at cruising altitude. I quickly throw on my breathing apparatus and hungrily devour some oxygen. My hands and extremities are numb, and the black spiders of frostbite are starting to inch down my skin. If I could feel it, I would be in excruciating pain from my cracked collarbone. I can tell it's cracked because it has a golf ball-size lump on it. What else? Definitely some broken toes and maybe a sprained ankle, but again, the numbness is masking any pain of injuries I might have.

My watch is telling me I have about one minute of air left in my breather, so I get my ass in gear. I pull my tools from my zips with shaking hands and go to work on the panel I was trained to be able to remove with my eyes closed. It's open within a couple of seconds. A blast of warmth hits me in the face but I don't linger because I know that this hull breach will eventually trigger an air pressure drop alarm. So, I shove myself through the three-foot-square access panel and find myself crouching in the aft baggage compartment. I quickly replace the access panel and seal it with marine repair cement.

With the panel secured, I take a moment to enjoy the finer things in life: oxygen, heat, light, etc. In the end, my midbrain tells me, *this is all we need. Everything else is just window dressing.* Hypoxia is still getting the best of me so I gobble up some more Acetazolamide.

Right away, the foggy feeling is gone and I feel like I have full possession of my physical and mental faculties.

According to my specs, there should be a transformer box that controls the lighting in the passenger cabin somewhere in the wall between the aft lavatory and the baggage compartment. I cut into the molded plastic wall until I find it. It *also* supplies the heat and AC controllers with juice, so I have to be careful not to cut those. If I did, all of us would freeze to death before the captain could descend to a more hospitable altitude. I tape those to the wall and cut the wires that power the lights.

The plane goes dark.

I hear them out there calmly discussing the problem. I put on my night vision goggles. I have a few seconds to get some work done before they find the emergency lighting switch, which is back here by me. I wait for the first guy with any brains to come back here for that. He is massive. A three-hundred-pound Samoan with his prodigious mop of hair trained into a lunch-lady bun on the back of his head. I am ready for him, holding pretty much the only gun that is safe to use on an airplane. It's composite and has a range of one foot. Remember what I was saying about the slaughterhouse? This is just like a slaughterhouse stun gun. In fact, it is based on an actual device called a free bolt stunner. Most modern stun guns have a pointed, retractable spike that pierces the skull but retracts. The free bolt was designed for emergency, in-the-field euthanasia of large farm animals that can't be restrained. Kind of like my new friend, Mr. Samoan. The bolt can actually release from the pistol so you can use it at short range, and it does not require contact. I designed this one to have a cylinder like a revolver, and since the bolts are thin, it can hold fifteen.

POP!

The first large animal, Mr. Samoan, is euthanized. He falls face-first onto the floor. One of his friends comes running to see what happened and *POP!* He falls on top of the Samoan's body and I duck as one of the security thugs starts chucking knives in my general direction. I pull one out of the wall and, like the true circus freak I am, I whip it about twenty feet right into Mr. Knife Thrower's forehead. He points to his head as if to say "Do I have something here?" and falls into a tray of cocktails. The boys are all taking cover, so it's hard to count them, but I estimate there are now nine security types left and my target is nowhere in sight. That's fine, because these guys have protocol to follow and Locke is probably hidden in some custom-built panic room.

I push my way into the passenger cabin. It's a fucking mess in there, broken glass all over the place, three dead bodies, and the fun has only just begun! One of the thugs pulls a water-based stun gun. It fires a stream of highly conductive water, made up mostly of salt and other minerals, and juices the stream of water with an ungodly amount of electricity. He shoots me in the nuts. I am wearing Kevlar, which wicks water almost completely and is not conductive at all, but it's still pretty painful to get shot in the junk with a few thousand volts. The disadvantage of these weapons is that, unlike the Taser I'm carrying, they don't shoot the razor-sharp barbs that sink into the skin like fishhooks and allow you to *volt fuck* some poor bastard for as long as your batteries last. I fire these into his balls to see if *he* likes it. Then I cram a wine cork in the trigger guard and the bro gets juiced until his head starts to smoke.

Now it's time for the thug that has "had enough of this shit" and wants to—you guessed it—"take me on *mano a mano*!" He is also a man mountain. His strategy is to rush me. I immediately go into bullfighter mode. Instead of taking any of the force that this heavier, stronger, and more insanely angry bull wants to deliver, I stylishly side-step like a matador and *POP!* He gets a bolt in the back of the head.

Now there is more electrified water coming at me and the stream gets me under the neck guard. It knocks me back and I fall right on top of the dead Samoan. I roll off him and land in the galley and another thug is instantly on me. This is what he wanted, a close quarters grappling match where he can suffocate me with his muscles and manhood. I see his face as he puts one of my arms in an exotic hold and pulls a combat knife that he intends to bury in my throat. My free hand stops it but not for long. He has leverage, weight, and strength on his side. I have half frostbitten fingers and I am totally exhausted.

There is something about his sadistic smile that fills me with uncontrollable rage. It travels under my skin like a wave of liquid heat. I am instantly sweating, and my ears are roaring from what I'm guessing is an adrenaline surge. Without hesitation, I move his knife hand and pull the blade into me. It sinks into the flesh above my cracked collarbone and goes right through to the floor. The pain is earth-shattering, but manchild's knife is stuck in me and in the floor and he now has no weapon. That's when he frees my other arm to reach for something. Big mistake. I grab his hair and shove my two fingers deep into his eye socket. He attempts to jump up off me but I use my knees to flip him over the top of my hand and onto his back. I pull the knife out of me and shove it in the spot behind his ear, severing his brain stem.

"Who's smiling now, asshole?"

I leap to my feet and rush the other three as they rush me. Instead of hitting them head-on, I dive into the knees of one of them with all of my body weight. Both knees buckle and I hear the telltale snap of ligaments and tendons. As the guy lies there whimpering, I laugh out loud at him.

"Oh, did that hurt fat ass?"

I pile drive his neck with my knee, crushing his windpipe and breaking his neck. Two left, and they pull guns. They are thinking that if they just fill me full of the low-velocity rounds that don't pass through, they can dispatch me quickly without endangering the aircraft and Locke.

"Go ahead, you stupid fucking meatheads. Shoot. You'll pop this plane like a shaken soda can and kill us all."

They say nothing, just quietly stalking me, pushing me back to the galley wall, which is thick enough to stop a bullet. I have to move quickly, so I pull my second Taser and fire it into the chest of one of the thugs. The juicing I give him causes him to jerk and fire his weapon into the floor. Oops. As he shakes and twitches, the other guy grabs a chair and braces himself for the plane to lose cabin pressure and plummet to the earth. I wrap the wires from the Taser around him and shove him to the ground. Then I see one of their water stun guns and I snatch it up.

"You ever play that carnival game where you shoot the clown in the mouth with the water pistol and blow up the balloon?"

I unload the fucking thing into his and his buddy's face, penetrating their nostrils, mouth, and ears. They fry like death row cons sitting on Old Sparky, their eyeballs bursting into flames. I cover their heads with a blanket to keep from setting the plane ablaze and assess the situation. The thugs are all dead. Locke is nowhere in sight. Then all of the plasma screens fire up and Locke appears.

He's piloting the plane.

"Hello, asshole," he says cordially over the intercom.

I say nothing, my head buzzing from near total exhaustion.

"The intern. Very clever. Who do you work for?"

"Judge Judy."

He smiles.

"Have you ever heard of the vomit comet? It's an airplane that they use to simulate antigravity environments for shows about space, et cetera. People get into what is essentially an empty fuselage and the plane does steep climbs with zero gravity stalls. Basically, they let the engines stall and the plane just plummets."

"Sounds like fun."

"Fasten your seat belt in case we encounter some turbulence."

He guns the throttle and we start rocketing straight vertical. I fall back into the galley wall and it cracks under my weight.

"Oops. That looked like it hurt."

Then he stalls out and the jet drops like a stone. I am instantly floating weightless in the cabin. I try to grab on to whatever I can and make my way to the cockpit door. Then he hits the gas again and climbs. I lose my grip and fly through the main cabin like a bullet, hitting every sharp or hard object along the way. I protect my head with my arms as I slam into the little cocktail bar and obliterate it. Glass shards explode in all directions.

"This is what you get when you fuck with someone like me."

Bam! Back to the plummet, but this time he is doing rolling turns at the same time, so I am like a fucking extra sock in the spin cycle. I don't know what is up or down but I do know I can't take much more of this. I feel the blood coming out of my nose and ears and know I have a very bad concussion and maybe even a burst eardrum.

I pull two knives from the dead guards and stick them into the floor. I use them as metal talons so I can claw my way to the cockpit. If Locke pulls more moves, I can quickly sink one or both of the blades into other surfaces. I am like a spider, inching my way along, so dedicated that my hands are bleeding.

"That door you're thinking about breaking down is quadruple reinforced titanium with a thick Kevlar sheath in the middle. Good luck opening it."

"I don't need to open it because you're going to open it for me."

He laughs and tries to shake me but I am dug in like a tic and getting closer to the cockpit door.

"Why would I open it for you?"

"Because your daughter is locked in the fucking bathroom and if you don't open it, I'll think up another carnival game."

"I don't know what you're talking about."

"You really are an asshole, Locke. I saw her take cover in there when I dropped your first goon."

"How do you know she's my daughter?"

"Really? That's how you're going to play it? She was on your passenger manifest, tough guy."

"That's my admin. And don't bet on me giving a fuck about her."

I claw my way back to the lavatory and kick the door open. Locke's little rich girl daughter is strapped to the jump seat inside. I pull her out of there and sit her down in a chair.

"Okay, I'll bet on this."

I take up one of the guns from the dead goon squad and point it at the back of her head.

"Daddy!" she screams.

"Looks like we have a winner!" I yell.

Silence from the cockpit.

"I think she has something on her mind. Let's see what it is."

I cock the hammer back for effect, and the cockpit door opens. Locke stands there looking at me, a gun in his hand.

"Lay the fucking gun down. Now."

"Fuck you."

He fires at me but misses and puts a hole in the fuselage floor, a few feet behind the left wing. Alarms go off. The autopilot drops the oxygen masks and dives down in a very steep descent. I roll down the aisle and into the wall near the cockpit door. Locke is waiting for me, his gun pointed at my face.

"Stupid motherfucker," I spit.

"Sometimes doing what's necessary seems crazy but it's the highest form of sanity."

"Tell that to your daughter over there, asshole."

When he looks at her sobbing in the chair, screaming and unable to breathe, he's struck by his actions. Then he's struck in the balls by my foot. He goes down, holding his crotch and gasping. I pull him up by his collar and drag him into the cockpit.

"Now you are going to land this fucking plane and I am going to kill you. But if you fuck with me, I'll kill her too, right in front of you. Understood?"

He nods and takes the controls. The plane is shaking like a motherfucker as he attempts to stabilize our descent. After fifteen or so harrowing minutes, we settle into an altitude of around 18,000 feet.

"Where are we?"

He looks at his satellite positioning system.

"About a hundred miles south of Miami. Looking for a private airport in Grand Cayman or maybe Barbados."

"Change course for Honduras. There's an airfield outside Puerto Cortés."

"Honduras? We may not make it with that hole in the fuselage."

"Just do it."

36

"LA CUCARACHA"

Two hours later, we're landing in Honduras. Locke taxis to the single building on the airfield and sees that it is empty.

"Stop here."

He stops the plane. I shove him out into the passenger cabin and sit him next to his daughter. I put the gun to his forehead and cock back the hammer.

"No! Daddy!"

"Quiet," I tell her.

"Please don't kill my dad."

"Do you know who your dad really is? Do you?"

She whimpers.

"He's been selling the names of people in witness protection to the highest bidders—mob, cartels, Aryan Nations, you name it."

She shakes her head and sobs.

"Leave her alone and get it over with!"

"Shut up!" I yell.

I pistol-whip him across the face, cutting a deep gash across his cheeks and nose. I turn to his daughter, who is sobbing.

"I'm sorry that you had to see this, but you need to know what kind of man raised you. You need to know he is a lowlife piece of shit and he has innocent blood on his hands. You need to know that he deserves to die."

I press the gun to his forehead.

"I was sent here to kill him. It's my job. . . ."

I press harder for a beat . . . then I take the gun away from his head.

"But I'm not going to do it."

Locke and his daughter look up at me, stunned.

"Because I just retired."

I grab what ammo and weapons I can from the corpses of the thugs and pop the passenger door.

"You have enough fuel to get you to Mexico. I suggest you get the fuck out of here now before the cartel army finds out an $80 million private jet is parked on their airfield."

Both of them are completely speechless as I lower the airstairs and walk out of the plane into the hot, humid morning. I am speechless too, just trying to navigate my way into uncharted territory. You're probably speechless because I allowed Locke to live. Don't worry. It wasn't because I found Jesus or saw the light or anything. It was because of the first commandment in my own personal bible: survival. With Locke alive, Bob will most certainly end up dead, cashed out by his clients.

Bottom line is: by leaving Locke alive, Bob is out of my hair for good and I am now officially retired. Disappointed? I'm sorry if I didn't deliver the Disney/Pixar ending you were expecting. It's like I've been telling you, you have to be prepared for anything. You never know where the bottle will spin and you've got to kiss the princes and the frogs no matter what. Those are the rules. If you don't respect them, then you have less than nothing and that's a lot of nothing for people like us. I may not be walking away from HR, Inc. with my gold watch and pension, but I am walking away. And the closer I got to this moment, the more I realized the unlikelihood of that happening. Why would I trust someone like Bob? That's just plain stupid.

As for you, my advice is to formulate an exit strategy quickly. The shit is about to hit the fan, and you don't want to get hit by the spray.

———

Rule #14: Know the fine art of the exit strategy.

On my tenth job, I was working a global shipping CEO who was big into human trafficking. He was bringing cargo ships into the ports of Los Angeles, New York, Miami, and Oakland filled with exports from Asia: rubber dog shit, back scratchers, and indentured servants. You've heard the stories before, so I won't bore you with the details. Suffice it to say that this motherfucker was supplying 90 percent of the sweatshops in the U.S. with cheap labor and making *a lot of money.* Butt fucking the American dream so you can buy cheap T-shirts at Old Navy. Isn't life beautiful?

So I weaseled my way into this guy's inner circle as an intern at his New York port. Then Bob threw a wrinkle into the equation. He told me he wanted to give a new recruit some "on-the-job training." He also blew sugar up my ass and told me that I was his protégé and he wanted the greenies to learn from the best. At first, I enjoyed the ego boost. But that faded quickly when I started spending time with a young woman I will call *Juno.* Oh, you've *seen* that movie, huh? Well, then you know that Juno is an annoying twerp who never shuts the fuck up. That's what I was dealing with. Bob got her into the gig as an intern too, and I showed her the ropes. She was probably nineteen at the time. In addition to making me want to strangle her, she had all of the office workers wanting to join me in a gang-strangle. But the thing was, this chick was a star when it came to combat. I've never seen anyone shoot, slash, or fight better than she did. So I instantly became paranoid that Bob was going to have her whack me.

Anyway, D-day comes for our white slaver and Bob planned a Triad-type hit as our revenge scenario. Party line on the street would be that the Triads wanted white slaver to pay hefty tribute money for operating in Asia. White slaver stupidly refuses. White slaver gets butchered instead so Triads can just take his business. Pretty clean. Unfortunately, an authentic Triad killing is about as far from clean as you can get. Let's just say it involves the use of heavy, rusty meat cleavers, the Triad signature weapon of choice.

The plan was to do the deed in the early morning when the white slaver arrived for work. He always came in at around 4:00 A.M. to deal with calls from Asia. Staff usually arrived at 8:00 A.M. So we would have a solid four hours to make a jigsaw puzzle out of him. I picked up Juno at 3:00 A.M. For the first time ever, she was *quiet*. Now my paranoia was reaching a fever pitch and I was fully prepared to kill her if she even looked at me the wrong way. And I had an exit strategy. With the rest of the gear, I had brought with me a bugout bag that would enable me to survive for up to four weeks at sea. After killing her, I could stow away in one of the cargo containers, like my human trafficking brethren, and go dark in Asia. A little chop-sockey plastic surgery and I'd be golden.

Juno and I slipped into the white slaver's office and waited for him to arrive. He was a little early, so we made our move inside. I won't bore you with the gory details (literally) of white slaver's demise. Let's just say I can see why the Triads have done hits like this for hundreds of years. The prospect of being horribly mutilated is an excellent deterrent against ever fucking with them. First off, it is not a quick, painless death by any stretch of the imagination. Second, you don't want your loved ones to have to bury pieces of you. That's just a bummer for everyone. Speaking of loved ones, Triads usually chop up your whole family too. Bob never entertained going that far for "authenticity" or he and I would have reached a moral impasse.

Somewhat surprisingly, Juno froze up when it came time to do the deed. I was pissed as hell at her and made her pick up all the body parts and bag them. After we were done, we were preparing to leave when I got a text message from Bob.

"Kill her."

Okay, so maybe my paranoia was not as based in rationality as I thought. I completely misread this situation and should have seen the signs, like the fact that Juno was nineteen and had not yet completed an assignment. I had completed seven by the time I was seventeen. Turns out it was because she was an annoying idiot whose endless mundane banter was getting her shit-canned from her intern gigs. Seen and not heard never really sunk in with old Juno.

So I was looking at her, covered in blood, gathering up gear, and I did something that, to this day, sort of escapes me. I showed her the text. She blanched and I could see her mind racing, thinking of what she would need to grab to defend herself. I held my hands in the air and told her that I wasn't going to kill her. She was confused. If I didn't kill her, Bob would kill us both. Bingo! Not as dumb as you look, Juno. Then I handed her my bugout bag and told her I thought Asia was nice that time of year. She started crying, hugging the pack much in the same way I'm sure she wanted to hug me. She told me no one had ever done anything this nice for her, ever. I told her I wasn't doing it because I'm nice. I told her I did it because she's one of us, and even though Bob does not have honor, we do.

———

Rule #15: We kill others, but we do not kill each other.

The fact that Bob asked me to do that should tell you everything you need to know about him. There are ways to deal with people like Juno among the ranks, but that is *not* our problem. It's Bob's problem. And as much as I wanted her to shut up, I had no desire to shut her up for good. We found her a nice empty container on a boat bound for Hong Kong and I bid her adieu. But before I saw her off, she asked how she could ever repay me. I told her she would have plenty of time to think of something. When I got back to the office, Bob never even asked how it went. Now, that's trust.

37

BLEEDING ON THE PAGE

Just as Juno's brief tenure at HR, Inc. came to an abrupt, yet inevitable, end, we have now reached the end of *The Intern's Handbook*. I've told you *almost* everything I know. One of you might be assigned to take me out, so I need to keep a few tricks up my sleeve. You have to make your own way. That's the only way you'll survive. Things that work for me may not work for you, and you can't allow your flexible mind to become rigid to someone else's dogma. I've tried to teach you that you are an exotic weapon all on your own. Like the swordsmiths of Japan, you need to temper that weapon with great patience and a mind that is open like the sky.

To those of you who are sick of my blathering and can't wait to make your mark on the glamorous world of human extermination, I wish you good luck and guns that don't jam. If any nuggets of wisdom you manage to dig out of my sprawling diatribe help you in any way, you can thank me by not getting your ass shot off before you're old enough to buy a six-pack.

To those of you who are like me and can't help but gawk at a train wreck or a twenty-car pileup, I invite you to read on, brothers and sisters. I am going to continue this more as a memoir now. I have enjoyed the process of "bleeding" on the page, as Hemingway so aptly put it. As a matter of fact, writing this handbook has been fairly cathartic. Maybe there *is* something to the whole confession booth thing. I sincerely doubt that God gives a shit if we whine to her about the transgressions she has given us the proclivity to commit and has clearly seen us perpetrate. However, I'm beginning to get the feeling that confession is what we need in order to forgive ourselves.

I have never told another soul what you've borne witness to in these pages. And although I don't feel absolved per se, a weight has been lifted. Evil deeds may not have actual mass, but they feel like they weigh a ton, especially if you're the only one trying to schlep them all the way to the grave. And then there's the matter of Locke and the fact that he's still breathing. Even though he probably "deserves to die" as much as any of my previous targets, *I didn't kill him.* It may seem like a small thing, but making that decision has made me feel free for the first time in my life. And right now, an ounce of redemption is worth more to me than a pound of the illusion insurance salesmen like to call "peace of mind."

So enjoy the rest of this train wreck if you like. Just don't expect there to be any survivors.

38

MARCUS

I'm in Honduras because this is where my father lives. Until recently, I was convinced he was dead. But throughout my life, I have always been driven by a compulsive desire to know where I came from. I'm sure many of you can relate to this, considering our similar pasts. And now, due to what is probably the only stroke of good luck that will ever come my way, I have found him and gotten a step closer to finding myself. To offer a brief history, which I am sure you can also relate to, I am the son of two junkies. My mother was murdered by her drug dealer while I was still in the womb. My father fled the country to avoid prosecution for being an accessory to her murder through his connection to the dealer. My father loved my mother. He did not kill her, but in the eyes of New York State, he was complicit in her death, as he was the killer's partner and they were wholesale heroin dealers. When you are a dealer of that caliber, the law is designed to completely own you if you are ever caught. Everything becomes part of the case against you. And, God forbid, if anyone should get whacked as a result of your dealing, you are an accessory to Murder One and you are looking at twenty years to life, depending on your three strikes status.

So, after my mother was killed, I took up residence in an incubator for several weeks so I could fully develop into a human from what probably looked like a fetal pig. While I was cooling my minuscule heels in the NICU, my father visited me a few times before the heat got to be too much and he had to hightail it to Honduras. It was those visits that were the key to me finding him. A Mormon family lineage consultant, recommended to me by Alice (R.I.P.), helped me with the process. Those people are good at helping adopted and disenfranchised kids find their bio parents. It's part of their religion I guess. Anyway, she was the one who had the idea to use the visitation list from when I was in the NICU. During the time I was writing this handbook, Alice and I both chased down the leads. And eventually I found my father. Nice guy. Feels bad for what happened to my mother. Wants my forgiveness. To tell you the truth, I'm not sure I want anything from him. Just knowing where I come from and even meeting him one time is all I've ever wanted.

So I hike into Puerto Cortés, a small coastal city about ten miles from the airstrip. So fucking hot in Honduras. My pores are hurting from the sweat they've been spraying out since the first mile. But I am light on my feet because I am done with Bob, I have a ton of cash hidden all over the world, and I am going to meet my biological father for the first time. It's a weird feeling, freedom. I have never been free anywhere other than my own head and having that extend into the rest of the world is almost overwhelming.

I arrive at my father's modest house by the sea in the late afternoon. He is not home, so I go and sit on a rusty beach chair behind the house and look at the ocean. Then I think I see him, surfing about a hundred yards offshore. I don't know for sure that it's Marcus yet because we haven't met, but I think it's a safe bet that he's the tall white man in a cluster of small brown ones. He rides a long wooden board and it's clear that he has been doing it for years. He walks up and down the board and "hangs ten" off the nose. Then he rides a wave all the way to the beach and walks up to me.

"Either you've come to kill me or you're my son." He smiles.

I know in an instant he's my father. He has all of the qualities I would have had in full if I had not been a premature baby and if

I had not been fed what amounted to cat food growing up. I am a smaller, slightly undercooked version of him.

This is the moment I have wanted ever since I was eight years old and I was getting ready to retire Mickey and Mallory with two plastic bags and a roll of duct tape. This is who I am.

And even if it ended right now, I would be satisfied. I *am* a real person, not a robot like I always fantasized about as a child.

"I'm John."

We shake hands. He does this kind of "fuck it" shrug and hugs me, soaking my shirt with warm salt water.

"Marcus Hunter. Good to meet you."

"You too."

"Beer?"

"I could murder one."

As the sun goes down, we drink a cooler of cold local beers and talk about surfing. Neither of us has much interest in rehashing the past. There is sort of an unspoken boundary that is raised, allowing us to build something for the future without ghostly distractions. After all, we are father and son, but we have never known each other until now. So, in many ways, this is our beginning. When night falls with the chatter of what sounds like a million parrots and monkeys, Marcus's housekeeper, Marissa, arrives and cleans and dresses all of my wounds. She is a trained nurse but makes more money cleaning toilets and I am impressed by her fast, efficient technique. She puts a homemade poultice on the frostbitten flesh, which instantly relieves the throbbing pain.

When she is done mending me, she cooks us dinner. It's a simple meal of fish and fruits and I think it might be the best one I've ever had. This is the taste of freedom. I hope you can experience it someday. Over dinner, I regale Marcus with my entire life story, starting with the time he held my tiny hand the last time in the NICU, up to now. To say that he is stunned would be a gross understatement.

By the end of dinner, he has a look of deep sadness that tells me he truly regrets leaving me in that hospital.

Marissa cleans up and goes home and Marcus and I retire to the beach to enjoy some hand-rolled cigars and a cold glass of Marissa's homemade *guaro* — a sugarcane liquor similar to silver rum.

"You really have something here, Marcus. A nice life."

"Why don't you stick around? You can have it too."

"As much as I would like that, I can't. Have to move on soon."

"Too bad. Would be nice to have you around."

"I want to stay. I just can't. It wouldn't be safe for either of us."

"Same people that killed Alice?"

"I think so. Maybe others. It's hard to tell."

We spend the rest of the evening drinking, smoking, and talking. Marcus has a way about him. A fatherly way. He keeps the emotional responses he can control to himself and *listens*. I have never experienced that before. All my life, people have been barking shit in my face and never listening to anything I said.

This is why I was so good as an intern.

I never fell out of character as the android order taker because that is how I was raised. But Marcus makes me feel like my story has importance and impact on someone else — him. And that makes the story more of a legacy. It's like the oral tradition. I have passed mine on to Marcus, and now it has a life of its own, regardless of whether I live or die. The burden of bearing witness to my life has been lifted.

When we're finished, he tells me he understands why I have to go and says that, in time, he will try to find a way to join me if I'll have him. I tell him I would like that. Then the *guaro*, the white noise of the ocean, and the miles I have put on my body over the past two days take over and we both turn in.

39

RAPID EYE MOVEMENT

I sleep deeply but am haunted by a horrific nightmare. In the nightmare, *I am the one that beats Alice to death*. It starts with the real fight that we had in her apartment the night she caught me there in my ninja gear. But then it changes into a different scene, a gruesome montage of us making love, covered in blood, and me pummeling her naked body to a pulp. I wake up with a start, completely disoriented in the unfamiliar bedroom, weeping. As I get my bearings and focus my eyes . . .

Alice emerges from the shadows, smiling at me.

I lose my breath. She looks so real.

"Alice?" I whisper hoarsely.

She says nothing. This is the most vivid dream I've ever had.

Then Bob walks into the room holding a gun to Marcus's head and the dream becomes a waking nightmare.

The lights switch on and reality comes in the form of a Honduran death squad standing behind Bob.

"Surprise," Bob says with a casual grin.

"What the fuck is this?" I hear myself say.

Before I can even think about getting up, Bob shoots me with a tranq dart that feels like it was designed to penetrate the hide of an elephant.

Lights out.

40

THE BAGGAGE HANDLER

When I come to, Marcus and I are both bound to chairs in Marcus's living room. We're surrounded by the Honduran death squad. They look like starved mongrels circling the last table scrap. Marcus appears to have taken a few shots to the face in the interim, but I can tell by his eyes that he's lucid. Alice stands in front of me, fully resurrected, and I'm still in shock that she's actually real. Add to that the fact that she's clearly working with Bob, who's smugly holding court from a bar stool, and we have ourselves a whole new definition of "coming out of left field." Part of me thinks I might have had a psychotic break and I'm in a brownish grayish green mental hospital somewhere rocking, mumbling, and scratching my fresh lobotomy scar.

But the worst thing is that I'd blow my own brains out right now for being such a dumb sucker if I could get my hands on a gun. In this moment I realize that I *actually loved her*. What a fucking shmuck.

"I know what you're thinking, John," she says.

"You do?" I inquire feebly.

"And the answer is yes. All of your worst nightmares did come true in ways you never imagined."

She smiles. Quoting the handbook. I can't let her into my head anymore. I find my anger. I think about Mickey and Mallory, how they were bound to chairs just like this. I can guarantee you there are plastic bags somewhere in the next act of Bob's production here. Never took him for a lover of drama. But I guess there are a lot of things I don't know about Bob. Maybe I'll open his head someday and peek around a bit. Meantime, I need to get into this game as a player.

"Alice, you're looking much better than the last time I saw you."

"Bludgeoning is the new beauty treatment."

"Who the fuck *was* that?"

"Does it matter?" Bob asks.

"Yes, it does, Bob," I say coldly.

"It was nobody." Alice smiles.

"Nobody is nobody, Alice."

"What she means is that it was not a person, John," Bob says.

"I thought you were a movie buff," Alice sneers. "That was a prop. We got one of those special effects makeup guys to build it for us. He's a fucking genius."

She laughs, gloating a little too much.

"That's enough."

Good old Bob. All business.

"I'll say it again. What the fuck is this?"

"This . . ." says Bob as he pats Marcus on the shoulder, "is your assignment."

"I don't follow."

"He's talking about me, son."

"My great white whale, right, Marcus?"

"Fuck you, baggage handler."

"Ouch." Alice and her two fucking cents.

"I found you, didn't I?"

"By using my son."

"What the fuck are you talking about!" I'm starting to lose it.

"Why don't you tell him, Marcus. I'm just a baggage handler."

Marcus looks at me apologetically.

"Sorry, John. I fucked up. I should have told you the truth the day you called. When you knew my real name . . . I knew I was in deep shit. But you're my son. And so much time has been lost. I guess I was hoping you had just found me on your own."

I think back on Alice's so-called generosity and the fact that Mormon Dorothy was just another fucking operative, and my head is swimming.

"Who are you, then?" I hear myself say.

"I'm not a former junkie hiding out from the police. And your mother wasn't a junkie either. We were both working with the CIA. Ghost ops. Way off State Department protocol. We disagreed with some—"

"He's a traitor, John," Bob blurts out almost too quickly.

Bob's jealousy of Marcus is clear. He is stung by the fact that I very clearly betrayed him to make a connection with my father, even though it is beginning to sound like that was the plan all along.

"We were disavowed because we refused to carry out a directive that we knew we couldn't live with. We planned to run, but your mother was pregnant and they . . ."

"They killed her," I whispered. "With me inside her."

"That's right. I stayed as long as I could, but it was untenable. And I couldn't take you with me. You were on life support . . . and . . ."

Tears. Even though Marcus was in a similar line of work, he is not like me. He has feelings. He has a conscience. I see how that can be considered a weakness, but it feels very powerful to me. Marcus was the master of his domain and his unwavering mission to stay that way altered his life in the worst kind of way imaginable. But he kept himself.

Sometimes, that is everything.

"So, they've been looking for you all these years?"

"We had found him a while ago," Bob chimes in. "But we could never get anyone close enough to kill him. With his training and experience, I knew we never would."

The red-headed stepchild of epiphany kicks me in the balls.

"Only *I* could do it because you knew he would trust me."

I think I might vomit.

"It's actually pretty genius if you think about it," Alice says.

I need to center. I need to get back in the game before I peter out. I focus on my rage and use it to push one of Alice's buttons.

"Why don't you shut your pretty little mouth and let the men talk?"

She backhands me. And now I'm in *her* head. My mind calculates her weakness: pride. She will risk her life to preserve her pride. She has something to prove. I'll give her a chance to do just that. And that's how I will take her down.

Bob smiles and steps in, gently moving her away from me. Thank you, Bob. You just turned her prideful anger up to eleven. Her judgment will now begin to slip. He kneels next to me, fatherly, gentle.

"I was looking for your father, but found you instead. I was humbled by your strength. You were so tiny but I knew you would scratch and claw your way into life. After Marcus was long gone, I visited you in the hospital. I paid the bills. I controlled your path from foster home to mental ward to juvenile detention. When I knew you were ready, I tempered you like a sword. Turned your thin skin to the hide of a reptile. Sharpened your teeth."

"My foster parents in San Francisco."

"Your first assignment. Helped make you what you are."

Indio and Diablito. On the fucking payroll.

"What I am? Nothing in my life is real. It's all HR. It's all you."

"Remember what the social worker told you when you were six years old?" Bob asks. "He said, 'You're nothing if you don't know where you came from.' Do you remember that, John?"

I nod. Suddenly I feel like Sean Young's character Rachael in *Blade Runner* when she finds out all of her memories were someone else's, implanted in her brain to make her think she is human, to stoke the fires of the Bullshit Express.

"Then you joined us." Bob smiles. "And our clients couldn't have been happier. At first, they wanted to try to set it all up themselves. But I told them you're a very suspicious fellow, that you would see through anything that was laid before you and consider it bait versus prey. So I put you through the wringer with the Bendini, Lambert & Locke thing. 'Highly irregular' was your term I think? You had no idea."

"And you gave me Alice. That was a particularly clever touch."

"Alice is the new generation," Bob brags. "She's smarter, tougher, and comes with a lot less psychological baggage. None of this ego-centric nonsense that I have had to endure with you."

"Yeah, when she shot me in her apartment and almost blew your whole game she looked a lot like the new generation of dumbass."

Alice starts to speak. Bob knows I'm trying to draw her out, so he holds up his hand to silence her. This drives her insane.

"Come on, John. It's okay to admit you fell for her. Look at her. She's amazing. And also very talented. She's basically the perfect woman for you. Without her, you would never have developed the kind of utterly irrational, emotionally driven path that brought you here."

The extent of Bob's deception hits me hard. It's one thing to be played, but something else to be the sucker in the middle of a long con that makes your whole life a fucking joke. For years I've been seeing only what Bob wanted me to see, riding the Bullshit Express straight to my own private hell. I wait for the numbness to come, but it doesn't. I open my eyes and see their smug faces and the blind rage surges through me like a heroin rush.

"Bob," I say, mimicking his trademark cynical grin, "what difference does it make if I know how smart you and your rubber doll over there are? You're just going to kill both of us anyway. Gloating is not your style."

"John, if I wanted to kill you, I would have done it. The reason you're still alive is because *I* am your family. You think this guy is your family? The man that abandoned you as a premature infant on the edge of death in some hospital? The guy whose country would execute him for treason if they ever saw his face again? No. He is nothing to you and I am *everything* to you. Which is why I'm going to let you walk away if you agree to kill him."

I laugh out loud. This gets a chuckle from the death squad.

"You're even crazier than I thought, Bob."

"Fuck this, Bob. Let's just waste them both."

"Shut up, Alice."

Nice. That really has her hackles up.

"I believe in you, John. You're brilliant, loyal, and have the ability to process the world at a higher level. This is why you're the best I've ever had. By now you know that trying to be a hero for *him* is a no-win situation driven purely by misguided emotions *that I created*. I'm giving you a choice. Kill him, show your loyalty, and live. Or refuse and die. We're going to kill him no matter what. If you play ball, you're on a private jet to Paris, starting a new life, if that's what you want. Or you can go straight to hell, which is probably where you are right now anyway."

"Do it, John," Marcus says calmly.

"No," I say bluntly. "You're my father."

"Bullshit. *I'm* more of a father to you than he will ever be."

For Bob, this is as personal as it gets.

Marcus ignores Bob.

"You need to do this, John," Marcus pleads. "I will not have *your* blood on my hands too. I want you to have a life of your own. Do it before he changes his mind."

"No fucking way!"

I close my eyes. I'm starting to lose it. My mind will not accept this reality and the seed of a psychotic break is quickly taking root.

In my defense, this particular reality is one that most people would have difficulty *believing* let alone accepting. It's like the end of a Scooby Doo episode written by the fucking Manson family . . . on acid. I half expect Velma to walk in, her orange turtleneck drenched in blood from a ritual killing, to jerk off the villain's mask and deliver a shrill indictment. Speaking of which, let me see if I can wrap my head around this bullet—Alice doesn't work for the FBI. She works for Bob. . . . Huh? I've been spooning with a sociopath sent to use and manipulate me? *Get the straitjacket.* Bob has been hunting my father, a former CIA spy, for over two decades. My mother was also a spy, assassinated by some cloak and dagger jagoffs while she was pregnant with me. *Fire up the shock treatment paddles.* Bob and Alice actually used me as bait (and other clichés) to get to my father, knowing that I am the only person he would trust. Everything else was just window dressing for the big shit show. *Fuck it, let's skip right to the lobotomy.* I open my eyes and see their smug faces and the blind rage surges through me like a speedball rush. *Do not pass go.* I try to contain myself, but I can feel everything slipping. I use the last shred of my sanity to address my father.

"I have been looking for you since I was eight years old. This is not how this is going to end."

"How is it going to end, John?" Bob asks casually.

"Let's just kill them both and get on with it," Alice says.

"Shut your mouth, you dirty fucking whore!" I scream.

She punches me in the face. I fall over and smack into the tile floor. And this, brothers and sisters, is when I totally fucking lose it. I spend the next few minutes screaming and jerking as hard as I can, the nylon sash cord cutting into my skin and drawing blood. I'm having a full-on fit and no one knows quite what to do. I can see the reactions of everyone in the room. They range from apologetic and empathetic (Marcus), to disgusted (Bob), to amused (Alice), to wildly entertained (death squad guys). While I have my temper tantrum on the floor, I find myself facing the sliding glass doors that lead to the back patio. Since Bob, Alice, and the death squad are facing the opposite direction, only I can see the small detachment of heavily armed Honduran soldiers racing up the beach to the house. I feel the adrenaline surge, clearing my head and locking my body into an objective—one that I will have only seconds to execute. I kick Marcus's chair legs and he falls down next to me. And I use every last bit of strength I have left to get one of my hands free.

"*Alto!*" the Honduran Army commander yells as he and his soldiers fill the rest of the room.

Nobody moves. The commander gives Marcus a look. Marcus gives me a look. I smile. The fucking cavalry has arrived.

"Stay down," he says.

41

CHOPPING OFF THE HAND THAT FEEDS

For what feels like a full episode of *Gunsmoke*, we all sweat it out in this Mexican—sorry, Honduran—standoff. Then, as you might expect, one of the death squad guys gets trigger-happy and starts spraying the Honduran soldiers with machine-gun fire. Next thing you know, the room is a black cloud of smoke, bullets, and chaos. Meanwhile Marcus and I are on the floor, tied to fucking chairs. I jerk my arm out of the ropes and pull a knife from a dead Honduran soldier. I quickly cut myself free then Marcus. A bullet grazes the side of his neck and blood soaks his shirt, but he keeps his focus. Fighter pilot instinct. Turns out we have a lot more than genes in common.

"Come on!" he yells and grabs my arm.

We crawl through the mayhem into Marcus's bedroom. He pulls up floorboards in the closet and grabs two MP7s. He throws one to me as the death squad guys come rushing into the room. We both open fire, expertly wasting those toothless motherfuckers before they can even get a bead on us. Like father, like son.

"Outside!"

I follow him out the broken patio door and head for the beach. As we get to the back patio, we are suddenly on the front lines of a massive gun battle between Bob's mercenary death squad and the Honduran soldiers. Machine-gun fire peppers the wall, and we barely make it to the ground in time. I see Alice on the beach, blazing away at us.

"You take her. I'll find Bob!" Marcus yells.

We split and I move to the beach, taking cover and firing at her from different positions. As we get closer to each other, the bullets are getting closer too, and I can't get a clear shot because of all of the fucking smoke. I take cover and look inside through one of the broken windows. Marcus has Bob cornered behind the kitchen island. Marcus has great cover near the fireplace. Bob has nowhere to go. It's only a matter of time before Bob runs out of ammo and has to try to run for it.

A round blasting in the wall, temporarily blinding me with plaster dust, reminds me that Alice is out there. Instead of continuing on my current path, I backtrack and come around the other side of the house. I slap a new mag in the MP7 and wedge it in between the wall of the house and the air-conditioning unit. It's pointed in her general direction, so I jam the trigger with a rock. While it continues to fire on its own, I sprint around the front of the house. On the way, I snag an AK-47 off a dead Honduran soldier and haul ass around the other side of the house. I find a good cover position behind a stucco wall and wait.

Then I see Alice peering down the side of the house, trying to make out my position. I aim carefully at her head and I am about to squeeze off a round when I *hesitate*. I can't do it. Shit. My hesitation and sudden distraction by that hesitation causes me to indiscriminately fire my weapon at nothing. Of course, this alerts her and others to my position and they all open up on the wall.

It's a grind, but I start taking out the death squad mercenaries one by one. Predictably, it comes down to Alice and me in another target-shooting competition. We nick and scrape each other, but we are both too good to open ourselves up to a kill shot. Meanwhile I catch glimpses of the gunfight in the house. Bob throws an M84 stun grenade and Marcus is blown back hard into the stone fireplace.

Bob sees an opening and takes it. I run toward the house, unloading the fucking AK magazine at Alice, pinning her down in the sand. When I make it into the house, I am out of ammo so I dive and tackle Bob. We fight like mad dogs while the Honduran soldiers battle it out with the death squad mercenaries. Bob tries his myriad fighting techniques, but none of them are a match for my blind rage. I am kicking, punching, biting, and gouging. I am the predator, driven by my desire to taste blood, to tear flesh, to devour my prey.

I lift him and throw him into the stone fireplace wall headfirst. My intention is to break his neck or crush his skull, but he is agile and tucks his head at the last minute. The impact is brutal but not fatal. He hits hard and lays there for a beat. I crawl to him under a hail of gunfire. When I get there, he pulls a razor and cuts my hand deeply. He struggles to his feet, holding his blade, a cornered animal slashing at the air to defend himself.

"So this is what you call honor, John?" he screams through bloody teeth. "Chopping off the hand that feeds you? That clothed you? That saved your life? You're just going to kill me like a fucking dog?"

"No," Marcus says. "But I will."

Marcus shoots Bob in the forehead. Bob stumbles backward with a surprised look on his face and smashes through the bedroom window. When I see him lying there, it's hard to believe he's dead. He has always seemed invincible to me, like the steel and glass of the city that he made my prison when I was twelve years old. Now, with his legs twitching on the edge of the jagged, bloody window glass, he's nothing but a stiff, toppled relic, shaken to his foundation by a better man and left for the rats to judge.

Marcus shows me an exit wound in his back. It's as big as a coffee cup saucer and oozing dark venous blood.

"I'm hit pretty bad," Marcus says.

Very bad indeed. Shit.

"Let's get the fuck out of here," I say.

"Watch out!" Marcus screams.

I see a flash of Alice's reflection in the window. She is holding an AK. I hit the deck as she opens fire. The Honduran soldiers open fire on her. She runs toward me, ducking their bullets. The death squad stragglers open up on the soldiers and we're being pummeled by crossfire.

I take Alice's legs out with a chair. She falls hard, hitting her head and losing her AK. This barely slows her down. She is off the ground and on her feet as quickly as she went down. I am dragging Marcus into the next room for cover and she follows. We square off. She slams her foot into the side of my face. I fall to my knees. This brings a very predictable front kick from her. Going for the throat, huh? After all we've been through?

I kick her right in the crotch. Yes, it hurts them as much as it does us. She doubles over, actually giving me a reprimanding look, and I wipe it off her face with the bottom of my foot. She flips backward and slides across the floor. Bullets explode through the room.

"We have to go now!" Marcus yells.

I turn to him. He's lying on the floor, pale from blood loss.

I look back at Alice, but she's gone.

"Wood chute. Behind the fireplace," Marcus directs.

We both crawl back there and stuff ourselves through the narrow chute that Marissa probably uses to deliver firewood in the cooler, rainy season. This puts us on the side of the house where the coast is reasonably clear. As we creep off into the darkness, Marcus stops and pulls a bloody iPhone from his pocket. He punches in a code and his house EXPLODES, shattering the earth and filling the sky with burning ash. We limp into a thick black cloud of smoke and disappear.

42

PENNY-WISE

After we make it to the street, I steal a car and take Marcus to a local hospital, which might as well be a butcher shop based on their total disregard for hygiene. We bribe a nurse to take us to a private room and then bribe a doctor that speaks English to help Marcus. The news is not good. The shrapnel destroyed part of his liver and tore a major vein on the way out the back. He has lost a lot of blood. He also has a small, but potentially lethal, brain bleed from the impact with the fireplace stones. The idea of having brain surgery in Honduras makes Marcus laugh out loud. The doctor is not amused. Finally, Marcus's heart is showing a strange arrhythmia, most likely due to the damaged vein and blood loss. We start doling out the dollars for blood, antibiotics, and pain meds. And more doctors.

While they stabilize him, I go out to the street, looking for people who might be looking for us. If anyone survived the blast at Marcus's house, they will come here to the only real hospital in a hundred miles. After scanning the streets on each side of the hospital, I see nothing and go back to Marcus's room. He's asleep at first but wakes up when I turn on the TV to see if we're all over the six o'clock news. Nothing. I guess gun battles are considered family entertainment in this part of the world. I can tell Marcus is in a lot of pain, so I try to keep him talking.

"Tell me more about my mother."

"What, now that you know she was a spy?" He laughs. "Wasn't good enough when she was a junkie?"

We both laugh.

"What can I say? I'm a fucking snob."

"Yeah, I hated playing all that junkie crap. I'm just glad, and lucky, that you didn't go ballistic and tell me to fuck off and die."

"Who am I to judge?"

We both break up laughing like crazy. Marcus starts coughing, and we need to take it down a notch. I am watching his blood pressure. It's getting low. I need for him to stay awake a little longer, at least until the transfusion is done.

"She was pretty incredible. No offense, but I never wanted kids. I didn't think it was the best environment to bring them up in. . . ."

More laughter. You can't help it.

"She told me if we didn't have children our lives would be totally meaningless. Otherwise, why would she want to be married to such a disagreeable old bastard?"

"She makes a good point."

"Yeah. As soon as she got pregnant, it all just clicked in my head. And in my . . . heart."

He fights back the tears and wins but not before I see the depth of emotion he has always felt for her and, as weird as it is to say, *for me.*

"Had you picked a name?"

Here come the tears again.

"We can talk about something else. It's okay."

"No. Give me a minute."

He takes a beat to gather himself. Then he laughs.

"We didn't start well. Your mom suggested Homer."

"What? Good Lord."

"Then I made it worse and suggested Titus."

"Jesus, humanities nerds."

"Yeah. We met at Yale. So I guess we were a couple of nerds."

"Yale, huh? Think they would take me as legacy?"

"Sure, if my identity hadn't been erased by the NSA."

Laughter again.

"Then we finally settled. We both agreed that we were not creative types and naming a person for the rest of his or her life was fairly important. So, we decided to use a family name."

Pause for Marcus to collect himself again.

"Marcus?"

He nods.

"That's not a cover name?"

"No. It's my real name. The irony is that after I was disavowed, I realized the best possible identity for me to hide under was my given name. Marcus Hunter had been deleted from all government databases when they gave me my cover name, so it was totally clean."

"It's a good name."

"Damn right. My great-grandfather—your great-great-grandfather—was a World War I hero, and his name was Marcus. He was a blood-and-guts son of a bitch, and that's why my dad gave me the name."

"I like it. John is officially dead. Nice to meet you. My name is Marcus."

I offer him my hand. We shake. I can see that this makes him proud and very happy.

"It's a good name. You wear it well," he says, beaming.

"I look just like you. Got gypped on the height though."

"Being tall in your line of work is not such a good thing anyway."

"My line of work. That's all over now."

"You got money?"

"Lots."

"Then you can do whatever you want. The world is your oyster."

"True. I just don't know what I want, you know?"

"You'll figure it out. Shit, compared to what you've been doing, the outside world is a piece of cake. It's like Keith David says to Charlie Sheen in *Platoon*, 'All you got to do is make it out of here. It's all gravy, every day the rest of your life, gravy.'"

"You like movies?"

"Obsessed with them."

"Sounds familiar."

We both laugh.

"What about *her*?" he asks.

"Who?"

"You know who I'm talking about. The blond nightmare with the machine gun. She couldn't decide if she came all this way to kill you or have your kids."

"Alice? She's dead. At least to me."

"Seems like a loose end for you, then. Might want to snip it."

"Yeah. Now that Bob's gone, she might go dark."

"You never know. Better safe than sorry."

I don't want to talk about her. Not now. Not ever. I choose to remember her as the bloated murder doll I grieved in New York.

"Tell me more about Mom."

We talk for a few hours about my mother, Penny. Like Marcus, she was a classic overachiever with many degrees and a very high IQ. But what strikes me most about her is her empathy, the exact thing I was lacking to the point where I became a good candidate to be a cold-blooded assassin. Whenever they were stationed in some godforsaken shit hole somewhere in the world, she would always take the time to help out its poverty-stricken people. Marcus thought it was ironic that the more she saw disadvantaged children and the horrors they endured, the more she wanted children of her own. I wonder if she would think it was ironic that I became one of those disadvantaged children. Marcus says it would have broken her heart. He gives me a photo of her, stained with blood, of course. She's standing by the ocean with a bump in her belly, looking like she doesn't have a care in the world. She's holding someone's hand, but that person is covered in blood. It's the photo the social worker had told me about years ago. And, of course, the person holding her hand is Marcus.

43

"YOU DON'T HAVE TO SAY IT."

I doze off midsentence sometime around 3:00 A.M. and dream about my mother. The beach photo animates to life, and she and Marcus are walking, talking to her belly, telling me how good it's going to be, and calling me Marcus. When I wake up, Marcus is sitting up in bed, staring intently at the full moon outside. He looks very pale but his heart monitor looks good and his pulse is strong. Then I notice that he has put his pulse and pressure monitors on *my* fingers.

"Marcus. What's going on?"

"That's my last moon, kid. It's a good one."

"No. Let me get the doctors."

I start to get up, but he puts his hand gently on my arm.

"I'll be gone by the time you get back."

"I'm not going to let you die."

"You're not letting me die, son. I'm just dying. And it's okay."

"No."

I can't speak. The words won't come. It's like I'm still in the dream and I'm walking underwater. I can barely see, my eyes are so swollen with tears and agony. I am back in that moment when I killed Mickey and Mallory. I am the jumper, falling but wanting to stop myself, to defy gravity, to go back to the ledge, run home, and tell my father, whom I have never known, that I love him.

"I know."

"What?" I choke.

"I know how you feel about me. You don't have to say it. From the first time I saw you yesterday, as the man you are, I knew that nothing, not even time, ever really came between us."

"This was the only thing I've ever wanted. I've waited . . ."

"And it was worth the wait."

"But now I have nothing."

"That isn't true. I want you to know something. Everything you've done. None of it is you. You did what was necessary to survive. Not just to save your body, but to save your mind."

He lies down on his pillow, the full moon still reflected in his tear-filled eyes, a smile on his kind, paternal face. Seeing that smile brings about the first feeling of peace I have ever known. He takes my hand.

"Everything that came with that survival, the violence and ultimately the betrayal, it all brought you right here. It brought you to me. Even Bob and all of his bullshit brought you to me. And now you can be who you really are."

"I won't . . . let go."

"Never. We will never . . ."

He is gone. His last breath sounds like a gentle sigh. The full moon outside is shrouded in clouds, and his room goes dark.

44

THE LEDGE

Five weeks later. This is my last entry. I am not in Europe, basking in the glow of my retirement. I was there for a month. I had settled on Prague and was about to go under for my facial reconstruction surgery when I pulled the IVs out of my arm and walked out of the hospital with my ass sticking out of the back of my gown. As I walked, feeling the smooth cobblestones on my feet, my mind never felt clearer. Over and over again, I could hear my own voice saying, out loud and in my head—

"I am Marcus."

Not John. Not the man that playing-it-safe was about to make me become. I am Marcus. And I will not destroy the only thing that reminds me of where I came from. I want to look at it in the mirror every day.

Now I am in New Hampshire in the middle of winter, driving through one of the worst blizzards on record. I feel like Dustin Hoffman in *Marathon Man* as my car slides all over the road. I know that I can trust no one. I know that death is around every corner, the smiling friend that invites me in for a hot cup of coffee to get out of the cold.

Is it safe?

The answer to that question doesn't matter to me. Not anymore. In fact, there is only one thing left in this world that matters to me and I am looking for it in a whiteout, a frozen landscape that is waiting to devour me if it can get its icy fingers under my skin. In the distance, through the four-inch circle on my windshield that is not covered in frost, I see it. It's a cabin in the middle of nowhere. The perfect place to disappear.

When I get close, I hide the car in a grove of trees and walk up. I make certain not to make any fresh footprints in the snow in the front of the cabin. Instead I approach from the back, concealing my tracks in the powdery snow with a pine bough. It's so cold I can feel the moisture in my nose and eyes freeze every time the wind blows.

I enter through the back door. It's dark and bitter cold inside. I sit in a chair, cover myself with a blanket, and wait. After an hour or so, I hear tires crunching in the snow out front, followed by the tread of boots coming up the steps. The door opens.

Alice walks in.

She's carrying a bag of groceries. I say hello by shooting her in the shoulder with my Walther P22. The groceries go flying and she falls back onto her butt, clutching the wound. She goes for her gun but then sees it's me and thinks better of it. Now I have her full attention.

"John? What the fuck are you doing here?"

"It's Marcus now. After my father. Actually he suggested I come. Take care of a loose end."

"Do you think I'd be up here if I was still after you?"

"You're up here because you're working a target. Based on the surroundings, my guess is it's someone in intelligence. CIA. Rogue. About five foot ten, a hundred and forty-five pounds. Josef Ricard. Am I getting warmer?"

"What have you done?"

"I told him to get the fuck out of Dodge before he gets his brains splattered all over Robert Frost country. I told him that his lovely assistant is really a cold-blooded killer who is using him to get close to his boss so that she can cut his throat with a Tanto knife—Yakuza style, of course."

"Congratulations. Now that you've destroyed my career, please say something cryptic about tying up loose ends and put me out of my misery."

"You're not a loose end, Alice. I am."

"Now you're making no sense."

"Neither did my father when he suggested I come here. But then I started thinking about it, and it made perfect sense. He knew that I could never go on with my life if I didn't know."

"Know what?"

I set my gun on the floor.

"I love you, Alice."

I kick my gun across the floor, well out of my reach.

"All I need to know is if you love me."

I roll the box with the Harry Winston ring across the floor, within her reach. She just looks at me, waiting for the punch line.

"You're fucking crazy. You know that?"

"Not anymore."

She pulls her gun and levels it at me.

"I don't love you," she says defiantly. "And I don't see how you could possibly love me."

"Believe me, if I could walk away from this, or better yet, put a fucking bullet in your head, I would. But I know who I am now. And I know that you're part of that."

"No, John. I'm not."

"Then pull the trigger," I say, ready for anything. I can hit the water now. And all of me can disintegrate into the depths.

She is frozen in this moment, completely torn between her true self and the put-on persona that fell in love with me.

"I can't do it."

"Just squeeze."

"I'm not talking about killing you. I'm talking about what happens if I don't kill you. What you want. I can't do it." She fights the tears that are now rolling down her cheeks, mocking her bravado.

"Neither can I. But I'm willing to die trying."

As we sit there staring at each other, wondering what to do next and thinking for ourselves for the first time, I think back to my first week of training. After Bob got me out of juvie, he took me to a cabin in the woods that was a lot like this one, made me a hot meal, and sent me to bed. It was the best night's sleep I'd had in years. But when I woke up in the morning, he was gone. At first I thought he had just gone out for supplies. Then the bullets came smashing through the windows, obliterating everything in the cabin. I spent the next three days doing everything I could to survive. When I tried to hide in the cabin, Bob burned it to the ground. When I tried to run, he sent dogs to hunt me down. When I tried to fight, he scorched the earth around me with bullets and explosives.

On the third day, as I cowered behind a rock, half-starved, frost-bitten, burned, bloody, and dehydrated, I screamed that I gave up, that he could kill me if he wanted. In fact, I begged for death. That's when Bob walked up and sat me up against the rock. Instead of killing me, he gave me a drink of water, covered me with his jacket, and told me I was *ready*. He saw the state of complete confusion on my face and explained that, until I was fully prepared to die, I would never be a true predator.

It was this statement that made me what I was at HR. And it's this statement that has made me what I am now. I'm not a predator. I'm Marcus Hunter. Who are you?

Acknowledgments

This book exists because of the guts and genius of Sarah Knight; the rock-and-roll soul of Hannah Brown Gordon; the help-you-hide-a-body guidance of Brad Mendelsohn; the Shaolin white eyebrow–style kung fu leadership of Marysue Rucci and Jonathan Karp; the earth-shattering love and support of Amanda D. M. Kuhn, Skoogy D, K Bear, Jo Mama Kuhn (best mum ever), Ky, Mary B, Big Bri (Ar dheis Dé go raibh a anam), Cherry, G. Vance, Suzie, Brad, Silver, and Nixon and Kennedy (canines representing political duality); the Boy Named Sue love and fearless support of my late father, Kenneth Kuhn (the tough got going, Pop); the heartbreaking love and redemption of my beautiful late sisters, Tina and Kara Kuhn (thank you both for making me the twisted maniac I am today); the professional support, dedication, and karaoke skills of Ed Wood, Stéphanie Abou, Kirsten Neuhaus, Rachel Hecht, Molly Lindley, Roberto de Vicq de Cumptich, Elina Vaysbeyn, Kate Gales, and Brad Pearson; and the ink, wood, metal, and muscle of Simon & Schuster in the United States, Sphere/Little, Brown in the UK, Dumont in Germany, Sonatine in France, Pantagruel in Norway, and Alnari in Serbia. A true disciple of life has many deities. These are mine.

About the Author

Shane Kuhn is a writer and filmmaker with twenty years of experience working in the entertainment business and the ad world. In feature film, he has written screenplays for Universal, Paramount, Sony, Fox, and Lionsgate. In the world of independent film, he is one of the original founders of the Slamdance Film Festival and currently serves as an Executive Board member of Slamdance, Inc. A shameless product pusher in the ad world, he has worked as a copywriter, creative director, and broadcast video director and producer for several notable brands and charitable organizations. As a college baseball player, he threw a fastball in the low 90s, but his career was cut short by a Bull Durham strike zone. *The Intern's Handbook* is his first novel. He lives with his wife and family in a bi-coastal/ mountain migration pattern that includes Massachusetts, Colorado, Los Angeles, and San Francisco.